V.A. Dold & Tori Austin

RICHIE

Le Beau Series
Book 6

By

V.A. Dold
&
Tori Austin

RICHIE: Le Beau Series

Table of Contents

PROLOGUE– THE PLAN	1
CHAPTER 1	4
CHAPTER 2	18
CHAPTER 3	41
CHAPTER 4	55
CHAPTER 5	72
CHAPTER 6	87
CHAPTER 7	102
CHAPTER 8	115
CHAPTER 9	130
CHAPTER 10	146
CHAPTER 11	166
CHAPTER 12	185
CHAPTER 13	204
CHAPTER 14	221
CHAPTER 15	237
CHAPTER 16	258
SETH	278
K.I.S.S SERIES	286
ABOUT THE AUTHORS	294
FOR ANNOUNCEMENTS ABOUT UPCOMING RELEASES AND EXCLUSIVE CONTESTS:	295

V.A. Dold& Tori Austin

The Five Shifter Rules

Always put your mate before yourself.

Respect another shifter's mate.

Do nothing to expose the existence of shifters.

Do no unnecessary harm to shifters or humans.

Respect all nonhumans.

RICHIE: Le Beau Series

Copyright 2014 by V.A. Dold & Tori Austin

ALL RIGHTS RESERVED. No part of this book may be reproduced or transmitted in any form whatsoever without written permission from the author–except by a reviewer who may quote brief passages in a review to be printed in a magazine, newspaper, or on the web.

This novel is a work of fiction. Any references to historical events; to real people, living or dead; or to real locales are intended only to give the fiction a sense of reality and authenticity. Names, characters, places and incidents either are products of the author's imagination or are used fictitiously and their resemblance, if any, to real–life counterparts is entirely coincidental.

ISBN–13: 9781943896035

V.A. Dold& Tori Austin

This is Dedicated

To all of my readers and fans of the Le Beau Series, I appreciate you more than I can say.

Thank you to my friends and family who cheered me on and believed in me even more than I believed in myself.

To the Bayou Babes, who jump right in and spread to word about every book I write.

And, a very special Thank You to Billie Jo Giles, Theresa Anderson, Helen Jack, Karen Clasen, Pam Altman, Amy Holcomb, Jessie Clinton, and Jackie Allison. You were such good sports to let me torment you in the book.

...You all helped make this possible.

...Enjoy the adventure!

RICHIE: Le Beau Series

RICHIE
Le Beau Series
Book 6

V.A. Dold & Tori Austin

Prologue– The Plan

With great care, Emma Le Beau placed a purple satin cloth on the altar she consecrated to the Goddess Luperca almost two centuries ago.

She carefully smoothed every crease and wrinkle until the altar cloth was perfect. Next, she pulled four white candles from her prayer satchel. One for lighting all the others, and one for the creator and source of all, another for the goddess, and the last for the god and lit them.

Gently, she touched each of her sacred stones until she decided on amethyst, citrine, and clear quartz. With great reverence, Emma placed them in a triangle on her altar.

She closed her eyes, centered her mind, and quieted her thoughts. After three deep breaths, she opened herself to her spirit guides, and to the Goddess, God, and the Source. She asked them to join her and invoked their assistance.

Emma was greeted by the Goddess's soft, soothing voice. "Blessed be, my daughter."

"Blessed be, Mother. How may I be of service?"

"My son, Richie Majors is on the verge of meeting his mate."

Emma's eyes went wide and her jaw dropped

RICHIE: Le Beau Series

open. "Richie? Is there anything you would have me do to assist you?"

"I have already set into motion the situation that will bring Richie and his mate together. His human friends who attend college here in Louisiana will make sure they meet. He will be invited to attend Theresa Anderson's wedding. He must attend. There he will meet Piper Sinclair."

"If it pleases you, I could have Isaac talk with Richie's place of employment to guarantee he is given the days off he will need to travel and enjoy the wedding."

The Goddess smiled at that. "It does indeed please me."

Emma loved it when the Goddess smiled. Her grin revealed laugh lines at the corners of her eyes and made her seem a little less like a deity and a little more human.

"Both Isaac and I will do everything we can to ensure he accepts the invitation and goes to the wedding. Is there anything more I can do to be of service?"

"I am very pleased with all you do. I am most pleased by the assistance you have provided: assuring these new humans are introduced to their destined mate and brought into the fold."

Emma lowered her head in supplication. "It's always my pleasure to be of service to my Mother Goddess."

"Take care, my most precious daughter. Blessed be."

"Take care, Mother. Blessed be."

Emma graciously thanked the Goddess, God

V.A. Dold & Tori Austin

and Source for partaking in her request and snuffed each of the candles. When working with a deity, politeness and care were always expected.

*****

By the time Isaac returned, Emma was on the verge of bursting. "Isaac! I have another name."

She danced from foot to foot excitedly while he removed his shoes. "Who?"

"Richie. He's going to meet his mate, Piper Sinclair, through his friends. Those college girls he befriended four years ago. The Goddess requested that we ensure he is given the time off from work that he'll need to attend the wedding. That's where he'll meet her."

He took her hand and they walked to the study. "Whose wedding is Richie supposed to attend?"

"One of the girls he hangs out with from the college, Theresa Anderson."

"I know that group of ladies. Richie talks about them all the time. He even suggested they be invited to a gathering, but without a shifter in their family, I can't take that chance."

"I agree. Inviting them would be too risky."

"I'll stop by the Crescent City Brewhouse and chat with him about the wedding. You know, get a few details for us to work with." Isaac grinned, rubbing his hands together like a mad scientist. Then he chuckled again and poured himself a scotch. "This is very exciting! Richie. That's just wonderful."

RICHIE: Le Beau Series

Chapter 1

One month later

Isaac hung up the phone and smiled.

Emma stopped wringing her hands. "Did it work?"

"Perfectly. Thank Goddess we checked his schedule. He'd asked for time off, but the restaurant was short staffed. Todd agreed to pick up Richie's hours so there's nothing stopping him from attending the wedding."

Her shoulders relaxed and she let out a long breath. "That was too close for comfort. I'm relieved it worked out. Did Todd ask for any favors in return?"

"None at all. He was more than happy to help when I told him the Goddess decreed Richie must go. The request coming from his king didn't hurt either." Isaac grinned and gave her a playful wink.

"I still won't get a lick of sleep until he gets on the plane."

V.A. Dold & Tori Austin

"Come here, mate," Isaac growled and patted his lap, his eyes glowing brightly with sexual interest. "I'm sure I can come up with a way to help you sleep tonight."

*****

Richie hit the time clock and turned to head behind the bar. He was prepping drink garnishes when a hand clapped his shoulder.

Todd one of the other bartenders, who also happened to be a shifter, removed his hand and leaned back against the bar. "Hey, Richie. I took a look at my budget and realized I was going to run short of funds before month end. Are your hours still up for grabs?"

"Yeah, man. They are." Richie frowned, a little confused. Just yesterday Todd turned him down.

"Great. I'll take all of your shifts then. Give me a minute to let the manager on duty know so they can mark the schedule and I'll help you prep."

Huh. Richie watched Todd walk into the employee area of the restaurant. Talk about luck.

Whatever it was, he wouldn't look a gift horse in the mouth. He had been sick over missing the wedding. Now he had to decide what to pack when he got home. He had a lot to do before heading to the airport tomorrow. Thank Goddess he hadn't cancelled his flight.

RICHIE: Le Beau Series

*****

The next morning, Richie rolled down the window of his vehicle as he neared the airport parking ramp, and inhaled the fresh air. It was early for a bartender to be awake, only six in the morning, but he didn't have a choice. He didn't care; it was shaping up to be a great day. The sun was up, the weather wasn't overly hot, and he was on his way to the wedding.

*****

Piper Sinclair woke to the sound of her own screams, drenched in sweat. Huffing out an exhausted breath, she fell back against her pillows. Once her heart stopped racing, she glanced at her digital alarm clock and swore a red streak. Midnight. She was going without sleep again.
Sighing, she headed for the shower. Experience taught her it was useless to try to go back to sleep. Once the nightmare made a visit, it was there to stay for the rest of the night. If she fell asleep, she was doomed to relive the horror of her parents' gruesome deaths. Once a night was more than enough.
The senseless tragedy happened twenty-five years ago. Both she and her little brother, Roger, were asleep. She'd been dreaming about getting a puppy for her birthday when she was jolted awake by something crashing in the living room.

V.A. Dold & Tori Austin

She'd just slipped her feet to the floor, ready to investigate when she heard her father cry out in pain and her mother screaming her name, begging her to get Roger and find a place to hide.

Even at the age of ten, she had a backbone of steel. Silently, she crept down the hall, flattened against the wall. From where she stood, she couldn't be seen. Carefully, she peeked into the living room and froze. Her parents were fighting someone and blood was everywhere.

Now she understood, and her mother had given her the responsibility of Roger's safety. Quickly, and just as quietly, she went to Roger's room and woke him. He was groggy, but blessedly, he did as she told him without making a sound.

As Piper opened his window and pushed the screen out Roger got the chair from his desk. She set it under the window and helped him climb through and then silently followed him.

"Come on, we need to hide under the front steps like when we play Hide and Go Seek," she whispered as she took his hand.

The wooden stairs was one of their favorite hiding spots. The only way under was on the side behind a thick bush. A fine wooden lattice covered the opening. It was easy to pull away, crawl inside, and set the lattice back in place.

Piper waited for Roger to crawl in, terrified the bad man would come out the door and catch her. She watched his tennis shoe covered feet disappear and dove to join him as quickly as possible.

RICHIE: Le Beau Series

She wrapped her arms around her little brother and rocked him. The sounds coming from the house were terrifying. But she had to hand it to Roger, even though he cried he didn't make a sound.

After a long time it became very quiet. Too quiet. She made Roger stay with her under the stairs while they waited and listened.

Then they heard him, the bad man. He was looking for them in the house. She knew when he found the open window from the cussing.

That was when he started yelling. Saying he would let their parents go if they came to him. She knew he was lying. She'd seen the blood and that was long before the noises had stopped. If her parents were alive, she'd hear them calling her or at least making some noise.

When they didn't do what he wanted, he started describing in great detail what he would do to them once he found them. Piper stiffened and held Roger tighter. His eyes were huge with fear, but he nodded when she put a finger to her lips.

Twigs snapped and leaves rustled as the man searched the yard. When his feet appeared outside the lattice, they both tensed, ready to fight him off. After what felt like a lifetime to her, he stepped away.

That was when they saw flashing lights bouncing off the house outside their hiding place. A neighbor must have called the police.

V.A. Dold & Tori Austin

Roger wanted to crawl out and have the policemen protect him, but she made him stay put. She listened hard, it sounded like some of them had gone into the house and others were searching for the bad man. It wasn't until she heard the bad man swearing at the police officers, and knew he'd been caught that she let Roger crawl out from their hiding place.

The policemen were shocked to see them emerging unharmed and rushed to get them to safety.

It was a complete accident that she saw into the house before they hustled her and Roger away to the police station. The front door entered directly into the living room and was standing wide open. What she saw still haunted her. She was grateful Roger never saw what was left of their parents.

The next thing she knew they were in the police station with suitcases filled with their clothes that someone else had packed, waiting for Uncle Harry and Aunt Margery to pick them up.

It was through the nightly news that she learned the man who'd killed her parents was an escaped murderer. He was supposed to be in jail. And the real kick in the teeth was he'd picked her house at random because it was convenient.

Her parents died for no other reason than a sick man wanted the rush of killing someone and her family was easy prey.

That was the day she decided she would hunt down bad guys when she grew up. She would never let another murderer destroy a family if she could help it.

RICHIE: Le Beau Series

*****

Yawning, Piper jumped in the shower to clear her head and then made a pot of coffee. Hanging her nose over the steaming cup, she came to a decision and powered up her laptop.

Ten minutes later, she plucked the sheet of paper from her printer. She'd been seriously considering retirement from the bounty hunting business for over a year.

The nightmare she had last night, the one she seemed to have every night lately, was the last straw. Chasing her bounties had taken a lot of horrible people off the streets, but it had never healed the pain of losing her parents.

The only reason she'd stayed in the business so long was the thought of the other little boys and girls who might lose their parents if she wasn't tracking down the dregs of society.

Today, she was handing in her resignation. Her boss at the highly secret organization that serviced the justice system was going to have a heart attack. She was his best bounty hunter and he wasn't going to be happy.

She brought a lot of power and clout to the organization. When a criminal escaped during trial or afterward from jail, her organization was called to quietly bring them in. Her name was requested more often than any other hunter.

V.A. Dold & Tori Austin

She waited for 8:00 A.M. to roll around and headed for the office. She didn't bother stopping at the front desk as she usually did, instead she walked straight into the director's office, slapped her resignation letter on his desk, and plopped into a chair.

Jerry glanced at the letter and flicked it with the tip of his pen. "What the hell is this?"

"I quit."

"You can't quit."

"I just did." She waved at it pointedly. "See, it's all right there in the letter."

He leaned back and cross his arms. "To bad, I'm not accepting it."

"You don't have a choice, Jerry, and you know it, so stop being difficult."

"Yeah, I know," he sighed heavily, "but I got a real doozy of a job this morning and I need you to pull it off. I'll make you a deal. You do this one last job and I will be forever grateful. Then I'll throw you a retirement party myself."

"I can't, Jerry, I'm burned out." She looked at her feet, and scuffed her tennis shoe on the floor before she met his gaze again. "I can't sleep. The nightmares are back and they're worse than ever. I need out."

Jerry reached across the desk and laid his huge paw of a hand over hers. "I'm sorry, kid. I just thought you'd be hot for this one. He's a serial killer that likes hacking up entire families. He took out five innocent families in their sleep before they caught him and now he's on the loose. But I understand, I'll give it to one of the guys to handle."

RICHIE: Le Beau Series

With every word her body stiffened more, and her jaw ached from her gritted teeth. "What's his name?"

"Ryker 'Qball' Quintrell."

She knew that name. Had followed his trial. The sick bastard was the scum of the earth. "I'll get him for you. But then I'm done, Jerry. I mean it."

"It's a deal, Piper."

Three weeks later, she was grinning to herself as she packed to attend Bob's wedding. She'd considered not going. Qball was sniffing around her, acting strangely. She'd never had a bounty act the way this guy did. It was like he was hunting her. The whole thing was worrisome. She didn't want this freak anywhere near her family.

She talked it over with Jerry and he promised the local law enforcement near the wedding would be working with her on the case. He didn't like Qball's behavior any more than she did. He assured her, there would be so many officers guarding the hotel, Qball wouldn't get near the place.

She hadn't seen her family in over a year and she really wanted to be there. So, she was going.

*****

A few hours later, Richie walked with the mass of people in the airport headed to baggage claim. The flight had been long and he was itching to leave the airport. Stretching his neck, he pulled at his collar and tie. He really hated wearing a suit.

V.A. Dold & Tori Austin

For the thousandth time, he regretted putting off booking his flight until the last minute. He hadn't expected the flights to be sold out two weeks in advance. His procrastination had bitten him in the ass. Now there wasn't time to change before the dinner. So, here he stood in a suit, feeling restricted and uncomfortable.

His fingers went to his collar again and tugged. Screw it, with an annoyed snarl he yanked his tie loose and popped the top button of his dress shirt. Relief flooded his body like a glass of sweet tea on a hot summer afternoon.

This was it. The first of the Tulane gang was tying the knot. All of the passengers gathered around the luggage carousel. Richie glared at the silent machinery as if he could force it to belch out his bag. Nothing. Any minute now, an annoying alarm would blare and the blue light above would flash, signaling his luggage would barrel from the metal shoot before him and onto the belt.

As he waited, his thoughts turned to Theresa. He imagined she was a bundle of nerves. In his mind, he could see her pacing across a room and wringing her hands while Helen tried to calm her. He smiled; he could already hear her jabbering a mile a minute with excitement.

Richie was a mixture of joyous thoughts and envy. He couldn't be happier for his friend, but at the same time, he envied the deep love she shared with her fiancé. He wanted that same happiness she bubbled over with every time she'd come into the bar.

RICHIE: Le Beau Series

First Anna had found Cade, and now Theresa was marrying Bob. He wanted his mate, too.

Richie was beginning to doubt he would ever find his mate. For every shifter, there was only one destined mate. Only one woman who held the other half of his soul. The odds of winning the lottery were about a thousand times better than finding your mate amongst the world's exploding population.

What if his mate had married a human? Anna had before she met Cade. He shook the unpleasant speculation off. Then for the hundredth time he thought *I need to start a dating service for shifters. I could call it Mates-R-Us*. Richie let out a derisive snort at his ridiculous notions as the light finally flashed and the siren blasted his sensitive hearing. Time to get the party started.

He squared his shoulders and dispelled his covetous feelings. This wasn't the place or the time. His friend was getting married in twenty-one hours. He would display nothing but joy and happiness while he was in St. Louis for her wedding.

Bag in hand, Richie went in search of his rental car. A quick check on the time, and he walked a bit faster. He only had twenty-five minutes to get his rear end to the dinner. If he hustled and broke a speed limit or two he would make it.

Thirty minutes later, he cursed and slammed the car into park, then ran for the reception hall, which was doing double duty as the rehearsal dinner location. He skidded to a halt outside the reserved space, straightened his tie and plastered a smile on his face.

V.A. Dold & Tori Austin

As quietly as possible he slipped in and searched for an open seat. A hasty scan of the room showed only one vacant chair. Great, obviously he was the last person to arrive. Without causing too much disturbance, he walked to the front of the room and took his seat between Billie and Karen.

Piper's gaze had swung to the double doors the instant they cracked open. She scrutinized the man slipping in. A relieved breath escaped the instant she got a good look at him, and verified it wasn't Qball crashing the dinner. But for some reason, the stranger raised a flock of birds in her stomach. She never reacted to strangers so strongly.

She didn't dare look too closely. The last thing she needed was this guy catching her gawking at him. Her aunt always said she started flirting the instant she left the womb. *Flirting, my ass,* she thought, shaking her head to herself. Her aunt never could tell the difference between profiling and flirting. She'd been profiling people her entire life. That was one of the reasons she'd gone into her chosen profession.

Experience taught her the best way to guard her heart was to thoroughly study the enemy and be prepared. And that was what she intended to do.

Too many of the opposite sex came armed with charm and playful banter. The problem was, most of the time the guy was faking it to get into the girl's pants. But this guy looked like no one she'd ever seen. For some reason he didn't fit her normal profile.

RICHIE: Le Beau Series

She glanced his way out of the corner of her eye as he took the empty chair at her table. His manicured five o'clock shadowed jaw was well defined and he had perfectly sculpted lips. But it was his eyes that captured her attention, a warm brown color with flecks of gold. To complete her assessment, she forced her gaze from his face.

Nice, he had a head of gorgeous dark brown hair. It wasn't long by any means, just long enough to sink her fingers into. *Where the hell did that come from?*

Richie was relieved to see Helen, Karen and Billie were seated at his table. Thank Goddess, he had someone to talk to. He smiled brightly and was nodding his hellos when a delectable scent tickled his nose. He smelled the most mouthwatering crawfish boil - ever. He glanced at the woman across the round table, his breath hitched, and his heart constricted. Holding her gaze, his nostrils flared as he breathed her in.

MATE!

Her eyes widened and she quickly looked around. She must have heard him telepathically and was searching for someone near who may have spoken. Odds were she didn't understand what she'd experienced and was suspicious.

Frowning, she turned her attention back to the table. Then she caught herself and carefully straightened her napkin in her lap while she fixed a pleasant smile on her face. Satisfied she managed to appear outwardly calm, she glanced up and froze.

V.A. Dold & Tori Austin

For the first time, she took in his entire face, where before she'd been analyzing each feature separately. The man who joined the table right before she swore she heard a voice in her head was gorgeous. Not just hot, but please God, let me strip him naked and lick him, gorgeous.

He must be an actor or a model. She racked her brain, but she couldn't remember her cousin, Bob, ever saying he knew someone famous.

RICHIE: Le Beau Series

Chapter 2

Try as she might to not ogle the man, she failed. Epically. *Maybe if I identify who he is, I won't embarrass him too badly. Ah hell, admit it, I'm the one who won't be embarrassed.* She told herself. Yeah, right. She wasn't trying to remember his name. She was too busy gaping at him.

He had broad, nicely muscled shoulders and a trim waist that she imagined led to an incredible ass. His suit, though slightly wrinkled was custom tailored and must have cost a mint. It fit him like a glove and showed off his incredible body. Oh yeah, she wanted to get him naked, horizontal, and take him for a test drive.

Piper was so busy drooling and sizing him up, she didn't immediately realize the table had gone silent, and now stared at the two of them panting over one another.

Quickly she looked away as a scarlet stain crept up her neck. Then she heard a soft chuckle rumble from across the table and blushed hotter.

Helen craned her neck and looked around the room to see what had amused him. "What's so funny, Richie?"

"Oh, nothing."

V.A. Dold & Tori Austin

Piper snorted. *Richie, huh?* She couldn't think of anyone famous named Richie. Without glancing at the problematic man, she sipped her water. The best course of action was to pretend he didn't exist.

Piper was content to allow the other members of their table to carry the conversation. Steadfastly, she ignored him, but the irritating man didn't make it easy. She could feel his stare and it was making her antsy.

Richie remained calm on the exterior, though he danced like a child inside. His wolf stared at their mate, panting and licking his chops. Both he and his wolf wanted to howl with joy, but that wouldn't be a good idea in the middle of a crowd of humans.

There was no mistaking what he'd seen. Her stare and interest had been evident for everyone to see. Secretly, and apparently at times not so secretly, he'd kept an equally interested eye on her. Her gray-blue eyes had a translucence he found fascinating. And the edges of her irises shimmered with an intriguing silver hue. *Goddess, her wolf's eyes will be heart stopping.*

He was enjoying the view when she bowed her head and her soft chestnut hair suddenly swirled over her shoulders and fell forward to hide her face.

A frown creased his brow. He didn't care for anything obscuring his view. His fingers itched to push it aside so he could see her again.

Unable to gaze into her eyes, his perusal continued over what little of her body he could see. Even with the table blocking much of her figure he could tell she possessed a womanly body.

RICHIE: Le Beau Series

Softly rounded, lush, full curves. The kind that would fit perfectly cupped in his hands.

"Richie? Hey. Earth to Richie." He heard Karen's voice calling from his left.

He broke his scrutiny of the beauty across the table and looked at his friend. "Pardon me. I didn't hear what you said."

Karen grinned and glanced back and forth between him and the woman. "You were a million miles away. I asked if you had met Bob's cousin, Piper."

Shit. Karen must have caught him staring. He forced a pleasant, friendly, but not overly interested expression.
He didn't want to scare his mate away before he had a chance to get to know her.

Smiling warmly at Karen, he shook his head. "No. I haven't had the pleasure." Then he turned his attention back to his mate. *Piper. What an interesting name.*

Karen took it upon herself to make the introductions. "Richie, this is Piper Sinclair. Piper, this is our friend from New Orleans, Richie Majors."

The ladies beamed at him as he reached to shake her hand.

Electricity zapped him the instant their palms touched. His wolf yelped and eyed her warily. Disregarding the strange electrical charge, he held her hand reverently, dying to place a kiss to each of her knuckles. Instant peace. It felt like he'd come home and the missing piece to his heart and soul clicked into place.

V.A. Dold & Tori Austin

He saw her eyes widen and she sucked in a breath. She'd felt that odd zap as much as he had.

"I'm very pleased to meet you, Piper." Richie's voice was suddenly husky and an octave deeper.

"Likewise."

He wondered if she'd met anyone at the table before tonight when Helen solved the mystery of her lack of conversation. "Piper lives in Portland. We all just met her before you walked in."

"I've never been to Portland. Did you grow up there?" The question was asked casually while allowing him to learn something about his mate.

"No. I moved there a few years ago."

Short and sweet. This lady held her cards close to her chest. She was proving to be a challenge and he only had two days to win her over. Richie could see he was going to have to work hard to get her to open up. His experience chatting up the customers at the bar was about to get a workout.

Piper stared into Richie's eyes. Absently rubbing at her chest with her free hand. An inexplicable surge of happiness had overtaken her. And the sensation was disturbing. There was no reason to suddenly feel like the nerdy girl who'd just been asked to the prom by the football quarterback.

Unable to stop herself, she stared into his smiling, twinkling brown eyes. Deep laugh lines fanned from their corners, which spoke volumes. Richie was a genuinely friendly person.
She rarely felt comfortable around strangers, but his impish grin and amused expression set her at ease.

Damn.

RICHIE: Le Beau Series

This guy was trouble with a capital T. The last thing she needed right now was a hot guy distracting her. Distractions were deadly in her profession.

When against her better judgment she'd finally agreed to come to the wedding, she fully intended to do her part as the personal attendant and keep a low profile until she could politely leave. She loved her cousin, and nothing or no one was going to endanger him.

She hung her head in defeat. Oh, who was she kidding, Aunt Margery and Uncle Harry would be crushed if she left early. Especially, with Roger deployed overseas and unable to attend.

Heck, they'd even tried to get her to sit at the head table. She nixed that faster than… well, really fast. To them she was their daughter even if she didn't call them Mom and Dad. Absently she rubbed her chest again. No one, not even them, would ever take her mother and father's place in her heart. There just wasn't enough room for that.

Now what the hell should she do? She couldn't leave. Stay and avoid him? No, it would be better to be polite and control her hormones. Shit, if not for Qball, she'd let her libido run wild all over his hot body. Just her luck, meet a sexy man when she couldn't do anything about it. Polite conversation and nothing else would have to do.

Richie grinned hearing her thoughts. Piper thought he was sexy. He could work with that. Only, what was she afraid of? What kind of profession put her in such danger? And who was Qball?

V.A. Dold & Tori Austin

Piper set down her fork and wiped the corner of her mouth. "How did you all meet?"

"I was mugged," Billie blurted out and shrugged.

Piper's gaze fastened on Billie. "What?"

"Yeah, Billie could find trouble in a convent." Helen nudged her friend good-naturedly. "Our first night in the French Quarter and she finds a mugger."

Billie stuck her tongue out at Helen then turned to Piper. "Don't listen to the peanut gallery. I was walking along minding my own business when a douche bag tried to steal my favorite purse."

Karen nodded and shivered. "It was really scary. The guy had a knife and everything. But Richie saved us."

Richie chuckled and shook his head. Here we go, the stories are about to fly.

"Yep," Billie leaned into Richie and batted her eyes. "My hero."

"So what happened?" Piper sat forward, intrigued.

"Like I said, I was just walking along, when I felt someone watching me. Then suddenly I'm yanked off my feet when this guy attacks me and tries to pull my purse off my shoulder. That was my favorite purse and there was no way he was getting it, so I hung on. The bastard hit me, too," Billie said with an angry scowl.

Karen touched Billie's arm to get her attention. "He also threatened to cut you with his knife, but I jumped on his back and stopped him."

RICHIE: Le Beau Series

Piper's eyes got bigger and bigger as they told the story.

"So how did you get involved?" she asked Richie.

He modestly shrugged his shoulders like he hadn't done much to speak of. "I was tending bar at Crescent City Brewhouse, when I heard a woman struggling with someone on the sidewalk. So I helped out."

"Helped out!" Billie squawked "You jerked him off me, and beat him up. And when he pulled his knife, you twisted his wrist until he dropped it and almost put him through the brick wall. And then Karen cleaned me up and we all hung out at your bar for the rest of the night."

"Wow, you really were a hero." She smiled, not just to be polite, but with interest, he thought.

"Naw, I just did what any guy would do if a woman was being mugged. Then I made sure they knew how to be safe in the French Quarter so it wouldn't happen again."

Billie set her drink on the table and winked at Piper. "Yep. He taught us all the rules and they really worked, too."

Richie was blushing a light shade of pink from all their praise. He knew what they were doing. They'd seen Piper's interest in him so they were talking him up.

The dinner had dragged on and the need to touch his mate skin to skin was killing him. He breathed a sigh of relief when dessert was served. It wouldn't be long now and he could get her someplace quiet to talk.

V.A. Dold & Tori Austin

Piper held her fork aloft over her cake ready to take her first bite. "Bob told me Theresa just graduated from college. Did you all graduate with her?"

"Yes, we did. But I'm staying on to get my master's degree," Billie said around a bite of cake.

Helen's fork stopped midway to her open mouth. "For gosh sake, Billie, swallow before you talk. You're going to scare Piper away before we can become friends."

Billie waved her fork at Helen. "Whatever. Piper isn't easily scared, are you?"

Piper chuckled at their antics. "Not generally."

Karen cleared her throat and quickly directed the conversation into safer waters. "So anyway, back to the subject of graduating. On our last night in New Orleans, we all went out and celebrated our graduation and had a bachelorette party for Theresa, at the same time. That way Richie could join in."

"That was a lot of fun. I can't believe four years went by so quickly. I'm really going to miss you ladies." He smiled, but it felt weak and he couldn't hide the tinge of melancholy in his voice.

"What am I? Chopped liver?" Billie blustered.

Richie's eyebrows rose as a smile crinkled the corners of his eyes and he pulled her into a rib-cracking hug. "Not even close. You have no idea how grateful I am that you're sticking around, cher."

RICHIE: Le Beau Series

She smiled broadly and hugged him back. "Well, all right then. You're forgiven."

"So what did you do to celebrate?" Piper asked.

Ready to fork another bite of cake, Billie's eyes twinkled with amusement. "We had dinner at Irene's, an awesome Italian restaurant in the Quarter and then took a vampire tour."

Helen made a sound that was a cross between a snort and a laugh. "Yeah, and good thing for Karen there weren't any vampires on the tour. She was afraid one was going to jump out and bite her neck."

Karen glowered at Helen. "Vampires are scary."

"It was great, the entire tour Karen kept looking around like one was going to jump out from behind a bush," Helen said still laughing. "But there wasn't much chance of that happening. There weren't even vampires mentioned on the tour, it was just a boring history lesson."

Richie leaned back enjoying the conversation, sipping his coffee. "I told you guys those tour guides didn't know shit."

Billie's face was alight with devilish delight. "Yeah, but those plastic fangs Theresa bought were fun. I had a blast flashing them at drunk people and freaking them out."

Richie raised his cup in salute to her. "It was nice to meet the new posse, too. They're going to be a lot of fun. Thanks again for that, cher."

"New posse?" Piper asked.

V.A. Dold & Tori Austin

"The new crew of ladies from college. Pam Altman, Amy Holcomb, Jessie Clinton, and Jackie Allison. We hang out with Richie and keep him company so he doesn't get lonely. They're sitting over there." Billie pointed out a table in the second row.

Piper laughed and shook her head. "I can see you ladies are a lot of fun."

Richie rolled his eyes. "You have no idea."

Karen ignored his comment and continued the stories of their last night of partying. "Oh, it gets better. After we finished the non-vampire tour, we went to the Cat's Meow to sing Karaoke. Richie's Y.M.C.A. was a riot."

Piper's eyebrows rose. "You sang?"

Richie hung his head in defeat. It was no use trying to shut his friends up when they were on a roll. "Yes."

"He did all the arm gestures, too," Helen quickly added.

Then all three girls broke out in the Y.M.C.A. song earning their table strange looks. By the end they were laughing hysterically. Even Theresa joined in from the head table.

Breathless from laughing, Billie said, "He got us back though, and made us sing two songs."

"What did you have to sing?"

Karen pulled her phone out of her purse and found the video Richie had taken. "Here, you can watch it. Richie is such a brat, he posted it to YouTube."

RICHIE: Le Beau Series

Piper watched as the girls sang "We Are Family" by Sister Sledge and then followed that up with "It's Raining Men" by the Weather Girls. They danced and pranced their way through both songs having a blast.

She laughed and started to hand the phone back when Karen said, you have to see Etienne and Billie, too." She scrolled through videos until she found the right one.

Billie was grinning ear to ear the entire time Piper watched Etienne sing "Love Me Tender" and "I Can't Help Falling In Love With You." During the second song, she'd joined him on stage.

"Holy crow, he's really good."

"I know, right. And isn't Etie cute!" Billie squealed.

"Yes, he is," she agreed as she handed the phone back to Karen. "Is he your boyfriend?"

Richie let out a soft growl. His mate didn't need to notice how nice looking other men were.

"We only met that night. I gave him my number and he's called me almost everyday since. We haven't really defined our relationship though."

Helen patted her friend's hand. "I hope it works out, Billie. I liked Etienne a lot."

Billie sighed. "Only time will tell."

Dinner was over and people were beginning to mingle. Richie had spent most of the time the girls were rehashing their last night together trying to figure out how to get Piper alone.

V.A. Dold & Tori Austin

As he pushed his chair back to stand, Piper sprang from the table like she'd touched a live wire. "It was great meeting all of you. If you'll excuse me, I need to say hello to my cousin."

"See you around," the girls chorused and went back to talking.

Richie's eyes narrowed, tracking her. He watched as she stopped next to the groom and hugged him. Then with a glance around the room, she slipped out the door.

The manner in which she monitored her surroundings raised his hackles and had a low growl rumbling in his chest. Exactly how close was the danger that worried her?

He lifted his nose to pull her scent deeply into his lungs, and used it to track her to the bar. The closer he got to her location, the tighter his fists clenched. Males. There were several men in the same location as his unclaimed mate. Pausing outside the entrance, he took a moment to calm his wolf. If he found his mate with another man, he'd lose what little control he held onto by the skin of his teeth.

He forced his fists open, took one last breath, and stepped into the darkened bar. A quick sweep located her at a far table, deep in the shadows.

Piper narrowed her eyes. *What is Richie doing here? Is he following me?*

"Hi, there. Mind if I join you?"

She studied him, hesitating. He interested her like no man had, but she was in no position to start anything with anyone. Although, Qball hadn't shown his ugly face so maybe…

RICHIE: Le Beau Series

Finally, she gave him a small smile. "Sure."

He took a seat and smiled brightly. His focused attention a little unnerving. Piper sat quietly while he ordered a drink.

She would have bet good money that the management turned up the heat in the bar. There was no other explanation for her feverish body, at least none she would admit to. She was hyper aware of Richie's proximity and his leg pressed against hers beneath the table. Her libido really wanted her to get up close and personal with this handsome man.

Then she thought about it. Other people gave into their urges all the time. There was no denying, she was unbelievably attracted to him. As long as Qball was keeping his distance, did it really matter she was on a job? She decided to go with the flow and see where the night went.

Then a thought crossed her mind, trying to derail her temporary confidence. *Don't guys like him go for ditzy bombshells with huge fake breasts and fluff for brains?* If he was like all the rest of the men on the planet, she was screwed.

As if on cue, a blonde wearing more makeup than Piper used in a year, sauntered over to the table. If her dress were any smaller she would be arrested. Smiling brightly, she looked right past Piper and leaned over Richie. *Good lord, how is she not falling out of that dress?*

Richie leaned away from the bleached blonde. She was so close, all he could see was massive cleavage. He forced down a cough before it escaped from his throat. *Holy mother! She must bathe in perfume.*

V.A. Dold & Tori Austin

"Buy me a drink, handsome?" the blonde asked in a high little girl voice and giggled.

Richie cleared his throat. "I'm sorry, but that wouldn't be appropriate. My fiancée sitting beside me wouldn't appreciate that."

Piper looked at him and raised an eyebrow.

The blonde clutched her bosom, and feigned surprise. "Oh. I didn't see her there." With that, she turned and zeroed in on her next victim.

Piper grinned and suppressed a chuckle. Richie was a really nice guy, and exactly the kind of man she would like to get to know better. But he was a puzzle she wasn't sure she had time to figure out. At least not until Qball was behind bars. Then she considered his fiancée excuse. Maybe she had a chance after all, unless she was reading too much into it and she was just an easy out with Miss Boob-a-lot.

She glanced around the bar and noted every woman in the place was eating Richie up with hungry eyes. Maybe she should give up now before she made a fool of herself?

He was Prince Charming and she was the frog. Like every young girl, she had dreamed of being loved and cherished by her prince, a man not unlike Richie. But at the same time, she wanted to be the only thing on her man's mind and the way Richie drew the attention of the opposite sex, she knew that wasn't ever going to happen.

RICHIE: Le Beau Series

Silence engulfed them, making her hyper aware of his scent. What an odd but totally sexy cologne. It smelled like gun cleaner and patchouli. The scent drew her like a magnet. She was tempted to press her nose against his neck and breathe deeply. It would be so easy to lean into him and take a good long whiff.

Holy moly, Piper. Get a grip.

Richie was in a panic. Piper's thoughts were way off base. He had no interest in any other woman and he intended to set her straight on her misguided conceptions.

"Sorry about that," Richie apologized, as he reached for her hand and smoothed his thumb across her knuckles. He was pleased when she didn't pull away.

"It's quite all right. Obviously she inhaled too much hair spray when she shellacked her hair into submission and became confused," Piper replied straight faced.

Richie barked out a laugh. He liked his mate already.

For the next hour they made small talk. He flirted with her shamelessly and at the same time tried to wheedle out a clue about the danger surrounding her, but she was an expert at dodging questions. He was no closer to protecting Piper from whatever it was she feared than he was the first instant he'd met her.

He glanced toward the bar to order another round when a woman he knew from New Orleans caught his eye. *Shit. What is that bitch, Lori, doing here?* He quickly looked away and tried to blend in.

V.A. Dold & Tori Austin

Too late.

"Richie? Richie, is that you?" an intrigued voice from across the bar yelled.

Her high, whiny tone grated on his nerves. What had he seen in her? *Oh, yeah. She was easier than getting a beignet at the Café Du Monde, and willing to do anything.* That was a long time ago and now, she made him cringe and he felt like he needed a bath in lye.

"Lori. What brings you to St. Louis?" Richie asked in a frigid tone that could have frozen hell over.

"I met a new guy at Logan's Backwater Bar. I thought he was a really nice guy; boy, was I wrong. That shit brought me here and abandoned me," she spat.

Piper cocked a brow. What was he? Bimbo crack? This one wore a long, tight, black dress with plunging neckline to her navel, and a slit that went so high on her thigh it ended only inches from her waist. She watched, strangely intrigued, as Richie expressed zero sympathy for the woman – hooker – whatever she was.

Who is this guy? Don Juan?

"Call your sister. I'm sure she'll help you get home."

"I already did. She's driving up in the morning." The bimbo's head turned and she fixated on Piper. "Who's the broad?"

Piper crossed her arms and raised both brows.

RICHIE: Le Beau Series

Time seemed to slow as he first glanced at Piper and smiled warmly and then turned his attention to the woman standing before him. Richie's eyes narrowed and his lip curled back. "Leave, Lori. Now. Before I forget I'm a gentleman and throw you out."

Lori's eyes bulged in fear when he flashed his wolf fangs at her. As always, he was careful. No one else saw his display of aggression. Next time she insulted his mate, he wouldn't warn her, he'd just heave her ass out the door.

"Yes, of course," she stammered. As she stumbled over her dress and backed away, never taking her eyes off his very sharp white teeth now hidden discreetly by his tightened lips.

Once Lori was out the door, he turned back to Piper. Concern shot through him as her eyes glazed over like a person in the throes of a memory or daydream. His brows pulled tight. What had he done to trigger such an odd expression on his mates face?

Piper was shocked, she'd never had a man make it blatantly clear to another woman that he was with her and not interested. They weren't even on a real date and he'd behaved more honorably than any man she'd ever known. His eyes hadn't wandered over her body like men normally did to a woman. She'd never seen anything like it.

When she first met her ex-fiancé, Jeff, he'd been sweet, romantic, and loving. He was good looking, but not what she classified as hot. He was just a regular guy who treated her like a princess. That was what made the difference for her.

V.A. Dold & Tori Austin

The problem was, as soon as he had his ring on her finger, his true colors emerged. He criticized everything she did, wore, or said. Every hint of romance evaporated like he hadn't a clue what the word meant. Then the secret phone calls and late nights began.

She should have seen that coming a mile away. But as they say, love is blind. She had been trusting, never expecting a law-abiding man to be as violent, manipulating, and secretive as the bounties she often tracked.

She'd used her numerous tracking skills to follow him and a short two weeks later sent him packing. Apparently Jeff had an insatiable need to share his manhood with any willing woman that crossed his path. And there had been a shocking number of willing ladies to accept his offer. Thank God for best girlfriends and her little brother. They came running the minute she told them what happened.

She could still hear his voice as he shouted. "I'm going to destroy your life for this." Evidently, he was much more consistent in his follow through of a threat than maintenance of their relationship. No one said no to Jeff and now he was obsessed with destroying her.

Over the past nine months, the few dates she'd gone on, mysteriously ended in inexplicable cancelled dinner reservations, a keyed or towed car, a threatening gang of hoodlums following them, or all of them combined. Once, the sick bastard left a gutted cat on her front porch. To her date's credit, he hadn't let it end the evening.

RICHIE: Le Beau Series

After that, she'd gotten a restraining order to keep him away from her and her house. The problem was, that didn't limit him from damaging her date's car when they were away from her property.

When messing with her dates began to bore him, he added rumors to the mix. He even went as far as to contact her boss at the organization claiming she was a drug mule.

Fortunately, no one believed his dribble, which really pissed him off. The problem was, unless she could catch him causing damage or collect evidence of it, she would have to wait him out. That brought her back around to Richie and how utterly polar opposite he was from her ex. She may have only met him, but she saw his inner radiance, he was the real deal.

Shaking her head, she shrugged her memories off and laughed softly. "What did you do? You scared the crap out of her."

He shrugged. "I guess I can be a scary guy."

"Sure you can," she snorted.

To her utter surprise, he flashed a charming grin and leaned toward her to kiss the tip of her nose. Then he settled back to continue gently stroking his thumb across the back of her hand. "I don't understand why a woman would degrade herself like those two do."

Piper shook her head. "For the most part, many of the women who use sex for attention were either abused mentally or physically growing up. They have no idea how to get positive attention because no one has ever given them any."

V.A. Dold & Tori Austin

His lips thinned. "What is wrong with parents these days? How could anyone treat their child with less than unconditional love?"

She drew a breath, sighed. "It happens much more often than most people realize."

"Now I feel bad. Next time I see Lori, I'll try to be nicer."

Piper studied Richie's inner radiance more closely. After seeing him with his friends and now Lori, a person he disliked, she was curious to see if her initial assessment was correct.

When she wasn't on a job, she tried very hard to see the world in a positive light. Too long with the nasty dregs of society, where most of her bounties hid, and a person's attitude could become skewed. And not for the better.

Shortly after she started bounty hunting, a mentor taught her to look for the inner radiance people possess. The unique inner energy or soul, whatever you chose to call it, that made a person good and shone from within. She once was told it was an aura, but she didn't care what label was attached to the phenomenon.

People came in a variety of core personalities and behaviors. Her favorite were the people who honestly loved everyone. Somehow those people found a little bit of good everywhere.

Lately she struggled to see a person's inner light. That scared her more than any bounty could. She was losing herself piece by piece. She shouldn't even be on this job. She needed to end this chase quickly and find a soothing, peaceful place to live before she was completely lost.

RICHIE: Le Beau Series

A smile tugged at her lips. Richie was one of her favorite kind of people. *I could really like this guy. This wedding may not be a bust after all.*

She'd never dated a man who so completely ignored other women, especially when said women threw themselves at him. This one definitely deserved a closer look.

She wasn't in a position to date today, but that didn't mean she couldn't have a little fun. If Qball showed up, she would gently let Richie know she needed to take care of a few things and she would call him when it was finished.

And then once her tag was in police custody where he belonged, she would be more than ready to put everything she had into the kind of relationship a man like him would offer.

She looked at him with new interest, really looked at him. Yeah, she wanted to get to know this guy in more ways than one. *He's not a Don Juan at all. I wonder what he would do if I invited him to spend the night?*

The two of them spent a few more hours, talking and laughing. As time passed, she found herself flirting outrageously. She couldn't believe how at ease she was with him. But tomorrow was the wedding, and she needed to head to her room. It was now or never.

"I've really enjoyed meeting you and getting to know you, Richie."

"And I as well. We seem to be the only ones left in the bar, perhaps we should relocate before the bartender tosses us out?"

V.A. Dold & Tori Austin

"I would like that. We could go to my room. I have a little time yet before I have to get to bed. If I don't get enough sleep, I wake up with the most unattractive bags under my eyes." She glanced up to see he was surprised.

"I can't imagine you ever looking less than beautiful. Come on, I'll keep you company until you turn into a pumpkin."

Piper smiled and nodded. "All right."

Richie was on his feet and at her side before she could stand. She looked at him speculatively for a moment before taking his outstretched hand. How had he moved so fast?

He retained his hold once she was standing and they rode the elevator hand in hand. The exhilarating calm that descended over her during the short trip to her room with Richie felt – right. "This is me." She pulled her keycard from her purse, then glanced up to see him gazing into her eyes.

Slowly, he bent until his lips were a breath from hers and waited. There was only a moment's hesitation before she closed the gap and kissed him. The kiss was only a light graze of lips across lips.

Before she could turn to open the door, he wrapped one arm around her waist and tunneled the fingers of his other hand into her hair. Tipping her head just right, he coaxed her lips to open to him and deepened the kiss.

A fire was about to ignite in the hallway from the heat they were creating when a wolf whistle broke them apart. Whoever had seen them was already slipping into their room.

RICHIE: Le Beau Series

With a gleam in his eyes, Richie lifted her hand to his lips and kissed her knuckles gently. "I guess we better take this someplace more private."

Chapter 3

Shaky fingers and fumbling hands made the simple task of unlocking her door a nightmare. On the third try the light blessedly turned green. *Thank God for small favors*, she thought.

She was thankful that Richie stood quietly behind her and didn't try to commandeer the key. That would have been more embarrassment than she could have handled.

"Finally." she breathed, and cracked the door open. Then she looked at him over her shoulder.

Richie gazed back. Something flittered across his expression closely resembling possessiveness, but was quickly replaced by a smile tugging at the corners of his mouth. With a gentle hand, he smoothed her hair back from her face and tucked it behind her ear. His fingers slipped from the delicate shell and traced across her cheek, then paused to cup her face.

Piper closed her eyes and sighed. Then she turned her lips into his palm. "Would you like to come in for a few minutes?"

"I'd love to, mon amour."

RICHIE: Le Beau Series

Richie followed her and locked the door behind them. Then threw the security bar to ensure no one disturbed them again. When he turned, Piper was there.

Licking her lips, she reached up and brushed her fingers through his hair. "I've been wanting to do that all night." Her gaze fell to his mouth and she pulled him down to her lips for a long, deep kiss.

Richie was all in. Whatever his mate wanted to do, he was game.

Scooping her up as if she weighed nothing, he walked to the bed.

"Hey!" Piper squeaked. "I weigh a ton. You're going to hurt yourself."

"Hush. You're as light as a feather."

"That's not what my bathroom scale tells me. I swear it groans in pain every time I step on it."

"That's how little technology knows about a woman's figure. You're perfect, and I wouldn't change a thing about you."

His comment seemed to silence her.

Stopping next to the bed, he continued to cradle her in his arms. He wasn't ready to release his hold, not yet, not now when he finally had her where he wanted her.

Piper threaded her fingers more tightly in his hair, waiting for him to make a move. Heavy lidded with their coming passion, his eyes held hers, strangely glowing. They burned with his intense assessment of her face, pausing at her parted lips. Slowly, they closed, stealing their hypnotic trance, as his mouth descended to hers.

V.A. Dold & Tori Austin

Her heart thundered in her ears, she refused to admit she was falling in love with Richie. She'd always scoffed at her friends and family when they spouted nonsense about love at first sight. She wasn't scoffing now. And truth be told, it scared the crap out of her.

But she would be sensible. If all she got was one night with this incredible man, she would happily take it. The memories would just have to sustain her. Even one night was preferable to a lifetime of regret. The chance she was taking with Qball on her trail was minimal. It wasn't like he was going to crash through the door. Right now there was just the two of them, and this moment.

Their tongues danced and caressed, teeth nibbled, as they tasted and explored one another, pouring all their pent up attraction from hours in the bar into the kiss.

It was odd, she felt like she was coming home, which confused her. Normally it took time for her to feel comfortable with a man. Not that she'd been with a lot of men. The few she'd known had never responded to her touch and kisses the way Richie did.

She felt exhilarated and powerful. Every quiver, every moan, every sound of pleasure pouring from him spurred her on. Made her more bold and assertive than she ever dared be. The way he trembled under her fingertips, she'd swear he struggled for control. She'd never made a man tremble before. Richie really brought out her inner vixen. She liked it.

RICHIE: Le Beau Series

His pleasure was an intense aphrodisiac. Piper couldn't get close enough, even though they were chest to chest. Her boldness shocked her and aroused Richie. When she abandoned his lips to trail kisses across his chin to his throat, he tipped his head aside and obliged her exploration.

Richie was in heaven and hell. He was bound and determined to make their first time together unforgettable for both of them. That meant letting Piper set the pace and lead the way.

The wolf wanted to toss her on the bed and tear the clothes from her body. The man wanted to let her do whatever made her comfortable and pleased her. So he let her explore at her leisure and prayed for strength.

The hands Piper slipped under the collar of his shirt kneaded his skin like a contented cat. His wolf pressed closer, wanting to rub his scent all over her body. He rumbled and shifted her weight, sliding her feet to the floor. The motion raked her hardened buds down his chest and wedged his throbbing cock in the crevice of her thighs. The erotic contact ripped a groan from his lips.

When they finally came up for air and allowed a breath of space between them, he urged her backwards until her legs met the edge of the bed.

Holding her gaze, he slid his hands to the hem of her blouse and pulled it free from her skirt. One by one, he undid the pearly buttons. As each slipped through its buttonhole he widened the gap in the material and placed a kiss to the exposed flesh.

V.A. Dold & Tori Austin

Trailing hot licks and nibbles across her breasts, down her rib cage, to flick the tiny gold hoop at her navel. He hadn't realized navel piercings could be such a turn on. Slowly he rose from his knees and stood again. Then he eased the silky fabric from her shoulders and reclaimed her lips. Her moan of pleasure satisfied his wolf.

Devouring her with his eyes, he skimmed a finger over the satin trim of her bra. "So beautiful." His voice was rough and husky.

He felt delicate fingers working at the buttons of his shirt as he reached behind her to caress the soft skin of her back and release the clasp of her bra. Shockwaves of desire shot through his body when her chestnut hair brushed against his skin.

Slowly he eased back to slide the straps down her arms, freeing her full breasts. His breath hitched at the first sight of her bared from the waist up.

Piper worked to unbutton his shirt as he lowered his head, and flicked one puckered dusky nub with the tip of his tongue. She growled in frustration when she couldn't get the sleeves from his arms. With a low chuckle, he accommodatingly adjusted his position. Thankfully, he never took his mouth from her inflamed body.

His shirt fell free and she rewarded him with a throaty moan as she arched further into his hungry mouth, needing more. He switched his attentions to her other nipple, and she felt his hands skim down her body to lower the zipper of her skirt.

RICHIE: Le Beau Series

He paused his adoration to slip her skirt from her legs and toss it uncaringly across the room. With that, she was left in nothing but barely there panties. In a flash his arms were wrapped around her again. His muscular naked body felt amazing against her exposed skin. Piper pressed closer, molding her soft curves to his hard form. Damn, now here was a real man.

"Mmm." She arched invitingly into him, then realized she couldn't move.

She squirmed, needing to touch him, but was held too tightly to get at him. Richie relented and gave into her demands.

Piper stood on tiptoes and kissed his neck again, then she nibbled her way down his chest. Her hands were just as busy, caressing and loving his body. Her fingertips followed and traced every line and curve of his muscular arms. Compared to her pale skin tone, his skin was a smooth, taut, perfectly golden bronze. It felt incredible to run her hands over his hard, muscular chest and shoulders.

She glanced up and saw him close his eyes and let his head lull back. He seemed to really enjoy her kisses and caresses. She grinned when she licked his nipple and he rumbled loudly.

Richie's legs threatened to give way from quivering. His breath hitched and teeth clenched as he wrestled his wolf. He shook with the effort to go slow and pushed his beast into submission with an inner snarl.

V.A. Dold & Tori Austin

Just when he thought he had himself under control, her hands drifted below his navel, and a growl hissed through his teeth. He moved so fast her head spun. One second she was standing, and the next, she was flat on her back in the middle of the bed.

"Piper." Richie's chest heaved as he worked to calm himself enough to continue without taking her like a rutting buck. "Mon amour, please, I need a moment."

She frowned. "Why? Did I do something wrong?"

"No, cher, just the opposite. I want to make love to you slow and easy, but you have me so worked up I'm about to explode."

He stood with his hands on his hips, dragging long, deep breaths into his lungs, drinking her in, and then quickly shed his clothes. Piper lay propped on the pillows watching him with an expression of appreciation. He eased onto the bed and knelt before her, then reached for her panties.

Slowly he eased them from her hips and down her legs until they disappeared to the floor with the rest of their clothes. Now that she was gloriously naked before him, he had to take a breath and admire the magnificent woman laid out like a personal feast.

The way he devoured Piper with his gaze was intense. The stark desire written in his expression made her stomach flutter. His eyes lowered, taking in every bit of her, and then rose again, leaving a trail of heat in their wake. His look was ravenous. Passionate. Needful.

RICHIE: Le Beau Series

Her entire body burned with heat that pooled low, making her achy and needy. She'd never been brought close to orgasm by a look before. Richie made her so hot, she was going to burst into flame.

Like a prowling animal, he crawled up her body, kissing and licking as he went. Then he glanced at her face and frowned. She felt the heat of her blush rush up her neck when he reached for the fist she'd jammed in her mouth to muffle her cries.

She sure as heck didn't need the people on the other side of the wall to hear her. Ever so gently, he removed it. Then one by one, he uncurled her fingers, kissing and sucking each into his warm, wet mouth.

"Oh God!" Her toes curled tighter with each digit.

"Please, Piper. I crave the sounds of your pleasure." He whispered in her ear, and her heart was lost, truly and completely lost to this man.

Piper blushed hotter, but nodded in agreement.

His lips claimed hers in a long panty-wetting kiss that made her head spin. He skimmed her cheek with the tip of his nose and buried his face against her neck.

"Mmm, you smell so good."

He lay beside her, propped on one arm, kissing and caressing his way from her breasts to her heated core. God, his hands felt good roaming her body. Then he slipped one large palm between her thighs and she almost came off the mattress.

V.A. Dold & Tori Austin

Her need was so strong, her body felt like it was vibrating. One finger traced the line of her sex, and slipped in and she was in heaven. Finally, some relief from the ache he'd built in her center.

Piper moaned and ran her fingers through his hair as he nuzzled and adored her body. He was magnificently put together. Muscular back, wide shoulders, lean hips, and the sexiest ass she'd ever laid eyes on. Mix that body with the man she was coming to know and she was about to spontaneously combust. She might turn into a pile of ash right there on the bed.

"I have to taste you."

She watched him reposition, easing her legs further apart to accommodate his wide shoulders. His eyes locked with hers, glowing more brightly than humanly possible. Then he lowered his head and the glow was gone.

Warm, wet lips, softly kissed her inner thigh. She shivered with anticipation when he blew a gentle, warm breath across her inflamed core before he began a slow delicious torture of unhurried licks.

His soft hair felt like silk brushing her thighs as he slowly drew his tongue through the slickness of her folds and swirled it over her throbbing nub.

Piper shuddered and moaned.

Richie's deep rumble vibrated in his throat, creating a stimulating friction like she'd never experienced before. Not even with her favorite vibrator.

Her hands reached for her breasts, to roll and stimulate her nipples.

RICHIE: Le Beau Series

Richie lifted his head slightly. She hesitated when she saw him watching with much too intent eyes and began to place her hands back at her sides. *There must be really strange lighting in here. His eyes are glowing like hot embers.*

"Please, mon amour. Touch yourself. Enjoy your passion. A confident woman is sexy as hell."

Bolstered by his words, her inhibitions evaporated. She brought her hands back to her breasts as he growled and lowered his head.

Richie was some kind of master with his mouth and tongue. Then he plunged inside, and flicked her clit with his thumb. She shattered.

She was panting so hard she couldn't form words, even if her brain decided to reengage. Before she could recover, he slipped one finger in. Holy hell, he was going to kill her with pleasure. And when he added a second, she knew her life was going to end right there in that bed.

"I want to see you cum for me again. You're beautiful in the throes of passion."

He stroked faster, and the pressure rose. "Please, Richie. I can't take any more."

"Let go for me, mon amour. I've got you." He used his free hand to stimulate her clit as he plunged into her clenching heat. Then he crooked them inside her, and rubbed a spot she never knew existed. Intense pleasure tore through her body, leaving her weak and shaking.

"I love your mouth on me," she panted.

V.A. Dold & Tori Austin

He made her feel like he was worshipping her. Slowly, his palms ran from her hips and along her waist. Dipping his head, he traced each rib with his tongue as he made his way to her aching breasts. Licking and suckling.

He made that strange rumbling sound again when her moans turned to cries of passion. He kissed his way back to her lips and feasted on her mouth before blazing a trail of kisses across her jaw and down her neck, pausing to nuzzle her there.

Piper skimmed her fingers down his back and around his hips. When her fingertips skimmed his erection, she felt it jump. She grinned when Richie sucked in a sharp breath next to her ear. Gently, she traced the length of him with her fingertips before wrapping her hand around him. Stroking him in a tight fist.

Moisture glistened on the tip. He was weeping in preparation for her. She slid her fingertips up until she held him just below the bulbous head. In slow circles, she rubbed the pre-cum across the crest with her thumb. He let out a gasp as she stroked to the base and back again.

The action sent Richie into a growling frenzy, arching off the mattress, pressing himself harder into her hand. He thought his head was going to explode in ecstasy. Mindlessly, his hips pumped, working him in and out of her fist. Damn, her hands felt amazing. He was in heaven.

Then she leaned over and took him in her mouth. He roared, unable to hold back his release, he emptied himself into her greedy mouth.

RICHIE: Le Beau Series

Piper's smiled with satisfaction as he slumped against the pillows. "Aren't paybacks grand?"

"It was fantastic, but I had other plans for you. Give me a few minutes to recover."

She raised her eyebrows and grinned at him. "It might take a little longer than a few minutes."

"Not for me," he panted.

Piper shook her head and he felt her disbelief. She thought he was exaggerating.

He wasn't.

About ten minutes later, he propped himself on one elbow and gazed into her eyes. "Are you ready for round two?"

"There's no way…" Then his erection twitched against her thigh. "Okay, maybe you are."

Chuckling, he kissed her hard, demanding everything she had to give. Slowly, he caressed his way to her heated core, nuzzling and feasting at her breasts.

Quietly he murmured against her flesh, "Will you give yourself, body and soul, to complete this man and his wolf?"

"What did you say?"

He slid his palm over her most intimate spot. "Are you ready to give yourself to me?"

"Please, Richie."

He kissed her lips, then laid hot, delicious kisses down her body, nipping and laving as he brushed his palm up her inner thigh to her weeping core. Gently, he ran his fingers through the seam, then slid one finger deep inside. Stroking her clit with his thumb in time with his fingers.

Piper whimpered, rocking her hips against his hand. She was right on the edge.

Before she could orgasm he removed his fingers. Held her gaze, and licked each clean. Then he cradled himself between her thighs.

He was painfully aroused, thick and long. Hard enough to pound nails. Slowly, he rubbed his erection through her damp curls. Richie locked eyes with her and entered her, sliding all the way to the hilt. With a slow, gentle rhythm, he rocked against her.

A groan of pleasure filled the room as he started a slow, deep pounding pace that drove her crazy, pulling almost completely out before filling her again. With each deep stroke, he heard her keening cries grow louder.

Piper wrapped her legs around him and pressed with her heels. He slid in a fraction deeper. He couldn't get enough of this woman and the pleasure she gave him.

As he felt her nearing her climax, he began thrusting in earnest.

"I can't believe you're mine. Piper! You're so tight, you feel so damn good."

His mate met him thrust for thrust. Suddenly, she was shattering with ecstasy around him. Her channel clamped down hard as she came, screaming his name.

She had him in a mind-blowing grip. One more glide and he joined her in release. The aftershocks quaked her body, milking him with rhythmic clenching. He held himself up enough to

RICHIE: Le Beau Series

not crush her as he gasped for breath. Then he collapsed to her side.

"That was amazing," she breathed.

"Yes, you are," he panted.

She looked at him quizzically, but didn't remark on his response, instead laughed at his satiated expression.

A few minutes later, Richie propped himself up and gazed into her eyes. "I would like to stay the night, but if you're uncomfortable with that, my room is only four doors down."

She chewed her lower lip for a moment. "Maybe it would be best if we stayed in our own rooms tonight. I've never been comfortable with someone else in my bed. Please don't be offended, I loved every minute of my time with you, but everything has happened so fast and it's a lot to get used to in one day."

He smiled warmly and pulled her tightly against his side. "No offense taken. I totally understand, just remember, I'm only four doors away. If you need me for anything, call and I'll be here immediately."

They snuggled for a minute before he stood to dress. Then he pulled her into his arms for a final long kiss. "Goodnight, mon amour. I'll see you in the morning."

"Goodnight, Richie, and thank you for understanding."

V.A. Dold & Tori Austin

Chapter 4

Richie woke with a smile on his face. He couldn't believe his luck; he'd met his mate! And they'd made love. He languidly stretched, and an image of her in his bed popped into his mind. *Now there's an idea.*

He tapped into his precognition to see the future. Maybe he would be able to see her in his bed tonight. Nothing came to him. He concentrated harder. Still nothing. Shit, it had been so long since he'd tried to see his own future; he'd forgotten it didn't work for his personal life. He was only able to see other people's futures.

Ah, hell. He might as well shower and find some breakfast. He would simply make his desire a reality the old fashioned way. He'd shower his mate with romance. That was the least she deserved.

*****

Piper was showered, and her hair was done, now for makeup. She was about to stroke her eyelashes with mascara when she got a very naughty idea. *I wonder if I can see what Richie is doing?*

RICHIE: Le Beau Series

Until now she'd only used her strange gift if she were in danger and in need of a little extra something to get out of it. Maybe it only worked if her adrenaline was pumping? She smiled and shrugged her shoulders. It couldn't hurt to try.

Closing her eyes, she concentrated on his hotel room. She pictured a floor plan identical to her own and focused her view four doors down. His empty rumpled bed came into focus. Slowly she turned three hundred sixty degrees. He wasn't there. Piper moved her focus toward the door, her plan was to search down the hall and as far as the restaurant just off the hotel lobby.

Her plan came to a screeching halt when she reached the open door to his bathroom. A new piece of information made itself abundantly clear, Richie showered with the door open. She was about to glance away and end her little spy caper when the curtain pulled back and exposed Richie in all his incredible glory. *HOLY CROW! He's well endowed even flaccid!*

After last night she knew he was built like a brick house. That didn't mean she was tired of looking at him, not by a long shot. And a dripping wet Richie was mind blowing.

Richie's gaze jumped to hers. *SHIT, I'm so busted. But how the hell did he see me?* Piper slammed her gift down. Shit. Shit. Shit.

V.A. Dold & Tori Austin

*****

Richie frowned. He'd swear he'd felt Piper's energy, but now there was nothing. *That was strange. I must be imagining things.* He wanted to see her and touch her so badly he could taste it.

Once he was dressed, he'd knock on her door. Maybe they could have breakfast together? Easily remedied, with a thought he donned dress pants, a white shirt, and casual leather shoes. Ready to go. The shifter power of dressing or undressing with a thought was his favorite thing at the moment.

He knocked and waited. Nothing. Not a sound was heard on the other side of her door. She must have gone to the restaurant already. Grinning excitedly, he hit the elevator. When he reached the only restaurant in the hotel, his shoulders slumped and his smile faded. She wasn't there either. The girls were probably still sleeping, so he ordered a table for one.

After breakfast, Richie searched high and low, and came up empty handed. He couldn't feel her energy either. She must have left the hotel. At least she was guaranteed to be at the church. He'd find her and then not let her out of his sight.

When he couldn't find his mate, he headed to Billie's and then Helen's hotel rooms. He knocked and waited, no one answered. Dang it, the hotel was like a ghost town. Discouraged, he returned to his room. He needed to change for the wedding anyway.

RICHIE: Le Beau Series

*****

     A couple hours later, his wolf perked up the instant he exited his car in the church parking lot. She was here, somewhere. Energized by thoughts of touching Piper again, he bounded up the church steps. The lobby was wall-to-wall people. Luckily, he was taller than most.
     He took a position along a wall that would afford a good view of the entire space. His initial search failed to locate her or his friends. Her scent was present, but faint. It must have been some time since she was in that part of the church. He called on his wolf senses; if he concentrated hard, he may be able to follow her energy.
     Slowly, he waded through the crowd. He was pretty sure she was down the hall on his left. He found the men's and women's restrooms and what must be a dressing room. He bet money on the dressing room, but he sure as hell wasn't going in there.
     Hell, nothing to do but wait. He hated waiting. Claiming a bit of wall at the edge of the lobby and hallway, he crossed his arms and leaned back.
     What the heck was taking the ladies so long? Thirty minutes later he still held up the same patch of wall. The lobby emptied as people were ushered to their seats. Richie had no choice but to leave his station, and join the crowd.

V.A. Dold & Tori Austin

The groom stood at the front of the church and still no Piper. Richie's wolf raged. The beast wanted to take action and track its mate. He braced his arms on the bench of the wooden pew, prepared to stand and leave the church when she hurried through the door and took a seat in the front row. *Finally*, he breathed.

Richie lost sight of her when everyone stood as Theresa, escorted by both her mother and father, walked down the aisle. She was stunning. He'd only ever seen her in jeans and a T-shirt. Wow, she was beautiful. His mind immediately pictured Piper in a wedding dress, walking toward him, as he stood proudly at the front of the church. The excited hammering of his heart about beat his ribs to dust.

Once they were seated again, he paid little attention to the wedding. His eyes were riveted on his mate. Like a lovesick pup, he held his breath, and willed her to turn slightly so he could see her face. What was he? Stupid? He could get her attention with telepathy. They were mates and as such were gifted with the ability to speak to one another telepathically.

Piper, he whispered gently into her mind.

He watched her shoulders stiffen. Slowly, she turned and searched the church.

Piper, it's me, Richie. Don't ask why, I'll explain later, but we can speak telepathically to each other.

Her shoulders rose slightly as she sucked in a breath and held it.

RICHIE: Le Beau Series

You can speak to me as well. Just think what you want to say and imagine saying it to me. Richie explained.

Is this for real? I'm not losing my mind, am I?

Richie's chuckle sounded in her thoughts. *Yes. It's for real.*

You can read my mind?

No, cher. I can hear what you direct at me.

Thank god! How is this possible?

Richie slapped a hand over his mouth to contain the laughter that threatened to erupt. *Like I said, I'll explain later, it's complicated.*

I'm holding you to that, because let me tell you, this is freaky.

You've got a deal. Tonight after the wedding dance when we can talk in private I'll tell you all about it.

Okay, I guess that might be for the best. This is too strange to talk about in public. People will think we've lost our minds.

Exactly. Hey, where were you this morning? I missed you at breakfast.

Sorry, I had appointments with the girls in the wedding party. She paused, then continued. *Will you save a dance for me tonight?*

How about I save all my dances for you?

There was a long pause. *Okay.*

I better let you enjoy the wedding. Meet me outside the church after the ceremony is over.

Okay, I'll look for you.

V.A. Dold & Tori Austin

Thank Goddess for a short service! The instant the bride and groom walked passed his seat and into the lobby, he stood and rushed from the church. His gaze fixed onto the huge double doors. His heart accelerated as he waited for Piper to emerge. Wedding guests flowed down the steps and still no Piper. Where had she gotten off to now?

Finally, he spotted Billie. "Hey, gorgeous." He greeted her with a smile and gave her a hug.

"Hi! Wasn't the wedding beautiful?"

"It sure was. Theresa was breathtaking."

"I know, right! Her dress was to die for." She narrowed her eyes on Richie. "What are you up to?"

Richie's brows rose. "What? Why would you ask me that?"

She narrowed her eyes further and poked his chest. "I know that look. You're up to something."

"Actually, I'm looking for Piper. Have you seen her?"

"No!" Billie covered her heart dramatically. "The Great Richie has a crush?"

Richie laughed and put an arm around her shoulders. "Shut it before I give you a noogie and mess up your fancy hair."

Billie stepped back and touched her fancy up do. "You wouldn't dare! It took forever for the beautician to create this man catnip."

Richie barked out a laugh. "Man catnip?"

"That's right." She nodded and leaned closer. "I've already gotten numbers from three guys."

"Sorry to break it to you, cher. But that's because you're a bridesmaid. Guys always hit on the bridesmaids. It's a thing."

RICHIE: Le Beau Series

Billie put her hands on her hips. "What kind of 'thing' are you talking about?"

"Ah, hell. You really don't know?"

She crossed her arms and tapped her toe. "If I knew, I wouldn't be asking you."

Richie cringed and leaned away from Billie before he said as quickly as he could, "It's kind of a bragging thing for guys to bag a bridesmaid."

She gaped at him, and blinked. Without a word she reached into her tiny bridesmaid purse and fished out three even tinier slips of paper. She ripped them once, twice, and then a final time before tossing the confetti sized scraps over her shoulder.

Then she lifted her chin and slipped a hand into the crook of Richie's arm. "Let's find Piper, shall we? I'll even let you escort all this sexy, man catnip."

Richie grinned and gave her a wink. "I'd be honored to escort your sexiness."

Before they could find Piper, Billie was summoned to join the wedding party for pictures. At first Richie hung around and watched. His hope was she would appear since the girls were here. She didn't. Apparently, the personal attendant wasn't required for the wedding party shots. Who knew?

After forty-five minutes of "look this way," "smile," or "could you move a little the other direction?" he'd had enough. The reception would be in the ballroom of the hotel so he headed back to locate a stiff drink. If the Goddess happened to be in an extra helpful mood, he might even find Piper waiting for him there.

V.A. Dold & Tori Austin

*****

  Piper had every intention to escape the wedding as quickly as possible. Her aunt, Margery, the mother of the groom, had other plans. Some of the wedding guests left their gifts at the church and now a small mountain of shiny packages needed to be relocated to the reception.
  With a heavy sigh, she glanced one last time at the double doors that would take her to Richie. Her fascination with their telepathic link would have to wait. Since she was parked next to the exit door at the rear of the church, the logical option was to get a couple people to help lug the gifts through the church and out the back.
  It took a few trips, but the task was done and her car was packed solid.
  Piper puffed a strand of hair from her face and shut the trunk of her car. "All right, that's the last of them. Could you guys meet me at the hotel to unload?"
  "Sure, we'll meet you at the front entrance with a luggage rack," one of the men said as he turned to find his own vehicle.
  Slightly overheated from the exertion of repeated trips back and forth loading gifts, she turned up her AC and got on the road. The sooner she was done, the sooner she could track down Richie.
  Fifteen minutes later, her assignment was completed and she searched the ballroom. It looked like most of the guests were either still at the church or somewhere in between.

RICHIE: Le Beau Series

Her heart sank. Where was he? Piper grimaced when she took a step to leave and search the lobby and bar. The shoes were pinching her toes something awful. A sadist with a grudge against women must have designed the heels she wore.

Grateful she always had a backup plan, she made a beeline for her room and the comfortable flats that waited there. Fashion be damned, she was attached to her toes and planned to keep them.

Once in her room, she grabbed the flats and kicked off the heels. Closing her eyes, she smiled and sighed. Blissful relief. She spotted her laptop sitting on the bedside table and powered it up. Qball was still out there and for some reason he was fixated on her.

Quickly she glanced down the list of unread emails, when she finally found the one from her employer she clicked it. Shit, her bounty was on the move and seen just outside of town by the local sheriff.

This guy must be truly insane; bounties didn't chase the bounty hunter. Behavior like that was suicidal. Several email messages, text messages, phone calls, and one pair of shoes later she was back in the ballroom. Her side trip must have taken longer than she planned. The reception was packed with guests and the party was in full swing.

At least she was forewarned about Qball. Along with her new shoes, she'd also strapped on her dress weapons. It was better to be prepared than caught off guard. The hotel manager had assured her security was on high alert and extra officers were posted in strategic locations. Ryker 'Qball' Quintrell wasn't getting anywhere near her family.

Her attention turned to the head table when she heard the tinkle of silverware on glass.

Her uncle stood and said, "Everyone please take your seats, dinner is about to be served."

Little table tents with names printed on them dictated where to sit. From her earlier visit, she knew Richie wasn't assigned to her table tonight. The string of delays, which kept her and Richie apart, had graduated from bothersome coincidences to full-blown annoyance. Unhappily she took her seat and placed her napkin in her lap.

Piper used her predicament to locate Richie. With everyone forced to remain in one spot for the next thirty minutes she would be able to systematically sweep the room. There, three tables over. He was directly in front of her, and dang, looking straight at her. Her breath hitched, she felt like a side of beef in front of a starved lion.

Richie was silent throughout dinner, his focus on his mate, not the inane chit chat people felt required to generate with complete strangers. He noticed Piper rarely offered a response either. They were both too busy watching each other to bother with the people at their tables.

His fingers itched to touch her. Forced to gaze at, but not touch one's mate was cruel and unusual punishment for a shifter. His fingers flexed again. If he was forced to wait much longer, his claws were going to make an appearance.

RICHIE: Le Beau Series

Helen's whisper of his name caught his attention. He glanced from Piper to his friends at the head table. They all sported blatantly curious smiles. Their faces were too alight with interest for his comfort. He'd seen them like this before, and it never ended well. Whatever they thought they knew was eating them alive. He was screwed. They'd never let up until they had the entire story.

Too bad. He had no intention of enlightening them. This was between him and Piper. Regardless, he couldn't tell them about mates or shifters if he wanted to. So, he cocked a brow and gave them a look. If they were smart, which he knew they were, they would back off.

He held his glare until each of them looked away. Then he turned his attention back to his mate. He captured her gaze again and held it. She seemed to be on guard. Why would a gorgeous woman at her cousin's wedding be so edgy? Who was she looking for? He scanned the room himself, ready for any threat to his mate.

Piper sucked in a breath, as heat surged through her body. She felt Richie's intensity like an intimate caress from twenty-five feet away. Her brows furrowed and she concentrated on his eyes. They appeared to glow like they had last night in her room. Memories of his eyes glowing made her blush like a schoolgirl with a crush. The effect excited her, which in turn worried her.

She swallowed hard on a bone-dry throat and blinked. The glow was gone. Either he'd turned and the light hit his eyes differently or she'd imagined it.

V.A. Dold & Tori Austin

Piper reached for her water, shook her head to clear her wild and crazy thoughts, and took a good long drink. The last thing she needed was a distraction and illusions. Qball was stalking her and he was far too close for comfort.

The past thirty minutes felt like a lifetime. Finally, the clamor of dinner plates and silverware being cleared filled the room. About time, too. She needed a drink to calm her nerves and clear her mind of romance.

Piper took a sip of her whiskey Coke.

Damn, that's good.

She nodded her approval to the bartender and stepped out of line. One well-mixed cocktail was exactly what the doctor ordered. She was on the job, which meant limited alcohol, so this would have to last the night.

After years as a bounty hunter the habit of locating every exit and potential danger was deeply ingrained. A wedding reception was no exception. She found a spot away from the crowd and stood to the side of the room, sipped her cocktail and secretly observed Richie.

He was genuine and courteous, his manners leaning toward old world and refined. In the short time she'd watched, two things she found incredibly sexy became evident. He was intelligent and had a sense of humor.

She eavesdropped on a conversation between him and the bridesmaids when she'd made the circuit around the room. It seemed last night hadn't been a fluke or an act. Richie was the real deal. Everything she'd ever wanted and smoking hot.

RICHIE: Le Beau Series

His suit jacket did nothing to hide his wide shoulders and sculpted chest. Piper leaned a little to the right to get a better look. Holy Moses did he have a nice caboose in those dress pants! She clenched her hands, her fingers itching to stroke his thick dark hair.

Taking a deep breath, she closed her eyes, remembering his scent. He'd smelled so darn good. Opening her eyes again, she longed to see his expression. If he turned around, she knew she'd see a twinkle of amusement in his deep brown eyes.

Richie shivered with awareness. The tiny hairs on the back of his neck stood at attention. They acted as a warning system when he was being watched or hunted.

And he was definitely being watched.

Intently.

Casually, he turned, ever so slightly. Piper stood hidden in the shadows of a large floor plant, with her eyes fixed on him. As if a thread were tied tightly around his heart, he was drawn to her.

Without thought, his feet began to walk him across the room. He'd waited one hundred and fifty years to feel like this. The intensity both intrigued and thrilled him.

He couldn't help but stare. He was both mesmerized by her beauty and afraid if he blinked she'd slip away and he would never find her again.

Like a mate should, she'd enchanted his wolf as completely as she had the man. In his mind, his wolf howled a sappy love song, rejoicing in the future that stood before them. He agreed with his wolf's assessment wholeheartedly.

V.A. Dold & Tori Austin

"Piper, I've been looking for you."

"Hi, Richie. I'm sorry I didn't meet you after the wedding. I was shanghaied into transporting a load of gifts from the church."

He smiled at that and reached for her hand. "I wondered what happened. If I'd known, I would have helped."

Piper swooned like a ninny when he gently kissed each knuckle. His lips were soft and warm, easing the zing that shot up her wrist. Heat flashed through her body with startling ferocity. The condition worsened when her gaze clashed with his ravenous eyes.

Wait...What? Ravenous? For me?

Maybe last night had meant more to him than a one-night stand or a wedding fling. This was getting out of hand. She really needed to find a way to tell him she couldn't be with him right now.

She allowed him to pull her from her hiding place and guide her to an empty table.

A server held her tray steady as Richie plucked two glasses of champagne from the cluster and offered her one. "What were you doing back there?"

What the heck was she going to say? Checking the room for a crazed killer? Spying on his total hotness? Both were the truth. Neither were things he needed to know. But he steadily watched her, studied her with his damn unwavering gaze, and waited. She had to think fast.

"Checking to see if the plant needed water."

RICHIE: Le Beau Series

Richie laughed, and his tempting lips curved into a contagious smile. "Goddess, I love your sense of humor."

"I'm here all night. Stick around, maybe I'll do a stand-up comic routine."

They chatted and asked a few casual questions about each other. The blasé thing two people do when they are getting to know each other. What's your favorite color? Do you like action movies? Etc.

The amusement from earlier continued to warm his gaze, only now it evolved into something hotter, and much sexier. He stole her breath without moving a muscle. With only his personality, he revved her engine.

Piper took a sip and tried to swallow. Which was a problem because her hand shook. Shit, her hands were always…ALWAYS rock steady.

She took a quick survey around the room. When Richie touched her, her hand jerked away instinctively. Expecting Qball to appear had her on edge and his touch set off her automatic reflexes.

His dark brows pulled closer and his jaw tightened. "What has you so rattled, cher?"

"Nothing," Piper answered tightly as she pushed from the table and practically ran to the other end of the room. She drew a breath, blew it out again. She couldn't allow her calm to be affected. And Richie shattered her calm like no one ever had. If she didn't pull it together, she was as good as dead. In desperate need of regaining control, she put a respectable distance between them.

V.A. Dold & Tori Austin

She needed a moment to catch her breath and survey the room, a habit she would not soon grow out of. The life of a bounty hunter brought a certain amount of - unease into a person's life.

A thorough search told her Quintrell hadn't magically appeared amongst the wedding guests. Regardless of the security posted around the hotel, she couldn't shake the feeling he was going to appear.

None of her marks had ever done anything of the sort. They always ran, as far and as fast as they could. For a criminal to come to her, was insane. The problem was, he WAS certifiably insane. By the courts, no less.

Damn, she should have retired like she'd planned. Why she allowed Jerry to talk her into one last tag, she hadn't a clue. The way this job was going, it could very well be the last thing she did, and that just pissed her off. She had plans, and they required she be above ground and breathing.

Richie sat back, confused. He could have been hit by a falling meteor and felt less shock. *What the hell just happened?* Piper fled as far from him as she could get. He knew better than to pursue her. That would only make matters worse. So, he stayed where he was and watched. One way or another, he was going to find a way to get close to her again tonight.

RICHIE: Le Beau Series

Chapter 5

After dancing the dumbass hokey pokey, it took a minute to catch her breath. Whoever made that dance up was a nutcase, too. If her cousin hadn't pulled her onto the floor, she sure as heck wouldn't have been caught dead doing it.

Then to make matters worse, the woman next to her was in mile high stilettos. She was so worried she'd need to call an ambulance, she kept putting the wrong foot in. Who in their right mind does that 'right leg in' crap in a full-length gown and four inch heels?

The juvenile dance ended while she moved along the edge of the dance floor. Her feet slowed as the DJ started a new song – a slow, romantic ballad. The kind that made her picture moonlight strolls on a beach, and candlelight dinners. Piper smiled as Bob took Theresa by the hand and commandeered the floor. It was apparent the bride and groom took ballroom dance lessons.

Their intimate contact unlocked her long-ago caged heart and opened the door a crack. Piper's attention was pinned to Bob's hand, clenched around Theresa's waist as he kissed her, passion permeating his every move. They were astounding. Until last night, no one had ever kissed her with such emotion. She'd never met a man she wished would kiss her that way, until Richie.

It wasn't long before others joined the happy couple. She leaned against the wall and smiled. Letting herself enjoy the reception and forget all thoughts of Qball, if for only a minute. Still grinning, she walked to the cash bar. A mirror hung behind the bartender, an attractive and welcomed touch. She could turn her back to the crowd and still see the room.

Piper was ordering a soda when she heard a familiar voice behind her. The one person she was avoiding. Richie.

"It's inspiring to see two people so deeply in love."

Her stiffened shoulders were the only evidence he'd surprised her. Her face flushed with heat, but her eyes remained firmly on her drink. "Yeah," she agreed with a sigh. "It is."

Slowly, she lifted her gaze from the drink she stirred to the mirror and met his eyes. He felt the impact like a punch to the gut and the tingle in his scalp made him want to scratch like he had fleas.

His pulse pounded through his veins, and flooded his groin. Even though he kept his expression composed, a slight tick began at the corner of his left eye. His gaze jumped to her mouth when an amused grin tugged at the corners of her lips. She was enjoying his failed effort and obvious discomfort. Damn, she was more intoxicating than an entire case of scotch.

RICHIE: Le Beau Series

She took her time, making him wait. Finally, she glanced at his reflection again and he was able to see her eyes. He loved the silvery blue color and the way they often gave her emotions away. Then, he swore he felt fingers feather through his hair like a sensual touch.

He held her gaze, felt a flutter of excitement, and his chest squeezed. The sensations made it difficult to breathe. She was teasing him, forcing him to work for every glance and touch.

Finally, she turned toward him and leaned back against the bar.

"Why aren't you dancing?" he asked.

"I was taking a break. Besides, no one asked me."

"I'm asking." Richie stepped onto the temporary dance floor and held out his hand.

She took a breath. He held his.

"Piper?" he prompted with a lopsided grin.

Piper stiffened. Shit, he'd caught her ogling him. She gave him a slight, reserved smile. Her gaze flicked to his hand and then his face. The moment their eyes met, she felt a flutter in her stomach. He definitely distracted her. Ah, heck. What could one dance hurt? Piper set her drink on the bar and asked the bartender to watch it, then accepted his outstretched hand and followed him to the floor.

He grinned at her, a quick, confident smile. The instant their hands touched, unseen sparks jumped from him to her and back again. From his inhaled breath, she knew he felt the zing of excited energy too.

V.A. Dold & Tori Austin

What the heck was that?
The tiny sting wasn't enough to hurt, more startling than anything. She'd never experienced anything like it. It was as disconcerting as his smile, or a glance from his dreamy eyes with their teasing twinkle. How did he send her body into a meltdown so easily?

A sudden, unexpected realization stopped her cold. She wasn't even aware she'd stopped dancing in the middle of the crowded dance floor. She felt alive. Richie made her feel alive. When had she stopped living life?

Like a far off voice, she heard Richie calling her name. "Piper? Are you okay?"

"Yes. Yes, sorry."

They began to waltz again, only this time, Richie directed their movements across the floor until they were on the very edge.

Quietly he whispered, "Want to tell me what happened back there?" With his lips close to her ear, his breath was warm on her neck.

"You made me realize something and it came as a bit of a shock. That's all." She shook her head, then tilted it to one side. "You're a dangerous man, Richie. At least to me you are."

His lips twitched into a mischievous grin. "Oh, cher, you have no idea. But I'm only intimately dangerous to you."

That wicked smile implied all manner of activities that had nothing to do with dancing and everything to do with behind closed doors activities. Intimate horizontal, hell against the wall, male and female calisthenics.

RICHIE: Le Beau Series

Before she could excuse herself and get her mind back on track, Richie swept her across the dance floor with an expertise only acquired through professional dance instruction. The man had skills. As Piper followed his lead like a pro, she asked herself, why his softly whispered teasing, revved her engine and piqued her interest, not to mention other things. There was something intense and possessive in his eyes. And dang, it was appealing.

They moved in unison, two people in a room filled with friends and family and yet completely alone. Not even a whisper from her gown or his suit was heard. For a moment, she wondered what his reaction would be if he knew she was covered in concealed weapons.

Unlike the rest of the guests, her formal attire included a thigh holster that came fully loaded with a 9 mm she could hide from view in the palm of her hand. And then, of course, there were her tiny throwing knives, two in her bodice and three strapped to her calf.
Not to mention the ornamental hair pins holding her chic messy up-do in place. Both honed to razor sharp points with lethal serrated edges. The protective sheath covering the deadly hair adornments took a full month to create. Like many of her weapons, she made them herself. Customized for perfect balance and weight.

And of course, thanks to a few military friends, everything was camouflaged with a high tech reflective shell that mirrored its surroundings so she could wear them in plain sight without detection.

V.A. Dold & Tori Austin

Under limited scrutiny, most people wouldn't even see a weapon, only skin or hair.

"Richie, I need to ask you a personal question. It's going to sound adolescent, but it's important."

"You can ask me anything, Piper."

"Are you playing with me? You know, just having a wedding fling. Or, are you truly interested?"

His gaze met hers. Burned into hers. "I've never been more serious about a woman, cher. Ever."

"In that case, since I can't keep my distance where you're concerned, and you don't intend to give me the space I need to get this job done, I need to brief you on a situation." Piper took his hand and led him from the dance floor.

"Let me get your drink and we can talk."

She took a seat and watched Richie cross the room with the drink she left at the bar. This man approaching had managed to capture her attention, ensnaring her in a web that caused her to be oblivious to everyone and everything around her. And that was the crux of the problem.

Richie prepared himself mentally for what she was going to reveal. Whatever it was, she had nothing that could compare to his wolfy secret.

"Okay." Piper took a deep breath. "Where to begin? Richie, I'm a bounty hunter. I'm contracted by a secret government office to catch criminals who have escaped and turn them over to the police."

RICHIE: Le Beau Series

"Really? I've never met one before. So, what's the problem?"

"You."

Richie's eyebrows rose. "Me?"

"Yes, you. I can't be distracted in any way. My loss of focus could be a death sentence for a bounty hunter on the trail of a murderer, like I am. Especially when my tag knows he's being hunted."

Richie took her hand and held it between his own. "You couldn't be more wrong. I can help you catch this guy."

Piper shook her head. "I can't afford the distraction, any distraction. And taking a civilian along on a hunt is out of the question. Attending my cousin's wedding was dangerous enough for all involved. I need my wits about me.

"When I accepted this contract, I took it knowing it would be my last. I'm tired of the constant travel and endless chasing. I know I can handle this mark if I see him coming, but this bastard is good, really good, and it will take everything I have to collar him without someone getting hurt.

"I can't risk you, Richie. I'm sorry, but I can't involve a civilian. It's too dangerous."

"What if I told you I have special gifts? As a matter of fact, I'm sure you do, as well."

Air whooshed into her lungs. *How could he know?*

"Look, I need to visit the men's room. Promise me you'll be here when I get back."

V.A. Dold & Tori Austin

"Sure, I'll be here."

"Good. We will finish this discussion when I return. I'll only be a minute." Finally, he knew how much danger his mate was in. His wolf was snarling with its hackles raised, ready to do battle. Nothing and no one would be allowed to harm their mate.

*****

Piper watched him go as she walked to the bar to refresh her drink. She was halfway to the table where he'd left her when a shiver ran up her spine. She was about to search the room when a hand clamped around her wrist.

"Dance with me, hunter."

Piper calmly turned, knowing who gripped her arm without needing to look. She forced a polite smile as her suspicions were confirmed. Qball. The man who'd murdered a family of four in their sleep. And they were only his most recent victims. He'd destroyed five families before being caught. His luck held when he was jailed in a facility with a corrupt warden. A large payoff to the right person and Qball was back on the street.

With her extensive training, he didn't pose much of a physical threat to her. He was average height and slightly built. For a woman like her, with police academy training, he would be easily handled.

His features were soft, almost cherub like which only enhanced his completely deceptive appearance that hid a monster from the world. He was a serial killer hiding in plain sight.

RICHIE: Le Beau Series

His grin widened, oozing evil, like the stench that drifted from a dumpster in one hundred degree weather. Clean-shaven and in a suit, he was camouflaged as a wedding guest. She watched as he blinked and waited. His green eyes were bright with excitement. Not a good look on him. To her, he looked manic, which she knew he was.

She fixed a blank expression on her face. "Sure."

She must be extremely careful, if she said or did the wrong thing she might set him off and someone would get hurt. As long as she danced with him, she knew exactly where he was and what he was doing. It was just one dance. She would get through it and maybe figure out a way to get him out of the room.

The touch of his clammy fingers made her wretch. Bile burned up her throat. Piper swallowed, forcing down her reaction, and allowed him to snatch her hand and lead her to the middle of the floor. Thank God her cousin and his new wife had already left the reception. With their departure, many of the guests had left as well. That meant fewer victims to worry about.

Remain calm and think, she told herself.

When Qball looked at her again, the intensity in his eyes had cooled to a calm, evil intent she'd seen too many times. The look a killer got before they plunged the knife into their victim. When she held his gaze he stepped closer and wrapped his arms around her back. Forcing her into close contact

V.A. Dold & Tori Austin

with him. Unable to avoid it, she lightly rested her hands on his shoulders, her skin crawling in objection to his touch. The very nearness of him was too many levels of wrong.

Alarms shrieked in her mind. She couldn't react to this monster, she needed to remain calm and think her way out of this without anyone getting hurt. She pulled in a deep breath, and considered her options. Nothing. She had nothing. She couldn't reach any of her weapons without tipping Qball off. That, and the dancers around her afforded no room for hand to hand combat. She was in a hell of a lot of trouble and saw no way out.

*****

Richie was washing his hands when Piper's fear hit him hard. In his rush to get to her, he pushed a man coming into the men's room out of the way without apology. His mate was in trouble and needed him.

He'd always been a calm, logical person with a healthy dose of confidence in himself and his shifter abilities. But as he rushed into the ballroom, his rage flared like a wild fire through him. He stared at his mate, held hostage before his eyes. He'd never felt so damned helpless. His chest clenched so tightly he could barely breathe.

He could smell Qball's intent. The man was blatantly testing him, craving a reaction.

He forced himself to calm his rage as he watched the man lick his lips, savoring the terror filling the room.

RICHIE: Le Beau Series

"Your woman is a delectable little thing, isn't she? I bet she has the most wonderful scream. I can hardly wait to cut her and find out."

Richie's nose wrinkled, the smell of the man's excitement was repulsive. This monster enjoyed terrorizing his victims. But his cocky attitude wavered when he noticed the unexpected result of his knife pressed to Piper's neck and his taunts. Richie knew the precise moment the man saw the sudden change in the color of his eyes from dark brown to glowing golden.

Sirens were heard as the parking lot filled with squad cars. Someone must have called the police.

Fear shivered across Qball's face. It was clear he didn't enjoy being afraid. Richie watched as he sneered an ugly smile and stepped toward the door, dragging Piper with him. With each step the man took, Richie stalked forward, step for step. He had Qball's attention, holding his gaze with his wolf's stare. Waiting for his chance to make a move.

With an accuracy that only came from years of practice, Qball flicked the blade at him and shoved Piper to her knees. Richie saw it coming, stepped to his left, and ignored the knife as it clattered harmlessly to the floor.

As soon as Qball retreated, the room erupted, women cried and men jumped into action, going to their families, some rushing to Piper's aid. In the melee, Richie was hampered from getting to her or tracking Qball. He snarled in frustration trying to get through the crowd suddenly in front of him.

V.A. Dold & Tori Austin

The people unwittingly gave Qball the distraction he needed to slip away.

"Damn it!" Piper growled. Once she extracted herself from the well-meaning people helping her to her feet, she charged after Qball.

Richie hustled to follow Piper. Her rage was bound to get her hurt or worse, killed. He'd never imagined his mate would be a warrior, of sorts. When he'd pictured his mate, he'd visualized soft, and sweet, and kind of a Suzy homemaker type. But he couldn't deny, Piper was damned sexy in action. Who knew he had the hots for Xena the warrior princess.

It took some doing, but he caught up to her when she stopped to catch her breath.

"What?" she barked, clearly angry she'd lost Qball.

Still leaning over with hands on knees she turned her head to glower at him. The moment their eyes met, he felt her anger recede.

Richie refused to back down and look away. This woman was his MATE. And she had been threatened.

She aroused his wolf; more than that, she enthralled him, but they were in a public situation, and he needed to control his wolf's demands. A thrill ran up his spine, both he and his wolf were captivated and more than willing to be imprisoned for eternity by her velvety soft, and enticing eyes. *Lock me up and throw away the key. Please!* But first he had a murderer to rip to pieces and feed to the gators.

RICHIE: Le Beau Series

Her steel blue eyes broke the mutual stare down they were trapped in and shifted toward the lobby, effectively snapping him out of his slobbering puppy trance. Yeah, that's not embarrassing. No, not at all. Casually he wiped the corners of his mouth to verify slobber wasn't actually hanging from his lips. *Thank the Goddess for small favors* he thought, as he brushed dry skin.

She raked her fingers through her hair, knocking the hairpins loose. "Dammit all to hell! I lost the bastard."

He stood, hands on hips, watching her. "What's our plan?"

"Oh, no, buddy. There is no 'our' plan. You can go back to the reception. I have a bounty to track."

Richie crossed his arms, eyes glowing angrily. "If you think you're going after that guy alone, think again."

Piper opened her mouth to tell him where to go, but before she could speak a swarm of humanity was headed her way as the wedding guests rushed to leave. She and Richie flattened themselves to the wall and waited. Finally, she was able to continue her search. He had to be somewhere in the hotel. There were too many cops in the parking lot and lobby for him to have gotten out.

Systematically she searched each of the smaller event rooms that made up the event center of the hotel. Finally she threw her hands in the air. "Where the hell did he go! There are officers everywhere. He couldn't just disappear into thin air."

V.A. Dold & Tori Austin

"Maybe that's the problem, if he blended into the crowd, he could have moved around easily. Let's make our way back toward the lobby. Maybe we'll pick up his trail."

"Maybe." She wasn't going to hold her breath. Qball was more slippery than an eel.

They walked slowly examining the floor, walls, and doors for a clue of Qball's passing. The horseshoe shape of the event center only compounded the difficulty. It took them about twenty minutes to search the entire center, dodging officers as they went.

As they turned the corner into the hallway that led past the ballroom and ended in the lobby, Piper saw Qball wearing a cop uniform, slip into the now vacant ballroom. How the hell did he get a uniform! That explained why no one found him, he was hiding in plain sight. She held up a hand to alert Richie and used hand signals to stop.

Without looking his way, she waved Richie off, as if he would sit and stay, like a dog. He let out an annoyed snort that earned him a glower. They approached the ballroom, moving with care and stealth.

There weren't many places for Qball to hide in that wide open room. The tablecloths only reached half way to the floor. That left only the bar and a heavy curtain along one wall as possible cover. Piper took a deep breath and tapped into her gift.

Standing in the safety of the hallway, she sent her spirit or whatever it was that gave her the ability to see, into the ballroom. Her non-corporeal

RICHIE: Le Beau Series

self inched to the edge of the bar and glanced behind. Not there. He was either behind the curtain or he was Houdini. As much as she wanted to, she couldn't use her gift to see behind the curtain. Even her gift couldn't overcome darkness. She gripped her gun, ready for action and entered the room, careful not to make a sound.

As she reached for the heavy, black curtain, Richie spotted a man among the hefty cloth. His heart jumped and his wolf snarled.

Before he got a good look at the guy, he dissolved into the fabric's pleats and folds. With an aggressive growl and a bit too much force, Richie yanked the curtain aside - then down. SHIT! He and Piper were about to be buried in hundreds of yards of velvet.

Just as his last glimpse of the room disappeared behind the falling weight, Qball pointed a gun at Piper. His wolf surged forward and slashed a huge hole in the heavy velvet. Using his wolf's speed and strength, he launched himself at Qball. The murderer managed to move sideways and avoid a full on collision, but his gun was knocked free and slid across the room and out of reach.

Richie tried to regain his footing on the highly polished floor, but he struggled like a dog running in place on linoleum. Not his manliest moment. Screw that, he'd just saved his mate.

Piper struggled from under the curtain as Qball disappeared out the door, cackling gleefully.

Chapter 6

Piper surveyed the damage. "What the hell just happened?"

Richie didn't blink. He glared at the doorway, eyes glowing with an angry fire. His expression was intent as his muscles flexed and rippled.

For a long moment, his gaze remained fixed on the door Qball had escaped through. Heaving from the rush of adrenaline, his chest rose and fell. His wolf pushed him to track the threat and kill it, but he also needed to protect his mate. As much as he wished he had the ability, he couldn't be in two places at once.

Finally, he turned on his heel and stalked toward her. Helped her to her feet and pulled her into his arms. "I'm sorry. I would have had him, but wearing these slick bottomed dress shoes, my feet slipped on this high gloss floor."

Piper knew his heart rate hadn't slowed. Somehow she was able to feel each beat. Her eyes widened and then her brows furrowed.

What the...

RICHIE: Le Beau Series

She couldn't prevent the rise of alarm that shook her body, nor her admiration that matched it. He truly was dangerous. Funny, she hadn't felt this side of him last night in the bar and certainly not in her bed. But for reasons unknown, she was absolutely positive he wasn't dangerous to her, only Qball. He was protecting her. No one had ever protected her before. She was always the one doing the protecting. She was surprised to find she liked it.

Piper shook with fury over losing Qball again. "I'll get that bastard next time."

Richie's hand cupped her cheek, stealing her attention from her anger and centering it on him.

"I'm sure you will."

She watched as he searched her face, looking for... something.

"I'm aware this is a wildly inappropriate request at a time like this, but I need to kiss you, Piper. I'm abundantly aware you're covered in weapons and could easily use one on me. But I can't help my reaction to the danger you were in, and at this moment, I don't really give a damn if you shoot me."

Piper's eyes widened as she unconsciously moistened her lips, but she didn't pull away.

"I'd never hurt you, Richie. You know that, right?"

She felt his breath hitch and watched as he focused on her lips.

Her thundering pulse, drowned out her mind's warnings that encouraging him before Qball was caught was a bad idea.

V.A. Dold & Tori Austin

Her body relaxed and responded to his need, a worrisome reaction for a woman accustomed to maintaining boundaries. But she chose to ignore her apprehension. Instead, she raised a brow as a teasing grin tugged at the corners of her mouth. "You'd better make it a really, really great kiss, because it might be your last."

Richie towered over her. There was hunger in his eyes, a desire that stole her breath and left her weak in the knees. She was hypnotized, imprisoned by his gaze, his need transparent in his expression. Desire for her, for Piper, bounty hunter and all.

His fingers tunneled into her messy up-do and raised her lips to his. Passionate and protective male energy engulfed her, sending desire rushing through her veins.

His lips touched hers and suddenly she couldn't process, or rationalize. Only feel. Her knees went wobbly and her body roared to life. His kiss was intense and edged toward demanding. Of their own volition, her lips parted and he dipped inside.

Piper wrapped her arms around his neck and Richie flowed into her thoughts, loving, cherishing, and determined to claim her as his mate. He opened his thoughts to her. Letting her in to see his hopes and dreams of their future.

Happiness and a sense of coming home burst through her like a hurricane making landfall. She clung to him, as they became what felt like one person. Sharing a heartbeat, exchanging breath.

RICHIE: Le Beau Series

Her mind whirled as she tried to process what was happening to her. She felt like a marionette with someone else controlling her body and emotions. It wasn't in her to behave like a horny teenager in the middle of a hunt. She needed to get a handle on herself.

Richie knew he exposed too much, too fast, but he couldn't stop himself. He had to have her. His wolf demanded they claim her for their own. The compulsion had been growing since the moment he'd set eyes on her at the dinner. He knew he'd have a lot of explaining to do, but for now he just wanted to feel her safe and alive in his arms.

His pulse thundered and blood pooled, causing his pants to tighten painfully. She was his salvation – his private paradise. Everything around them became nonexistent; there was only Piper with her soft curves, and scent that drove him and his ravenous beast crazy. The only thing that mattered was kissing her, the world could crash down around his ears and he wouldn't have noticed.

He was on fire for his mate, needing her intimately, but also as a companion. A best friend and confidant. He'd been unaware anything was lacking. Hell, he loved his life. He'd thought his life was full and happy. Surrounded by friends and pack.

Sure, he'd prayed there would be a mate for him, a woman who would turn his heart to mush and his body to stone. He just hadn't imagined it would happen so suddenly, like a bolt of lightning from out of the blue.

V.A. Dold & Tori Austin

Piper turned his world upside down and at the same time completed him. She made him whole. Regardless, she needed him to be her partner right now, not her lover. And certainly not her mate. At least, not yet. So he ended the kiss and took a breath.

Her thoughts told him of her determination to protect her heart from ever feeling pain again. Someone had hurt her – badly. She was drawn to him and it intrigued her, but also terrified her. She wanted to trust him, and yet wasn't sure if she could. Most of all, she was determined to hold him off until Qball was apprehended.

He felt her inside his mind, searching for answers and seeing more than she should, at least until he could explain what he was and what she was to him.

Her body stiffened. "What's happening to me?" she whispered against his mouth when they both came up for air. Her soft steel blue eyes searching his face.

He rested his forehead against hers. "I have a lot to explain to you, but not here. Not in public."

"I think I was reading your mind, but how is that possible?"

A slow smile curved his mouth. "You were. I let you in." He held up his hands to stop her when she opened her mouth to speak. "I'm sure you have a million questions. But I think we should take a little time to collect ourselves. And before you become consumed with what you've learned, we need to check the hotel for Qball."

RICHIE: Le Beau Series

She blinked, and moistened her lips again. "You're not getting off the hook that easily. I have to tell you, I'm more than a little concerned that you think you can turn into a dog. But you're right, I need to check the hotel and its perimeter. The last thing I want is an innocent victim. It looks like Qball thinks this is a game of cat and mouse."

Richie pushed a hand through his hair. "Where do you want to start?"

Piper blinked. Stunned. A hint of indecision crept into her eyes. She frowned, and he bent his head to swallow her protest before she could utter it.

"Piper, I'm going with you," he whispered against her lips.

She narrowed her eyes at him, then nodded. "Fine. You'll follow me anyway, so I might as well know where you are and what you're doing. I'd hate to accidentally shoot you. Keep in mind, I'm doing this under protest. I'm in charge and you'll do exactly what I tell you to do or the deal is off."

"You got it. I can assist you though. I'm an excellent tracker and I can handle myself."

She pressed her lips together, still worried. "Let's get started before my sanity returns and I send you packing."

He grinned, very pleased with himself.

She rolled her eyes. "Oh, shut up, dog boy."

"I saw him turn right," he said, and then pretend growled under his breath, making her laugh as they walked to the doors that led to the hallway.

V.A. Dold & Tori Austin

A foot short of the hallway, Piper silenced them and signaled Richie to the side of the opening. She sent her gift out into the hall to verify Qball wasn't lying in wait. The coast was clear.

"Stay close and don't make a sound," she ordered before stepping through the door.

She didn't see Richie shake his head and grin.

If she only knew what I'm capable of...

One by one, she tested the doors that lined the hall. Everything was locked down tight. Good. Less places for Qball to hide. She glanced back to make sure Richie stayed close.

Each time his eyes met hers, she felt a peculiar brush of butterfly wings. She glanced away and frowned, the sensation made it difficult to breathe. She didn't need nor want butterflies or any other wings right now. But she had to admit, she loved his dark eyes and the way his gaze drifted over her like the lightest touch of fingers. She just didn't want it this very moment. Stupid hormones.

There was no sign of Qball in the lobby or bar either. The perimeter of the hotel was the only area left to search. The long summer day would be helpful. Even at seven PM the sun brightened the sky.

She mustered the nerve to slide a sideways glance Richie's way. He was gazing back at her, his expression rapt, but not in a creepy way. His hand was strong and yet gentle. Curiously, it felt right to hold his hand—as if they'd been together for some time.

RICHIE: Le Beau Series

Did that mean she really was his 'mate' as he claimed in his thoughts? Whatever a mate was. She assumed it was another word for girlfriend or something along those lines. At least Piper hoped it was.

She gave herself a mental shake. *You're getting a little ahead of yourself. He danced with you, heck he made love to you, but he never asked you out on a date. Girlfriend... as if.* She snorted at herself and her thoughts. Men went to bed with women all the time without getting emotionally involved. Regardless, the odds were, there wouldn't be a repeat performance.

The entire time they had searched, Richie strove to only breathe through his mouth or while facing away from Piper. Every time he got a lungful of her, he lost the ability to form a coherent thought. As enjoyable as that was, he needed his wits about him.

He retained hold of her hand the entire time they'd walked the exterior. Piper hadn't resisted or shied away. As soon as they'd cleared the exit doors, a light wind had touched their skin, floating her scent his direction. He'd suppressed a groan. And when she had stepped from the shadows into the light. The sun bathing the entrance of the hotel had played seductively over her flawless skin like a lover. Damn, she was killing him. Now he needed a cold shower. *Get ahold of yourself, man. She needs a partner not a lovesick pup.*

V.A. Dold & Tori Austin

With his wolf and libido once again under his control, he considered her thoughts. How was he going to get her alone, and once he had her alone, how the hell did he tell her how much she meant to him and what he was?

If only his brain cells functioned around the gorgeous bounty hunter. He couldn't blame his deficiency on her beauty alone. Hell, no. She had an amazing mind and personality to go with her looks. How had he gotten so lucky?

And when she kissed him, he was completely screwed. His brain clocked out, closed up shop, and said adios amigos. It was a blessing he hadn't tripped over a chair in the lobby or walked into a wall. At the rate he was going, he would be wearing a hazard sign by the end of the day.

He needed to focus. If he didn't look at her and concentrated on where Qball was, he might make it back to his hotel room without the addition of the hazard sign. But damn, he liked looking at her.

*****

Nearing the automatic doors, they joined others coming and going. It was easy to see Qball wasn't among them. Besides, there were officers everywhere. The hotel was more heavily guarded than Fort Knox. She knew because she'd spoken with every police officer on the scene and informed them that Qball was posing as a cop.

RICHIE: Le Beau Series

They'd told her they would be processing the scene and hanging around through the night in the hopes of apprehending him. It was obvious with so many officers milling around Qball wasn't going to come near the hotel again tonight.

"He's gone… for now anyway," Piper sighed. "I don't know about you, but I need a drink."

"Yeah. I could use one, too."

"I'm going to change out of this dress. Do you want to meet me in the bar?"

"Sure, I'll get us a table."

"Great, I'll only be a minute." She left him outside the bar and hurried to the elevators.

During the walk from her room to the bar, Piper lectured herself. No more kissing! She would stay strong and keep Richie at arm's length. This was just two people having a stiff drink after a near death experience. Nothing more.

Until Qball was apprehended anything remotely resembling romance was downright dangerous. She had no business considering ideas like if he'd called her his girlfriend or going out on dates for that matter. Piper nodded to herself, she would be brave and avoid forming an attachment to the smoking hot Cajun. For now anyway.

A short five minutes later she had just taken her seat when he took her hand.

His eyes searched her face. "Penny for your thoughts."

"What?" She blinked in surprise. Did he know she'd been thinking about him… them… whatever?

"You seemed very far away. Care to share?"

"Not really." Despite her intention to maintain an emotional distance from Richie, she found herself smiling and playing along with him.

"You have a great smile. You should wear it more often," Richie teased.

"Thank you. You have a nice smile, too. But it's way too distracting." And dang it, she couldn't stop herself from gazing into his smiling, twinkling brown eyes, either.

Richie was like a decadent chocolate set before her that she couldn't resist. His impish grin and amused expression set her at ease. Too much at ease. Dangerously at ease. She had no defenses against this man.

He chuckled softly. "I'll take that as a compliment."

The waitress delivered their drinks saving Piper from having to respond.

Richie took a sip of his and set it on the table. "So, do you have any idea where Qball got off to?"

"Not a clue. He's a wily one, that's for sure. I'll feel better once the wedding party leaves the hotel. He's notorious for the perverse pleasure he gets from targeting the people around the person he's pursuing and I want my family out of harm's way."

Richie seemed to consider that for a minute. "If you were to leave the hotel, do you think he would follow you?"

RICHIE: Le Beau Series

Yes. But not something he necessarily needed to know. If she told Richie that, he'd follow her. She knew it all the way to her bones. But he was staring at her, reading her, waiting for a reply. Did she tell the truth? She'd have to fudge it, he would be safer that way.

"Maybe, maybe not." She shrugged, suddenly very interested in her cocktail.

Richie tipped his head back and barked out a laugh. Heaven help her, she was officially doomed. Laughter looked good on him. Really, really good.

"You don't lie very well."

She scowled still not looking at him. "Good to know."

They sipped their drinks staring at each other. Piper knew she was in trouble when the amusement in his gaze morphed into something hotter, a lot hotter. Determinedly, she fought her own heated response.

She needed to stay strong. Silently she ordered her body to behave. She meant to sit back, to lean away from the temptation across the table. So, why was she suddenly leaning closer to the sexy man?

She watched like a deer caught in headlights as Richie leaned in, not stopping until their breath mingled, and heat surged through her body, waking all her female senses from the tight grip she'd held them in.

Dang it! She was toast. She might as well wave the white flag because she'd lost the battle good and proper.

V.A. Dold & Tori Austin

Just when she thought it couldn't get any worse, his gaze dropped to her lips. Her breath hitched in her throat and she stopped breathing altogether. Holy hell. Her entire body started to quiver in anticipation of touching him. Everywhere. Naked. Again.

Something in the back of her mind pushed and elbowed its way to the surface. She knew it was what little was left of her common sense warning her to save herself while she still had a chance. Getting involved while Qball was on the loose was irresponsible and reckless. She just needed to get her body onboard with her mind.

She shouldn't be doing this. But dammit all to hell, deep down, she'd never wanted anything as badly as she wanted this man.

Richie wanted, no he needed, to kiss this woman. He glanced around the bar. This was not the place for what he wanted to do. Before he could suggest they retire to his room, Piper had another round coming. Each time her glass was empty someone in the bar bought her another. The bar was full of wedding guests and everyone wanted to buy her a drink tonight.

She gave him an apologetic look and sipped the drinks slowly. "I'm sorry, about this. I'll just drink them really slow and avoid anyone sending more to the table."

Two hours later, Richie and Piper still sat in the bar as Piper slowly sipped the last of the drinks.

RICHIE: Le Beau Series

She'd only had three, but it was evident she wasn't a drinker and she was a little tipsy. Richie was trying to figure out how to get her out of the bar and upstairs to her room when Piper started getting friendly. Very friendly.

Around the second drink, Piper had moved from across the table to a chair next to him. Not that he was complaining, but he wasn't the type of man to take advantage of a woman.

Piper finished her drink and giggled, scooting closer. At this rate, if someone sent one more drink to the table she'd be giving him a lap dance. She batted her eyes and ran her hand down his chest, then proceeded further south.

Richie sucked in a breath. Thinking became a problem. A whopper of a problem. He needed to get her to bed before he did something both he and Piper would regret. She'd never forgive him if he acted on his desire regardless she was the one pursuing him.

Fighting both his wolf and his need, he grabbed her wandering hand and went to place it in her lap. Then he thought better of it and retained possession of her roving fingers. She'd stretched his self-control to its limits. Who knows, she might go for his belt buckle next, and then he'd be a goner.

When she frowned, and glanced from their clasped hands to his face, he almost gave in to temptation. Taking a deep breath, he cupped her face with his free hand and brushed her cheek with his thumb.

"Cher, please believe me, it's not that I don't want you more than anything in the world, but you're in no condition to be doing this right now.

V.A. Dold & Tori Austin

When I make love to you again, it will be because you want me as much as I want you, not because your inhibitions are down.

She grinned and blinked her big blue eyes at him. "You want to make love to me again?"

"Hell, yes."

"Even though I'm a bounty hunter and might get you killed?"

"Sweetheart, you're not going to get me killed. If anything, I'm the one who is going to keep you safe."

"Sure I am. Qball's not only dangerous, but downright insane. That's a deadly combination even if you're a professional like I am. Besides, look." She took the hand he was holding hers with and placed it on her left breast. "Feel that? Those are throwing knives. I'm covered in weapons. If you skulk around following me when I'm hunting him, I might mistakenly stick you with one of these. And that's if he doesn't kill you first." Piper sighed unhappily. "You really should stay away from me."

Chapter 7

Goddess give me strength! Her warm, supple breast was too much to withstand. He wasn't made of stone, dammit. The day had been trying for both himself and his wolf. Denying the desires of his mate was going to kill him.

The confounding woman wasn't helping matters, pressing his palm against her hardened nipple. She'd finally pushed him to his limit and one step over. No more fighting the need. At least to a limited extent, he was a gentleman after all.

"Woman, you're testing my resolve. I'm trying to respect you and you're not helping matters," he said, tracing her lower lip with the pad of his thumb, watching her eyes round as he pulled her lips to his. "I'd love to strip you naked and worship you the way you deserve, Piper. Please, help me be the man you deserve and stop tempting me," he whispered against her lips.

"Y-you want me naked?"

"Oh yeah. More than you can imagine." He continued to kiss her softly, forcing himself to not deepen the kiss. "And you know what else?"

"What?" she gasped.

He brushed his fingers down the length of her neck and wrapped his hand around her nape. "When I finish tasting every inch of you…I'm going to make love to you so thoroughly, you'll forget every man you've ever known."

She trembled and whimpered, the sound fraying the little resolve he'd held onto.

Son-of-a-bitch. That was it. He'd surpassed his limit. Richie slammed his lips down on hers and devoured her mouth like a starved man. Piper moaned and wrapped her arms around his neck, kissing him as frantically as he kissed her. Her palm was a hot brand against his skin and she had the other in his hair. Tongues tangoed and danced, as they tasted each other's sweetness.

A throat loudly cleared next to their table ending his loss of control.

"Maybe you guys should get a room?" Billie stood inches from them, hands on hips with the biggest grin Richie had ever seen on her face.

Richie blushed and put space between himself and Piper. Then he sucked in a long shaky breath. Damn, that was close.

"You're right, I shouldn't have done that."

Billie glanced around the bar. "I'm looking for Helen. Have you seen her?"

"Sorry, cher. I haven't seen any of you gals. I'd keep an eye out for them, but we're just getting ready to call it a night."

"Oh, okay. I'll check the restaurant. Maybe she's there. Goodnight you two."

RICHIE: Le Beau Series

Piper and Richie wished Billie goodnight and left the bar. They didn't speak all the way to her room. Piper took a deep breath, opened the door, and waved Richie inside. She took a seat on the end of her bed as Richie triple locked the door. When he turned, he looked more like an animal stalking her than the gentleman he'd been all night.

She raised a hand to silence him before he could speak. "I would like to apologize for my behavior, I'm sorry."

"There's no reason to be sorry, cher. But I must admit I enjoyed your behavior, more than I should have. I don't make a habit of taking advantage of a woman who's been drinking."

"Yeah, sorry about that, too. I guess I should have turned down the drinks. I was trying to be polite. Dealing with this hunt in the middle of a family wedding is throwing me for a loop."

"I can understand that. From what you've told me, your bounties don't normally come after you."

Piper's shoulders sagged. "That's putting it mildly. Usually they try to lay low and draw as little attention as possible."

"So, what's your plan of action?"

Piper sighed heavily. "A good night's sleep and then try to pick up his trail in the morning." She seemed to consider saying more when she looked him directly in the eye and asked, "What is a mate?"

V.A. Dold & Tori Austin

Richie's eyes widened. "That's quite a subject change." He joined her at the end of the bed and took a minute to collect his thoughts. "What I'm about to tell you is pretty far out there. Are you sure you want to talk about this tonight?"

"Now that you've said that, there is no way I'll sleep a wink unless you explain yourself."

"Fair enough. But you must promise to hear me out and not scream or freak out. We're in a public place and if you scream someone is going to call 911."

Piper eyed him warily and he felt her reach for her thigh holster. He hadn't even said anything and he was scaring her.

He bent his head and closed his eyes. How to begin?

As he sat trying to figure out what to say, his animal soul hopped around like an excited pup. Maybe he should start with the subject of telepathy and her gift? With his course set, he raised his head. Just as he opened his mouth to speak, Piper slumped against his shoulder, sound asleep. *Thank Goddess!*

He had at least tonight to figure out what he was going to say the next time she asked. And he knew without a doubt, there would be a next time. He also knew, he didn't have much time before she demanded answers.

Richie grinned; even asleep she was adorable, although she looked mighty uncomfortable. He slid one arm behind her neck and the other under her knees and lifted her to his chest.

RICHIE: Le Beau Series

Damn, she felt good in his arms. Reluctantly, he laid her head on the pillow and pulled the covers over her.

Straightening, he gazed at her longingly. He didn't want to leave, but he couldn't crawl into bed with her either. That was when he caught sight of the notepad next to the bed. He wrote her a quick message, kissed her gently and turned out the light as he headed for his own room.

The Next Morning

Piper moaned and clutched her head. It felt like an entire drum line was banging around in her brain. When she rolled to bury her face in the pillow a crunching noise stopped her short. Carefully, she cracked one eye open. A sheet from the hotel notepad was stuck to her.

She shook her arm until she managed to dislodge the paper, then pulled the covers over her head. Just as she released a sigh of relief a loud knocking sounded at her door.

"Go away, I have a gun and I'll use it," she mumbled into her pillow.

"Ah, cher. You wouldn't shoot me, would you?" Richie tried to keep the smile from his voice.

Piper groaned. "Just go away and leave me to die in peace."

"No can do. I have the cure for your agony in my hot little hands as we speak. I promise, you'll be happy you let me in if you open the door."

V.A. Dold & Tori Austin

Richie pressed his lips together to suppress his grin. He could hear loud grumbles and complaints as she unlocked the door.

Cracking it open she narrowed her eyes on him. "What do you want, evil man?"

"Here." He handed her a glass of brownish liquid. "Drink it all, and if I may suggest, you might want to plug your nose while you do it."

Piper eyed the concoction suspiciously. "What's in it?" She took a sniff and pulled her head back. "OH, hell, no!"

"Trust me, I'm a bartender. This will cure what ails you."

Piper studied him, scowling fiercely. "If this kills me, I'll haunt your ass forever."

Her suspicions rose when Richie bit his lip and struggled not to laugh.

"Go on. Drink it."

One last squinty scowl his direction and she plugged her nose, then downed the entire glass in one gulp. "ACK! That's nasty!" she snatched the hem of his white T-shirt and wiped her tongue with it. Sputtering and gagging she allowed Richie to push her toward the bathroom. Without a word he ran a glass of cold water and handed it to her.

"Here, swish and spit, it'll help."

Piper latched onto the glass with both hands like it was a life raft and she was a Titanic survivor bobbing in the ocean. Several swish and spits later and the color returned to her cheeks.

"Better?" He chuckled, grinning ear to ear.

RICHIE: Le Beau Series

Piper frowned and shook her head. "Better. What the hell was in that shit and who came up with the concoction in the first place?"

Richie helped her to the bed and sat next to her. His eyes still dancing with amusement. "It's an old family remedy. If I told you what was in it, I'd have to kill you."

"Yeah, right. Next time I have more than one mixed drink, shoot me. It'll be less painful."

"How about, next time I give you something more pleasurable to distract you from a bad day?"

"Like what?" Piper eyed him suspiciously again.

"Me, of course."

She laughed so hard she actually snorted. "Full of yourself much?"

"No, just stating the facts, ma'am." He pretended to straighten a nonexistent collar.

"Hmm." She pursed her twitching lips to keep from laughing. "So, Richie, what brings you to my neck of the woods. And don't tell me you just wanted to bring me a drink from hell."

"Well, that and I'm here for our breakfast date."

"What breakfast date?"

"Didn't you see my note?" He looked around for the slip of paper.

"Oh, that." She waved at the bed. "I think it's lost in the sheets. I didn't get the chance to read it yet."

V.A. Dold & Tori Austin

Richie frowned at the mountain of bedding, no way was he going to hunt up the note. "Well, then I'll sum it up. You have a date with me in the restaurant downstairs for breakfast."

"Oh, I do, do I?"

He nodded and stood with his hand extended.

"Yes, ma'am."

"I guess I have no choice, seeing as you saved my life and all with your nasty cure."

"I love your attitude. Now get dressed, the breakfast buffet closes in twenty-five minutes."

She disappeared into the bathroom with her clothes and a few minutes later emerged dressed, fresh faced with her hair brushed.

"Perfection. Let's go." Richie took her hand and led her out the door.

Piper snuck glances at Richie as they walked to the elevator. When she'd opened the door and met his gaze through her half opened eyes, her mind had instantly filled with images of sweaty, entangled bodies and mind-blowing sex. If her head hadn't been about to explode, she would have stripped him naked. She prayed he hadn't picked up on her out of control fantasizing while she'd stood there practically toe-to-toe with him.

She huffed a breath and ran a hand through her hair. Shit, why hadn't she packed her vibrator? If she was going to stay in control of her hormones and keep Richie safe while she apprehended Qball, she needed to blow off some steam. Sooner rather than later, and without Richie's sexy body involved in said activities.

RICHIE: Le Beau Series

They each sat with steaming cups of coffee when Richie cleared his throat.

"Piper, I have a suggestion and I hope you'll hear me out."

She took another sip, speculating about what he wanted to suggest. "All right. What's on your mind?"

"I was thinking over what you said about Qball possibly targeting your friends and the guests of the wedding. I believe, if you leave the hotel he'll follow you. That would take the civilians out of the equation."

"I was thinking the same thing. If I leave, he'll follow me. I just haven't decided on the best place to leave, to."

"I have a suggestion for that as well." He grinned, his eyes sparkling with excitement.

"Okay, I'll bite. Where?"

"My cabin in New Orleans," he announced proudly.

A frown wrinkled her forehead, and her eyes narrowed. "No," She stated emphatically, and shook her head.

"Why not?" he asked incredulously.

"I won't bring this trouble to your doorstep. Besides, there are way too many people in New Orleans. He'd start shooting them like goldfish in a bowl."

"Not the city. I have a secluded place in the bayou. We could stay there while we hunt him down."

"No."

After the disagreement, they finished their breakfast in relative silence.

Piper pulled her phone from her pocket and glanced at Richie. "Please, excuse me while I call in. The local law enforcement might have new leads on Qball's whereabouts."

The table was cleared and they sipped a third cup of coffee as she made her call. She ended the conversation and frowned, the local PD hadn't gotten any new tips since last night. She'd lost his trail when he disappeared yesterday and she wasn't sure where to begin looking. Piper tapped her phone against her chin. If she were Qball, where would she be?

*****

She hadn't noticed Richie's silence or his rigid posture. He was caught in a precognitive vision of the future. Images of Piper's cousin the groom flashed through his mind in sharp clarity. Piper was right; Qball was going to target her family.

Richie shook his head to clear the vision from his mind and return fully to the present. He was reaching out to touch her arm and warn her when all hell broke loose. Screams were heard in the lobby. He and Piper scrambled from the restaurant and skidded to a halt as the lobby came into view.

RICHIE: Le Beau Series

Sure enough, just as he'd seen in his vision, Qball stood before them sneering. Everyone in the lobby had shrunk back from the maniac wielding a knife. Bob was held tightly against Qball's chest as the man searched the room until his eyes landed on Piper.

"Ah, there you are." Qball grinned evilly. "I knew if I raised the stakes, you'd come out to play."

Piper shook with fury, but she didn't allow her emotions to enter her voice when she spoke. "Oh, I'll play all right. But we really don't need extra people in the game. Why don't you come on over here all by your little lonesome and we'll do this, one-on-one?" She really hated that little prick and was going to enjoy taking him down.

"I think I'm good right here with my new toy." He giggled and pressed the knife deeper.

Bob was trying to maintain his cool and hold as still as possible. There was no fear in his eyes as he held Piper's gaze. The expression on his face said it all. Kill the bastard.

Theresa stood a few feet from her new husband shaking with a mixture of terror and fury. "Richie, kill this fucker before I do."

Richie glanced to Theresa and growled, "Back away and let us handle this."

"Yeah, Piper. That's a good idea. Why don't you back away, and let us MEN handle this?" Qball mimicked, and then laughed like only a crazy person could. "Of course, I know you won't. You'd never let a man do your job for you, now would you?"

V.A. Dold & Tori Austin

Without acknowledging Qball's remarks, Piper pulled her gun. "Let him go, and slowly set the knife on the floor in front of you."

"That's not playing very nice, Piper. Someone could get hurt, you might miss and hit one of these other fine people." Qball giggled as he pulled Bob with him and backed toward an exit.

With each step he retreated, Piper and Richie advanced. "Let him go and take me instead," Piper demanded.

Richie snarled at her angrily.

Qball, stopped his retreat and considered her for a moment. His eyes took on a sheen of insanity. "That's not a bad suggestion. We could have all kinds of fun. Put down your gun and walk to me slowly."

Piper laid her gun on the floor and stepped toward Qball, never taking her eyes off the blade at Bob's throat. When she was two steps from him, she stopped. "Let him go and I'll go with you quietly."

Qball appeared to consider her offer, then without warning shoved Bob to the floor and lunged for Piper. He grabbed her by the neck and slammed her against the wall.

Richie growled helplessly.

Anger erupted in the pit of her stomach and roared through her chest, as she placed both hands against the wall and shoved Qball back. Then she bent forward and slammed her head back with a vengeance, head-butting him with every ounce of energy she could pack into the blow.

RICHIE: Le Beau Series

A crunch resounded as she made contact. Bright red blood dampened her hair and splattered the wall. Damn, she hated the irony smell of blood.

Qball howled and released his hold.

Richie reached for his mate and steadied her, but before Piper could regain her footing Qball was out the door.

"Godammit!" Piper yelled as the door clicked shut.

She tore loose of Richie's grasp and dashed after her prey, but he was long gone. She and Richie followed his blood trail for a few blocks until he must have stemmed the flow.

Richie tried to follow his scent without her knowing what he was doing, but the bastard took a short cut through a small creek a few blocks over and he lost Qball's scent. If he spent a little time searching the area, he was sure he would pick it up again, but how would he explain that to her? Plus, the last thing he wanted was his mate walking into an ambush unprepared.

"I'm sorry, cher. We lost him again."

"Shit." Piper breathed heavily, glaring at the creek with her hands on her hips. "All right, I'll admit you had a good idea. I need to leave the hotel and find an unpopulated area to finish this."

Chapter 8

Piper's body language left little doubt she was furious, and the steel in her voice confirmed it. Her frosty blue glare shot daggers at the offending water.

Richie took her hand and kissed her knuckles. The act was second nature to him; apparently she wasn't in the mood for it.

She pulled her hand away. "What are you doing?"

"I'm sorry, cher. You're upset and I felt…I was compelled to soothe you." He'd almost let the cat out of the bag that he could feel her emotions.

"Oh. I'm sorry, Richie. I flew off the handle. I'm just so frustrated."

Richie took her hand again and started walking back the way they had come. "I know. So, do you want to check the available flights to New Orleans when we get back to the hotel?"

Piper pulled her hand away a second time. "Who said anything about New Orleans?"

Richie frowned at her. "I did during breakfast."

RICHIE: Le Beau Series

"And I told you no." She scowled and turned to walk away.

He grabbed her arm before she could take two steps. "I think we should at least discuss it. Think about it, there wouldn't be anyone Qball could use against you."

Then it hit him, it wasn't the location he suggested, it was him. She didn't want the temptation of being in the same cabin with him. "I have two bedrooms, you can stay in the guest room. What's the problem?"

Instantly her expression changed to one of interest. "I'll think about it. But I don't like having you in the line of fire either."

"Don't worry about me, I can more than take care of myself," Richie assured. "Besides, we have things to talk about and privacy is warranted for what I have to say."

Piper's eyebrows rose. "Are you talking about the fact you believe you can turn into a dog?"

"Not a dog…something – else," Richie hedged. "I'll tell you what, come with me to the bayou and draw Qball away from the wedding guests. Once we're there, if you change your mind about staying at the cabin, we'll go to town or think of something else. What's important here is the safety of the people in the hotel."

Piper drew a deep breath, held it a long moment, and nodded. "You're right. The safety of my cousin and the guests come first. All right, let's get back and after we insure Qball hasn't doubled back to the hotel or the grounds, we'll talk."

V.A. Dold & Tori Austin

Two hours later

There was no sign of Qball. He was still in the wind. At least the hotel guests were safe for now. Richie took Piper's hand and nodded toward the elevators. "Let's go to one of our rooms. We have things to discuss in private."

She met his eyes, held them. Then nodded. "All right, it looks safe enough for the time being." She hadn't pulled her hand away, but during the trek to her room, she was much too quiet for his comfort and her walls were up so he couldn't tell what she was thinking.

He glanced at her out of the corner of his eye and watched as she worried her lower lip. He wouldn't mind her nibbling on him with those little white teeth. He prayed to the Goddess she would consent to accompany him back to Louisiana.

Piper's stomach felt as if hummingbirds had replaced the butterflies that had taken up residence ever since she first laid eyes on the handsome Cajun. *He's like my knight in shining armor come to life,* she thought. And he wanted to take her to his home and protect her from the bad guy? Not just protect her, but also help her catch her bounty. The second worried her more than the first. Not that being alone with him in his house didn't make her pulse race and her knees quiver.

Expelling a breath, she opened her hotel room door and preceded him through. She watched Richie as he took his time locking the door before

RICHIE: Le Beau Series

joining her at the small breakfast table with its two chairs. The simple kitchenette and table made the room a little less hotel like and a little more homey.

Once he seated himself, she sucked in a breath and began to speak. "So, why don't you fill in the details of your idea? If I go to the bayou, how do you suggest I inform Qball where to find me?"

Richie rubbed his chin in thought. "I've been thinking about that. He may be getting information from someone, possibly an employee of the hotel. But I'm not sure that explains how he tracked you here in the first place. So the question is, how did he know you were coming here?"

Piper frowned. How had he known? "I didn't tell anyone at work, except my boss, Jerry. Other than him, only my family knew I was coming. Maybe he's tracking my credit cards?"

Richie snapped his fingers. "Tracking. Now there's a thought."

He stood and began searching the room. Nothing smelled like an electronic bug, but he was sensing a low frequency hum.

"Do you have a purse you normally use every day?"

"Yes, why?"

"Did you bring it with you?"

"It's in the closet. What's this about?"

"Would you mind getting it for me?"

She pulled it from the shelf. "What are you thinking?" Then she handed it to him.

He gave it a perfunctory sniff and smiled. "A bug," he said, handing it back. "You're being tracked."

V.A. Dold & Tori Austin

Piper tore into the bag and found a tiny tracking device tucked inside the lining.

"Damn." She began to remove it.

"No. Leave it there. It will lead him to us and he won't be alerted we found it."

She nodded and put the purse back on the shelf. "All right. We still need transportation. I'll check with the airlines to see what's available for a flight, my ticket was for Tuesday and it's not exchangeable."

"Okay, if commercial flights are an issue I have someone I can call."

Piper looked at him warily, then grabbed her phone and called the airline. Within twenty minutes it was apparent getting a commercial flight out before midweek wasn't going to happen.

Richie gave her a charming smile and winked. "Let me see what I can do." He made a hushed call and returned a few minutes later.

Isaac Le beau was number one on his speed dial. It was always, ALWAYS wise to have the king of the shifters quickly and easily accessible. Speaking quietly, he laid out the situation and requested the private plane Isaac kept on hand. Without missing a beat, Isaac assured him their transportation to the bayou would be waiting for them on the private strip outside of St. Louis in three hours.

He was positive Piper would be in a hot mess temper over this, but it was much easier to ask forgiveness than permission. He didn't have a choice. Not even if he'd wanted one.

RICHIE: Le Beau Series

In his precog dream, she died. He had to be there, at the exact moment he'd seen in the dream in order to intervene and save his mate. Since the horrifying vision took place inside what looked to be a warehouse, he had no way of knowing if it was daytime or night. That meant he had to be with her twenty-four seven until that fated moment revealed itself.

Richie shoved his phone in his back pocket and turned to find a scowling Piper ready to blow. "Did you just arrange for a private plane?"

The fabric of his shirt rustled with his shrug. "Um…yeah." He was confused. Why would that make her so angry?

"You had no right to do that without asking me."

"Okay. Would you like to elaborate? I'm not sure what I did wrong."

He watched as she considered sharing one or two of her reasons with him and discard them just as quickly. Based on her scent, he smelled fear and the underlying scent of insecurity.

She must be afraid of flying, he guessed. Maybe she didn't want to admit a weakness and was fearful he would scoff at her? Not that he would, especially not with her life at stake. But it was interesting that she hadn't tried to explain herself. She was his mate and once he was able to explain that to her, she would see things differently. He hoped.

She stiffened her spine and snarled, "Fine."

V.A. Dold & Tori Austin

Dang, she had a sexy snarl. Only one word, but it spoke volumes. She may be scared spitless to fly, but she was going to handle it like a pro. With her head up and chin high. He knew showing no weakness was very, VERY important to his mate. His Piper had more moxie than any person, shifter or human he'd ever met.

Richie stood desperately trying to keep a straight face. The last thing he wanted to do was grin. That wouldn't go over well. "Okay, then. I better get packed. The plane will be on the runway in three hours."

"Right," Piper agreed without looking his way. "I'll get on that as well."

He let himself out without another word. Best to let her calm down before he opened his mouth again and found himself tasting his own foot.

He could hear her slamming drawers all the way in his room, several doors down, with the door shut. She was really upset. Rubbing his jaw, he racked his brain for a way to get back into her good graces. Nothing. He had nothing. Maybe Billie would have a suggestion?

She answered on the first ring. "Hey, Romeo. How's Juliet?"

"Angry. Very, very angry."

Billie busted out laughing.

"Not helping," Richie growled.

"What did you do now?" she asked still laughing.

RICHIE: Le Beau Series

"We need to get to the bayou ASAP. The problem is there's no commercial flights offered by the airline she flew in on until midweek so I have a private plane flying us. Who knew that would send her into orbit?"

"That does sound a bit extreme. Is she afraid to fly? Little planes are scary for most people and petrifying if you are already afraid."

"That was my first thought, but I'm not about to ask her."

"If I were you, I'd get her butt into the bar and ply her with a few cocktails to take the edge off."

"That's not a bad idea. Once she stops slamming drawers, I'll invite her for a drink."

"Slamming drawers?" Her voice rose a couple octaves.

"Oh yeah. She's pretty mad."

"Your goose is cooked, my friend. Good luck with all that."

"Nice, cher. Really helpful."

"I aim to please. I'll see you back home in a couple days." Billie said laughing.

"Take care and travel safely."

"You, too. Gotta go, Helen's calling."

"Okay, I'll talk to you later."

Richie waited a full ten minutes after he heard the final drawer slam. *Was it safe yet?* he wondered. *Why am I being such a chicken? I'm a big bad wolf, right? Yeah, right.* He snorted.

V.A. Dold & Tori Austin

Might as well get this over with. He set his luggage just inside his door and headed to Piper's room. His fist was raised to knock when she yanked the door open, still hopping mad.

"What?"

There was no way on God's green earth she would admit to being terrified of flying. Anger would do just fine to mask the real issue, and she planned on holding onto that lifeline until they landed in Louisiana.

"We have a couple hours before the plane gets here and then it needs to refuel. I'm headed to the bar for a drink. Would you like to join me?" he asked in a shaky voice.

The edges of her lips turned up in a small smile, *the big, tough guy is afraid of little old me.* "Yeah, okay," she answered, then under her breath, she grumbled, "I could use a drink."

*****

Two hours and a bottle of wine later, he poured Piper into the seat next to him on the Le Beau aircraft. He'd been drinking scotch and soda, which left her to drain the vintage by herself. He knew she wouldn't thank him tomorrow morning.

Breathing a sigh, he resigned himself to his fate. *Better make a batch of my hangover cure the minute I get her home.*

The flight attendant was readying the galley for takeoff as he struggled with his mate to latch her seatbelt. As much as he would have enjoyed her amorous attentions at any other time, he needed to

RICHIE: Le Beau Series

get her belted in. If she remembered any of this, he was a dead man. Piper didn't do embarrassed. She would cover it up by being mad at him again if she recalled anything of the last ten minutes.

Shortly after takeoff, she passed out. Thank Goddess! By the time they were circling to land she came to. He watched her out of the corner of his eye, afraid if he made eye contact she would detonate or something worse.

Instead, she stretched, leaned her head left and then right to crack her neck and smiled at him. "Are we there yet?"

He gaped at her. He was never going to understand women.

She shook her head and laughed. "What? Cat got your tongue?"

Richie shook the shock from his mind. "No. I figured you would wake up hung…with a headache," he quickly corrected.

"Sorry to ruin your fun. I know how you like to torture people with that nasty remedy you make, but I only get hung over from whiskey."

He grinned and nodded. "Good to know."

"So, how do we get from the airport to your place?"

"My car was at the international airport and this is a private strip so I had a friend fetch it for me."

Piper eyed him. "Private airport?"

"Breathe, cher. It's not my airplane or my private strip. I'll explain everything once we're settled in at my place."

She continued to study him for a few seconds before she turned her attention to her window to admire the landscape.

Damn, she really didn't like being left out of the loop. His Piper was all about being informed.

*****

By the time Richie drove to the pier he used to store his boat and then piloted them to his cabin, the silence had become unbearable. Piper hadn't spoken another word once she'd turned her attention to things other than a private plane and airstrip. She also had her walls up so he couldn't hear her thoughts.

The instant he pulled up to his pier, she was on the dock pulling her bags behind her. There was only one cabin in sight so he didn't need to tell her where to go.

"Let yourself in, it's open," Richie called after her as he tied off the boat.

She turned to look at him in surprise. "You don't lock your doors?"

"No need. Everyone knows me and would never steal from me, or the people I know. Plus, in the bayou we look out for our neighbors. If someone was on the water and got caught in a storm, they know to go to the nearest shelter. Lightning strikes are dangerous when you're caught unexpectedly. The people of the bayou leave their doors open for those who may need shelter."

RICHIE: Le Beau Series

"In Portland I never leave my doors unlocked even if I'm home. Your way of thinking makes sense, but I can't help my worry over how unsafe it is. There are dangerous people everywhere in the world, even the swamp." She turned again and continued toward the cabin.

Richie entered lugging his own luggage and closed the door with his foot before setting his bags beside the door.

With hands on hips, he glanced at the suitcases still sitting at Piper's feet. "The guest room is down the hall on the left."

He watched her leave the room, still not speaking to him. He had to think of a way to get her talking again. Until then, he had luggage to take care of.

It didn't take either of them long to finish and return to the cozy, main room that made up the kitchen, dining area, and living room. This was a cabin, not a fancy house, and the open floor plan suited him.

Piper didn't waste any time before she began to question him. "You said you would explain the plane and private airstrip once we were here."

He scrubbed his fingers through his thick dark hair. "Where to start? If I explain this poorly I might confuse you more than you already are. I've never explained myself before."

He paced the room a few times and then looked her directly in the eye. Maybe he should start with the subjects of telepathy and her gift? With his course set he raised his head.

V.A. Dold & Tori Austin

"I'll start with our ability to speak through telepathy."

With his last comment, Piper sat a little straighter. He could tell he'd caught her attention.

"I'm a little different from any of the other men you've met and there are reasons for that. To explain the telepathy let me ask you a few questions and in the process I will explain that as well."

"Okay," she agreed calmly.

"When you're near me, do you smell anything unusual? It would be a scent you enjoy."

"Yes, why?"

"Please, Piper just play along. What do you smell?"

"Gun cleaner and patchouli."

Richie's brows rose and he chuckled. "You never cease to amaze me with your uniqueness. To me, you smell like the best crawfish boil ever made."

She frowned. "How is that possible? I've never been anywhere near a crawfish boil."

"Give me a minute and I'll explain. But first, when you first saw me, were you unusually attracted to me? So much so that the attraction may have been confusing or even a bit scary?"

One brow rose and she crossed her arms. "Where are you going with this?"

Richie raised his hands in surrender. "Don't get upset. Personally, I was bowled over by you. I couldn't stay away from you and had to be near you. I'm betting you felt somewhat the same."

His admission seemed to ease the discomfort of his question.

RICHIE: Le Beau Series

"Yes, okay. I admit there was a strangely powerful attraction. It's not like I jump into bed with every man I meet the day I meet him. As a matter of fact, I've never done that before. Normally, I take my time getting to know the man before I take it to the next level."

Rubbing the back of his neck, he admitted, "There's a reason why you're attracted to me and smell what you do around me and can speak telepathically to me. I'm not like other guys, Piper. I'm human - but more. And you're my mate."

"Okay, that is another thing I don't understand from your thoughts. What the heck is a mate and how does your smelling really good and being my sexual kryptonite have anything to do with it?"

"For my kind, there is only one true mate. There are three specific signs that you've found her. A strong, undeniable attraction, the ability to speak telepathically, and a scent made specifically to attract you.

"That's why you smell like a crawfish boil to me, it's my favorite thing to eat."

"And I have all of those," she whispered to herself.

"So do I." He let her absorb what he'd explained for a couple minutes.

Finally, she looked at him again. "What do you mean, your kind?"

He gave her an uncertain smile. "Let me try something."

V.A. Dold & Tori Austin

Instantly, Piper felt overwhelming, unconditional love swamp her. Her eyes widened. "What you just experienced was me sending you emotions," Richie explained, his voice soft and calming.

She searched his face for the truth of what he'd said. His unwavering gaze was filled with the very emotion she'd just felt. "You did that?"

"Yes, I can send you emotions and physical touch." Then he lowered his eyes and more softly said, "It's because of what I am. And what you are to me."

She was even more confused than she'd been before. "Maybe you should draw me a picture because I'm not getting it."

Chapter 9

There was no way around this. He was going to have to show her and hope for the best. Explaining his gifts and hers would have to wait a few more minutes.

Richie closed his eyes and prayed the Goddess would help him through explaining what he was without losing Piper for good.

"You've heard of vampires, fairies, and such, right?"

She scowled at him. "Yes, everyone has."

"Where do you think those stories came from? There are tales of mythical creatures in every country of the world."

Piper glanced at the floor and then back to him. "I've never really thought about it. I guess I assumed it was people from the past trying to explain things science hadn't yet."

"Don't you think the stories had some merit? There had to have been something people saw or experienced that caused the legends to appear in every civilization. A grain of truth to the tales, so to speak."

She pursed her lips, tilted her head. "I hadn't really thought about it, but I guess so."

V.A. Dold & Tori Austin

"Hold onto that shred of belief for a little longer." Taking a deep breath, he sent her an image of his wolf.

She threw her hands in the air in frustration. "You still think you're a dog? What the hell does that have to do with legends?" she asked incredulously.

Richie knelt at her feet and took her hands in his. "I'm not a dog, I'm a wolf. A shifter."

Piper pulled her hands free and scooted away from him. "Are you telling me you're a werewolf like in the horror movies?"

"No. No, not at all. Shifters aren't werewolves. We're men born with a human soul and a wolf soul. I can shift into my wolf anytime I want. It's not like the myth of a cursed man forced into a wolf at the full moon. When I'm my wolf, I'm still me, just in another form and I don't need the moon to do it."

"Ah huh." She drew out the words and eyed him skeptically.

"I'm still a man, a human man, just one that can shift into a wolf."

"I think you should take me back to the airport."

"Mon amour, I know I sound crazy, but I can prove it to you if you think you can handle it."

"And how do you propose to do that?"

"I'll shift for you," Richie said hesitantly.

Piper snorted. "Whatever, dude. I'm going to pack."

Richie sighed resignedly. He looked miserable as he got to his feet.

RICHIE: Le Beau Series

Piper thought he'd given up his crazy talk and was going to do as she wished and take her back to the airport. She couldn't have been more wrong.

One second Richie stood a few feet away and the next a huge black wolf with amber eyes appeared. Even though she knew Richie hadn't had the chance to hide, she still looked around the room as if he were hiding somewhere.

Finally, she gulped hard and looked back at the wolf.

The beast wagged its tail and whined. Still watching her intently, it lay down near her feet and put its nose close to her toes.

Sucking in air like a fish out of water, Piper thought she was going to hyperventilate. Very carefully, she eased her gun from the holster she wore under her clothes.

The wolf gazed up at her with an expression of profound sadness as an overwhelming wave of defeat and sorrow hit her full force.

Piper clutched her chest and tears streamed down her face. She'd never felt such intense grief before. She wrapped her arms around her middle and stared at the floor as she rocked herself.

Startled, she jerked when arms enfolded her and warm, soft lips kissed away her tears.

"I'm sorry, mon amour. I didn't mean to cause you pain."

Piper wiggled from his hold and paced across the room, she had to think. There was an explanation for this. She just needed to find it.

V.A. Dold & Tori Austin

When Richie reached for her again, she panicked and bolted from the cabin.

"Piper, please don't go." But she was already out the door and disappearing into the trees.

*****

Richie hung his head. Now what should he do? Suddenly, an image of Anna flitted through his thoughts. His immense grief lightened slightly. That might work.

He snatched his phone and dialed his friend.

"Hello? Richie, are you back already?"

"Hi, Anna. Yeah, I'm back and I brought my mate with me."

"That's wonderful."

"Well, maybe not so much. I was trying to explain shifters to her and she freaked out. Now she's running through the bayou, terrified of me."

"Oh, hun. What can I do to help?"

"Could you come to my cabin and talk to her. Once we find her, of course."

"Absolutely. I'll be right there."

"Bring Cade or one of the men with you for protection. She has a serial killer after her and he could show up at any time."

"O...kay," she said slowly. "Are you in danger, Richie?"

He snorted. "Not from that idiot."

Anna sighed in relief. "I'll get Cade and we'll be there as fast as we can."

RICHIE: Le Beau Series

*****

Thirty excruciating minutes passed before Richie heard Cade's outboard motor. Finally!

He rushed to the dock and helped Anna from the boat while Cade tied off.

"Richie, I haven't seen you since Abbi was born." Anna hugged him tightly.

"I know. I'm sorry I haven't been to see her, but I've been pretty busy."

Cade shook Richie's hand "Congratulations. I hear you've joined the mated club."

"Yeah, well not quite yet. I still need to convince her I'm not a monster."

"Leave that to Anna. She'll explain everything to your mate. My mate has an uncanny way of knowing just what to say."

Richie's shoulders slumped in defeat. "We need to locate her first. She hasn't come back."

"No worries, I'll track her down and then stand guard while Anna does the talking."

Richie sighed, looking from the trees to Cade and back again. "What should I do?"

"Wait here," Anna said, hugging him again. "We'll bring her back and then the two of you can discuss your future."

"Thank you both for coming. I don't know what I'd have done."

"We'll let you know when we head back your direction. And once you have things settled with your mate, I want to hear all about this killer," Cade said, as they headed for the dense underbrush.

V.A. Dold & Tori Austin

Anna ducked under the fronds Cade held aside for her and stepped onto a faint game trail. Piper's scent was strong, indicating she'd gone this way recently and was probably not far.

Not more than thirty feet away, sat an agitated woman on a fallen tree trunk.

"Hello," Anna called out. She didn't want to startle the woman and make matters worse than they already were.

Piper leapt from her perch and crouch low, making herself as small a target as possible. Anna could tell she had some kind of training.

"My name is Anna. My husband, Cade and I came to talk to you." She stood just out of view and waited for Piper to answer. Richie's mate had a gun and knew how to use it. No sense in making herself an easy target.

She watched as Piper quartered the area with her eyes. This woman had skills.

Piper couldn't see anyone. Whoever they were, they were good. She sent her gift out and located them ten feet to her left behind two large trees.

Pointing her gun directly at them, she demanded, "Show yourselves."

"Lay the gun on the ground in front of you and we'll come out," Cade instructed.

"I don't think so."

Anna rolled her eyes at Cade and without warning, stepped into view.

RICHIE: Le Beau Series

Cade snarled and leapt in front of her, putting himself between the gun and his mate. "Don't ever do that again."

Anna shook her head and patted his chest. "Sure, hun, whatever you say. Now get out of my way, you big oaf."

She pushed past him and smiled as he made angry noises.

"I'm Anna, a friend of Richie."

"Piper." Was all she offered in response.

"Do you think you could put the gun away? I'm not going to hurt you. I only want to talk."

Anna saw Piper eyeing her and Cade as he continued to snarl angrily behind her.

Piper lifted her chin toward Cade. "Yeah, I don't think that would be a smart idea."

Anna whirled on her mate. "Go cool off somewhere. You're not helping here."

Cade put his hands on his hips and drew a deep calming breath. "Sorry, mon amour. My wolf gets cranky when a gun is pointed at you. I smell her reluctance to hurt anyone, so I'll leave. I'll just be a few feet away at the edge of the forest. Call me when you're finished here."

Anna stood on tiptoes and kissed him. "Thank you, babe."

She waited for him to leave before she spoke again. "Sorry about that. The males can be a bit over protective."

She hopped up on the tree trunk Piper had been sitting on and waited for her to sit as well.

Piper sat again. "Males?"

"Male shifters."

She looked around quickly then back at Anna. "He's one too?"

Anna leaned in and conspiratorially whispered back, "Yeah, and so am I."

Piper fell off the fallen log and scrambled back until she hit a tree trunk.

"Don't be afraid, I won't hurt you. I understand your fear and confusion. I was a human woman without knowledge of shifters not too long ago."

That got Piper's attention. "You were? Wait. What do you mean you WERE?"

"Once you agree to accept Richie, there's a ritual that binds you together. After that, you will be a shifter, too. But I'll let him explain the ritual."

"Are you all from the same nut house?"

"No," Anna laughed, "but sometimes it appears that way. What would you like to know?"

Piper shook her head. "I'm not sure about anything anymore. He turned into a wolf in front of me. But I still can't believe it. I'm pretty sure I imagined it or was maybe seeing things."

"How about I shift for you, like he did. That way you will know it wasn't just Richie and you weren't imagining things."

"Okay..."

Anna hopped to the ground and scented her for fear, finding none she shifted.

RICHIE: Le Beau Series

Piper staggered back a few paces and eyed the beautiful red wolf. There was no way she was imagining the same thing twice. But how could this be real? Crazy explanations raced through her mind, each more ridiculous than the last. Finally, she took a deep breath and thought of the old saying: after every possibility has been discarded, what is left is the truth. Holy Mother! Shifters are real. Once her heart slowed, she took a closer look at Anna's wolf.

"You're gorgeous," she breathed in awe.

Slowly, Anna stepped closer to Piper and sat within touching distance.

"I feel really stupid asking this, but can I pet you?"

Anna nodded, her tongue lolling to the side.

Tentatively, Piper touched the top of the wolf's head with her fingertips. "Holy crow, you're soft."

Little by little, Piper's confidence increased and her fear dissipated. After a few minutes, Anna stepped back and shifted to human.

"I can't believe shifters are real," Piper whispered to herself.

"Seeing is believing. Feeling a little better?"

"Yes, thank you. At least now I know I'm not crazy." She paused for a moment and then quietly asked, "Can I ask you a personal question?"

"Sure, ask away."

"Are you happy as a shifter? I mean you could have stayed human, right?"

"I'm blissfully happy. My life before Cade and our relationship was dismal compared to what I have now."

"That ritual thing you mentioned, does it hurt?"

"No. You'll find the ritual quite..." she paused and tilted her head, searching for a word, "exhilarating."

"Are shifters, especially the males, dangerous?"

"Only to someone threatening their mate or family. They're really just like you, regular people. They just have something extra."

Piper nodded and was silent for a bit. "Do you ever wish you hadn't accepted Cade?"

"No, not for a second. I'm sure you're confused about just about everything. I know I was. Perhaps it will help if I tell you about the little talk I had with myself before I accepted Cade. Would you like to hear it?"

"Yes, I would if you don't mind."

"I asked myself if I loved him, and I had to admit I did. At first I was concerned how people would react to my jumping into a relationship in a matter of days. You know, concerned about what they would think and say.

"But let me explain something about the mate relationship. It isn't like normal human dating and getting to know the other person over time. Richie is human, but more, and the more changes everything.

"Mates aren't just a choice, they're destined. He has one half of the soul and you have the other. The phenomenon of mating creates an instant attraction between two people that would never occur if he were just human. I'm sure you've felt the draw. Where mates are concerned, the individuals involved instantly want and need to be together."

Piper blushed. "Yeah, I know what you mean."

"As a human you may take your time before taking intimacy past kissing as you get to know each other. Mates don't have that luxury, the bond creates a very strong sexual need. You might find yourself making love to Richie much sooner than you ever would with any other man."

"Yep, been there, done that." She shook her head and blushed hotter.

"Don't be embarrassed. The need isn't something you could have easily denied. With a shifter relationship, the getting to know your partner part often comes second."

Piper was listening and nodding, that was a good sign.

"Don't worry about jumping into the relationship too quickly and then regretting it. Mated pairs are a complete match in every way and encompass all the aspects the other person wants and desires in a perfect life partner. You actually couldn't have chosen a more perfect match for yourself."

"Is this all for real?" Piper asked in a small voice.

"Yes, it's very real. And when you find yourself ready to accept Richie in what very well may be only a few days, that is normal, too."

"A few days!"

Anna laughed and wrapped an arm around Piper's shoulders. "I know, crazy, right? But that's the way it usually happens. Your soul and his are drawn to each other and demand the ritual be completed to unite the two halves. From what I've seen and experienced the mating is usually completed within days of the two people meeting."

"What happens when one of the people wants out of the relationship?"

Anna shook her head. "That would never happen. The ritual is stronger and deeper than a marriage ceremony. The soul actually becomes one and the bond is unbreakable. That's why the two people are purposely made to be exactly what the other wants and needs in a loving relationship."

"How are they purposely made? And where did the two halves of a soul come from?"

"The wolf goddess, her name is Luperca, is the original creator of the wolf shifters. A long time ago, she blessed a village of humans with powers and gifts. Basically, she gave each person a wolf soul. This second soul gave the human the ability to change at will into the wolf living inside him. She has set it up that the shifter has one half of a soul and the human is born with the other half. In the same manner, the shifter and human are created with the specific personality, beliefs, likes and dislikes, etc. to be an ideal match to the other. There are powers you will be blessed with too, but I'll let Richie explain those."

RICHIE: Le Beau Series

Piper was quiet for a long time. "That's a lot to take in. I'm not sure what else to ask."

Anna patted the tree trunk for Piper to join her again. "Okay, then let me ask you a few things,"

"Do you have feelings for Richie?"

"Yes, I think I do."

"Do you want to be with him all the time? Miss him when he isn't with you? Think of him first when you have news you want to share with someone?"

"Yes."

"Does he turn you on? Light your fire so to speak?"

Piper lowered her eyes, and the color in her cheeks deepened to rose. "Yes."

"All right, I want you to take a minute and imagine Richie gone forever. You will never see him or speak to him again."

Anna patiently waited a few minutes and then asked, "Now, how do you feel?"

Piper absently rubbed her chest over her heart. "I feel lonely and miserable."

"You just answered your question."

Piper frowned. "What question?"

"The question, do you love Richie and want to spend the rest of your life with him."

Comprehension dawned on Piper's face.

"Are you ready to go back and finish talking to him?"

"Yes, I think I am."

Anna called telepathically to Cade and led Piper back to Richie's cabin.

V.A. Dold & Tori Austin

******

Richie was wearing a path across is living room floor, pacing anxiously. Frustrated and terrified he'd lost his mate before he ever had a chance. He raked his fingers through his hair. When he pulled his hand away, his fingers were covered in dark strands.

At the rate he was going, he'd be bald before Anna returned with Piper. He shook the hair from his fingers and crossed the floor to gaze across his expanse of lawn toward the tree line Piper had disappeared into. His heart stuttered as Anna and Piper walked into view.

Frantically, he used his wolfs eyes to search her expression. She didn't look scared, that was good. He hoped.

Hands shaking, he opened his screen door and stepped out. His wolf wanted to race to her side, but Richie stood fast. He wouldn't be stupid and rush her. That would only insure her flight or fight reactions. No, he had to let her come to him, and it was killing him.

He scented the air and smelled interest and curiosity. He breathed a little easier. Anna must have gotten through to her.

"We're back," Anna called cheerfully.

Moments later, Cade, Anna, and Piper stopped at the bottom of the stairs of the cabin. He couldn't take his eyes from his mate's face as he held his breath and waited for the verdict.

RICHIE: Le Beau Series

Anna grinned up at him. "Cade and I will leave you two to talk in private."

Richie was so relieved, his knees barely held him upright. "Thank you so much, Anna. I owe you more than I can say."

"Nonsense. That's what friends are for. We'll see you and Piper soon."

Cade paused as he turned to go. "Richie, don't forget I want to talk to you about the trouble following her when you have the time."

Piper looked at Richie sharply, then gave Cade a hard stare.

"I'll call you later, Cade." He needed to talk to Piper about disclosing information before he said anything more.

Cade gave him a quick nod and turned away.

When Richie looked back at Piper, her eyes were narrowed. Shit, he didn't need more friction between them.

"What did you tell him?"

He held up his hands in surrender. "I told Anna to bring Cade or one of the other males for protection because you had a murderer after you. That's all I said."

She searched his face, then nodded. "Okay."

Shuffling his feet like a nervous schoolboy, Richie asked, "Would you like to come back inside?"

"Yes, it seems we have a lot to talk about."

He waited until she was seated and asked, "Would you like a soda or bottled water?"

V.A. Dold & Tori Austin

"A water would be wonderful. It was pretty hot out there and there wasn't much of a breeze. I feel a little dehydrated."

Richie grabbed two waters from the kitchen and joined her on the couch. He opened hers and offered it.

"Thank you," she said and gave him a little smile.

His heart sang. Maybe this would end well after all. "I guess I better ask what you ladies talked about before I continue. I'm not sure what you know and what I still need to explain."

Piper relayed everything she knew about shifters and mates. Little did she know that new information barely touched the tip of the iceberg.

RICHIE: Le Beau Series

Chapter 10

Richie nodded along, taking note of what she already understood. And thankfully, seemed to accept.

"All right, based on what you've been told, what would you like to know first?"

"Could you explain the difference between a mate and a girlfriend or wife?"

He drew a breath. "That's a good place to start. When a human man finds a woman he is attracted to, he decides if he wants to pursue her. That decision may lead to a happy life together or heartbreak. A mate is destined and created by design to be the man's idyllic life partner and lover. Because the two people are so perfectly matched, there can be no mistake or heartbreak. It is virtually guaranteed happiness."

"Anna explained something about that and two souls."

"Did she tell you the two people were created to complete each other? That you hold the other half of my soul and I, yours?"

"Yes, she mentioned that, but at the time my head was spinning and I'm afraid I may have only caught bits and pieces. She explained the Goddess and how shifters were created, that's when she mentioned the two souls."

"Right. There is a ritual that binds the two halves together and gives the human involved all the gifts and powers of a shifter."

When she remained silent with an attentive expression, he continued. "Would you like me to explain the ritual now or would you prefer to wait? There are quite a few other things I need to tell you."

Piper chuckled, shook her head, and placed a hand on his arm. "I think we should wait on that. I have a feeling I'll need a clear head when you explain it."

Richie rumbled happily at his mate's touch and grinned. "Fair enough."

Her eyes locked with his. "What is that sound you make? Are you mad when you do that?"

His smile was broad, but gentle. "No, mon amour, that's my wolf's way of purring. It's a happy, contented sound."

"Oh, good." Her shoulders relaxed and she let out a long breath. "If it's not too personal, can you tell me about your wolf?"

"Absolutely. My wolf is average in size, as far as shifters go. He's about one hundred thirty five pounds. The wolf gives both the human and the animal the ability to hear, smell, and see far better than a full human. This might be a good time to

RICHIE: Le Beau Series

explain a shifter's gifts and powers. If you agree to complete the ritual with me, you will have the powers as well."

Her jaw dropped. "I would get powers?"

"Yes, all the powers I have plus your natural gift you have as a human would be enhanced."

"Holy crow!"

"Do you want me to continue or have you had enough for one day?"

Piper crossed her arms and raised a brow. "You can't dangle powers in front of me and then not tell me about them. This I want to hear."

Richie chuckled and put a hand to his heart. "How dare I tease you in such a manner. Let's see, you know about telepathy and sending feelings and touch. I explained the enhanced wolf senses, so that leaves zapping clothes and shifting."

"Zapping clothes?"

"As a shifter, you will be able to dress and undress with a thought. The only caveat to that is you actually have to own the clothes before you can zap them. It's not like you can decide you want to wear a fancy gown and zap it on if you don't have that gown in your closet."

"That makes sense that you would need to possess the clothes. So you just think it and it happens?"

"Yes and no. You would need to practice a bit before it comes easily, but all you do is picture the clothes you want to wear in your mind and see yourself wearing them."

"Huh, that could be handy."

Richie let his wolf enter his eyes. "It is."

"You mentioned shifting, are you telling me I would be able to be a wolf, too?"

"Yes. During the ritual you will receive a wolf soul and gain all the gifts and abilities. Even the ability to shift."

Piper sat back and stared at him for a heartbeat. "Wow, I wasn't expecting that."

"Oh shoot, I forgot two gifts that I'm sure you'll find very appealing. As a shifter you will heal ten times faster than a human, and you will be able to move so fast, the human eye won't be able to detect you."

"Shit. I sure could have used those powers the last few years."

"I'm sure they would have been very handy as a bounty hunter. I know you have a gift. Would you like to explain it to me?"

"It's hard to explain. I can sort of send myself outside my body and look around corners or into other rooms. But I have to have an idea of what the room looks like to do it."

"That sounds like remote viewing. I'm sure that was a useful gift to have in your profession."

Piper grinned. "It does come in handy and has saved my bacon a few times."

"I have a special gift as well. Each shifter is born with one special gift. I have visions, both while sleeping and awake."

"No way!"

"Way." His face broke out in a wide smile. Her excitement was infectious.

RICHIE: Le Beau Series

Piper grinned as she imagined taking down bounties with the powers Richie described. After a few minutes, she shook off her daydreams and focused on the issues at hand. *Wolves, we were talking about being a shifter.*

"Okay, I'm trying to wrap my head around being able to shift. Talk about surreal. Does it hurt when you change?"

"Not at all, and it's very fast, not like in the movies where the man agonizes for what seems like forever as his body contorts. When you shift, you just imagine the change and allow it to happen. It's instantaneous; one minute you're human and the next you have the body and senses of a wolf."

"That's good. I was imagining all kinds of horrible pain and gooey oozing stuff."

Richie barked a laugh. "Gooey oozing stuff?"

"You know, exposed muscles, and bones, maybe entrails."

He continued to laugh until he couldn't breathe. "Entrails? You have quite an active imagination."

She giggled along with him. "How was I to know?"

"You weren't, but it's still funny."

Piper caught her breath and got serious again. "I suppose I'll be a black wolf, too."

Richie took a good look at her hair, it was mostly chestnut, but she had a generous amount of red and gold highlights throughout. "I doubt it. You would likely be a rich brown. Red or golden are possible as well, or a mixture of all those colors. But I'm pretty sure you'll be brown."

"How do you know that?"

"A person's wolf is always some color of the human's hair."

"Really? So shifters come in different colors?"

"An entire spectrum. When the pack gathers and shifts for a run, it's an awesome sight to see. We usually do that sort of thing at the plantation you saw when we landed."

"Do you think I'll get the chance to see that?"

He took her hand in his and gazed deeply into her eyes. "I'm sure of it."

"Excellent," she beamed. "Hey, you never did explain the private plane and airstrip."

"You're right, I got a little side tracked. Shifters have royalty, a king and queen. Our king, Isaac, is a direct descendant of the original shifters created. His mate, our queen, is Emma. I think you'll really like her.

"She was a gypsy from the old country a couple hundred years ago, and when she settled here with Isaac she added voodoo to her magical talents. Her power is off the charts.

"She is the main healer for the shifters and the local humans, using natural herbs and crystals and such. She comes off kind of ditzy sometimes, but I think she does it on purpose. I've seen her do things that would curl your hair, but she prefers to be benevolent and kind.

RICHIE: Le Beau Series

"Cade, their oldest son is their investment advisor and has amassed a huge fortune for the family. They are billionaires several times over, but you would never know it. They act like everyone else in the bayou, friendly and helpful, never snooty or pompous.

"The king owns the airplane and airstrip, I just borrowed it."

"Holy crow."

"Yeah, accumulating wealth tends to happen when you live a long time." Richie winked.

Piper's eyes grew large. "What do you mean, live a long time?"

Richie gave her a good long look. "Are you sure you're ready to hear more?"

"There's no way I'll sleep tonight wondering what that statement meant, so you better tell me."

"Okay, scoot over close to me so I can hold you while I tell you the rest."

The way Piper smiled and snuggled closer, she looked like a little girl ready for a bedtime story.

"A shifter isn't immortal, but we do live a long time. A normal lifespan is fourteen hundred years. At maturity, we appear to be around twenty-five to thirty years old and we remain that way until we are about nine hundred years old, and then we start to slowly age again. I was born on July twenty-third, eighteen sixty-six. I turned one hundred forty nine this year.

"When a human completes the ritual with a shifter, if the human is past thirty, they go through a regression of sorts where their body returns to the way they were in their mid to late twenties. Anna,

V.A. Dold & Tori Austin

who you just met was in her forties and had a pretty dramatic regression. I know better than to ask a woman her age, but I'm guessing you're around thirty so you may not have to go through much of a regression."

Piper laid her cheek against his chest and played with the front of Richie's T-shirt. "Thank you for the compliment. I'm actually thirty-five. That's pretty old for a female bounty hunter and another reason I'm retiring. Age and wanting to start a family are my two big factors. It would be difficult to chase a perp down if you're nine months pregnant. Not that I have a husband to start a family with. I learned really early on, it's hard to maintain a relationship if I'm never home. Getting a nine to five job and finding a husband were my goals after I caught Qball."

"What are your goals now?" Richie asked quietly and held his breath.

"To catch Qball and get to know you," she said matter-of-factly.

"Good answer," he said into her hair as he breathed her in.

"How do shifters stay hidden from the world if they live so long? Someone is bound to notice."

"It's a combination of the magic which allows us to appear to age for the benefit of humans as well as making people believe we are our own descendants. After a normal human lifetime, a descendent inherits the property and investments we have.

RICHIE: Le Beau Series

"Of course, this person is actually just us pretending to be our own relatives. Since the invention of computers, it's much easier to get into public records and manipulate identifications or create new ones. Isaac has a hacker on payroll and all he does is maintain shifter identities."

"If you're over one hundred years old, you must have had at least one other name."

He smiled, and rubbed his chin across the top of her head. "Yes, I was born Raoul. I faked my death and left the area for about twenty years, then came back with a new identity."

She raised her head and studied his face, then nodded. "You look like a Raoul. The name suited you, you should take it back for your next alias."

"Good idea, I think I will. I liked that name."

She laughed and flashed him a smile.

Damn, she had a killer smile that made his heart race. He watched as her eyes went soft and inviting. As if touched by a tuning fork, her laugh vibrated through his body. It wrapped around his heart and made his wolf sing with joy.

Richie's focus centered on Piper's beautiful face. With each breath he inhaled, her unique bouquet filled his lungs. Wherever her hair brushed his skin, tingles rose. He moistened his lips and quietly said, "Kiss me, Piper."

The request was spoken so softly Piper almost missed it, but her mind registered the words as her heart and soul filled with his longing and love. Without hesitation, she slid her palm around his neck and urged him toward her parted lips, pressed her mouth to his, gliding her tongue into his warm welcoming depths.

Heat and erotic energy flashed from her to him and back, sending all the blood from his brain straight to his groin. His breathing became ragged and he held on to his control by a bare thread. He slowly pulled his lips away and pressed his forehead to hers. "I need a moment if you plan to ask any more questions. Mon amour, you destroy my control like nothing else can."

She grinned playfully and brushed her lips across his jaw. "I didn't know my kisses made such an impact."

"Impact is an insipid description of the way your kisses affect me."

Piper looked up at him, feeling flirtatious and mischievous, and heard him exhale a breath. The air left his lungs in a rush. He gripped her shoulders to put a few inches between them. "You are one hell of a dangerous woman, Piper."

"I'm only intimately dangerous to you," she said, repeating his words from the wedding dance.

"Touché."

She slipped her hand from his neck to rest on his chest and held it there, wanting the connection. Anna was right, she was falling hopelessly in love with him. Surprisingly, the depth of the emotion wasn't as alarming as she had expected.

"I don't have any more questions right now, but I would like a tour of your property so the next time I take a walk I don't get lost. That is, after you kiss me again, of course."

RICHIE: Le Beau Series

Richie wanted nothing more than to kiss her again. He didn't just want to kiss her, he had to kiss her. "You don't have to tell me twice."

He slipped his arm around her waist and hauled her onto his lap. Piper squeaked, but she didn't complain when his mouth came down on hers. He kissed her as if his life depended on it. His tongue plundered and explored her mouth hungrily, dancing and sliding along hers. She tasted exactly like she smelled.

They devoured each other until air became a priority. He broke the kiss, his body hard as a rock, and out of breath. "I love you, Piper. I've never wanted anyone as badly as I want you. Not just in my bed, but by my side for the rest of my life. I want to hold you as you fall to sleep every night and wake up next to you every morning," he panted in a husky voice.

Piper remained silent for what felt like an eternity. Her eyes searching his face, and gazing deeply into his own as if she could see clear to his soul. She took a deep breath, taking his scent deeply into her lungs. "I never thought I would say this only days after meeting a man, but I love you, too. It scares the daylights out of me. Thankfully, Anna explained feeling this way is normal for mates, but I'm doing my best to not freak out."

"You're right. The intense emotions you're experiencing are normal. I feel your confusion, and as much as I hate to say it, we should spend the remainder of today getting to know each other rather than falling into bed."

V.A. Dold & Tori Austin

She covered her mouth with her hand and tried to suppress a giggle. "Wow, I bet it really hurt to say that."

He rose from the couch and held out a hand. "Cher, you have no idea. Come on, let me show you around the place."

Richie owned ten acres, which felt like a heck of a lot more when wading through bayou brush. And it was stifling with such little air movement in the dense foliage. He noticed she was breathing hard in the heat and humidity. She wasn't acclimated to the life in the bayou.

"Do you see that snake over there?" He pointed to a multicolored snake in the brush. "That's a Texas coral snake, you want to avoid those. There are also rattlesnakes, cottonmouths, and copperheads around here, so be careful where you step and what you touch."

"All the snakes kind of take the fun out of exploring. I have to tell you, I'm not a fan."

"If you keep to the paths or game trails, and watch yourself, you'll be fine," he instructed, as he showed her every available option. He didn't want to take any chance of her wandering off or getting bitten.

"Holy crow, this is a workout."

"I'm sorry, cher. Just a little further and we will be back at the yard."

"Awesome," she panted.

True to his word, they stepped onto his manicured lawn a minute later. "Let me get you a bottle of water, and then why don't you cool off on the pier while I make dinner? You can catch a nice breeze down there."

"That sounds like heaven, thank you." She accepted the water, gave him a kiss and headed for the pier.

Richie watched her until she was settled then turned to the task at hand. His mate needed sustenance and he and his wolf longed to care for her. He opened the freezer and took stock of what he had on hand. Steak or chicken? Steak with baked potatoes and a salad sounded perfect. He had a tasty red wine to go with it, too. He grinned to himself as he thawed the beef recalling the last time she had wine. She was adorable when she was tipsy.

He wanted her glued to his side, but at the same time, he wanted her to love the bayou as much as he did. That was why he sent her to the river instead of keeping her with him in the cabin. If she found the peace she so desperately wanted here, she just might stay. He would go with her wherever she chose to live, though he prayed she would agree to live here after they completed the ritual.

*****

Qball checked his handheld tracker. She was here. Based on the blip on the screen, she was just around the bend. He glanced at the black murky water. There wasn't a gator in sight. As a matter of fact, he hadn't seen one for over a mile. He wasn't

V.A. Dold & Tori Austin

sure why there weren't any here when they seem to be plentiful everywhere else, but it worked to his advantage so he wouldn't look a gift horse in the mouth.

    Quietly, he worked the boat he'd stolen toward the water's edge and tied it to a low hanging branch. He set the tracker aside and stripped off his shoes and socks, no need to get them wet. Then he went into the water and quietly swam toward his quarry, keeping close to the edge where he could stay out of sight.

    As he rounded the bend he spied her on the end of the dock with her feet in the water. He wanted to laugh. The bitch was making this too easy. He inched his way along, staying under low hanging branches and hiding in the floating plants. Just a few more feet and he would be able to grab her ankle.

*****

    Piper swished her feet back and forth, feeling the water flow across her heated skin. The coolness felt wonderful and helped her relax and think. If she weren't afraid of what might lurk under the surface, she'd dive in. She took another sip of water and enjoyed the view. The beauty of the bayou surprised her. She had spent her life as a city girl and hadn't given this part of the country much consideration.

    Her mind wandered to Richie and her future. Could she commit to one man for hundreds of years? God, she hoped she could. The intense feelings and attraction were terrifying. Even as she stared at the water her thoughts turned to him in the cabin and she found she wanted to jump up and run back. No, she would stay put, she couldn't think straight when she was close to him.

Okay, Piper, what are you going to do? she asked herself.

Pros and cons, she needed to weigh her options. She had never met a sexier man or had a better lover. Check and check. She enjoyed his company and he made her laugh, more checks. He didn't pressure her to be something she wasn't or try to change her.

And if she was really going to be honest with herself, she loved his cabin. Although, it could use a few more bedrooms. She was shocked when she realized she could see herself settling down and having children with Richie.

Her heart hammered in her chest, there had to be negatives. She searched her mind and came up with nothing. She had nothing. Damn, Anna was right, he was perfect for her. She needed to hear the rest of what Richie had to say about shifters and that ritual before she made a final decision.

She was lifting her feet from the water when something latched onto her ankle. Before she could scream, she was yanked from the dock. Terrified a gator had gotten her, she lashed out thrashing to get free. When that didn't work, she balled her fist and pounded on what had a grip on her. That was when it dawned on her, it wasn't a gator's jaws that held her under the surface, it was a hand.

V.A. Dold & Tori Austin

A solid kick with her free leg loosened the hold on her and she broke the surface coughing and gasping for breath. Before she could escape to shore, she was grabbed from behind and pulled under again.

The case file she'd read said Qball wasn't the best swimmer by any means, but he was determined. Add insanity to that and she had a fight on her hands. He wouldn't let her escape if he could help it.

She was preparing an offensive when he seized a fist full of hair. He pushed her further under using his body weight, but she was strong and had trained for water combat.

Piper struggled under the water. If she lost a chunk of hair so be it, Qball was going down. She twisted and wedged her feet against the body of her attacker. Mustering all her strength, she pushed with her well-developed thigh muscles. Her scalp burned and it hurt like a mother, but she was free again. This time when she broke the surface she faced the asshat and gasped. Qball sneered and went for her again.

Too slow.

She was ready this time. Her feet were planted and she put everything she had into the punch. Qball's head lurched on his shoulders an instant before he crumbled into the black, churning river. Piper reached for him, but her hands found nothing but water. Carefully, she felt around with her feet; he had to be here somewhere. Nothing.

He'd gone down, literally at her feet. How the hell could he not be there? She dove under and continued to search.

RICHIE: Le Beau Series

*****

Mid chop of the salad Richie was preparing, he went rigid. A vision overtook him and held him in its grip. Piper was being attacked. Qball was here. He came out of the vision in a cold sweat and rushed from the cabin.

He smelled the intruder the instant he cleared the door. The scent of Piper's fear was heavy in the air. When he didn't see her on the pier, he panicked. The water boiled and churned as if a gator rolled with its prey below the surface. Richie dove in blind, unsure what he would find.

A body banged against his legs. Thinking it was Piper, he grabbed hold of what felt like a shirt and tried to pull it to the surface. The rough cotton yanked from his grasp. He meant to suck in a breath and dive again, but when he opened his eyes, Piper stood before him searching the water.

She hadn't seen him yet and continued to search for him below the surface. "He's here somewhere, dammit."

"Piper! Thank goddess, I thought I'd lost you." He yanked her into his arms and buried his face in her hair.

He held her tightly as she struggled to get free, running his free hand down the length of her hair. When she flinched, he pulled back to examine her. "Where are you hurt?"

Instead of answering his question she pulled away and began searching again. "Don't worry about me. We need to find Qball's body."

"His body? You killed him?" Richie asked as he helped her locate her bounty.

"No, I wish I had. I only knocked him out. He went under and I can't find him. I need to retrieve the body."

Then it dawned on him, the shirt he'd had hold of must have been Qball's. "I'm pretty sure he's gone, Piper."

She paused and turned to stare at him. "What? How?"

"I felt a cotton shirt when I dove in and it was yanked out of my hand. I'm pretty sure it was him making an escape."

He took a deep breath and smelled the water and the air for a sign of Qball.

"What are you doing?" she asked as she watched him breathe in and out with an expression of total concentration on his face.

"Smelling for him. He's no longer here, his scent has dissipated."

"Well, shit." Qball getting away again really burned her ass and that stuck in her craw something fierce.

"Come on, I want to get you cleaned up and check you for injuries." He heaved his heavy frame from the water and gave her a hand onto the pier.

Now that she was on a dry surface, he couldn't see any gaping wounds. That was a good sign. "Anything broken?"

"No. The little bastard didn't get a chance to do much damage."

RICHIE: Le Beau Series

His brows drew together and his breath caught in his chest. "Then why do I smell blood?"

She reached for the back of her head. "The asshat ripped out some of my hair, my head burns like crazy. That bastard fights like a girl. I hope it grows back. The last thing I want is a freaky bald spot that makes me look like a monk."

He took her by the shoulders and turned her. "Let me take a look."

"Is it bad?"

"Not too bad. I think it will heal and be fine. Besides, even if it didn't grow back, you wouldn't have a bald spot after the ritual."

She turned back. "Really? Why?"

"I've been thinking about it and I'm convinced you'll go through a minor conversion. Only a few years younger than you are now. Regardless, anything that's happened since you turned about twenty five will be reversed as if it never occurred."

"So the scar I have from a knife wound I received last year will be gone?"

"Yes, ma'am." He led her way from the pier and toward the cabin. "Was it a bad injury? If so, that will be painful when it heals during the conversion."

"Not too bad. And getting rid of the ugly scar will be pretty cool." She eyed the water and shoreline again, searching for a sign of her bounty's passing. He had slipped away without a trace again.

V.A. Dold & Tori Austin

"Dinner is almost ready, why don't you take a shower and wash the blood out of your hair. I'll watch for Qball in case he doubles back."

"Okay. Make sure you keep a gun handy. If you get a glimpse of him, shoot his pansy ass. I'm tired of his games," she groused and stomped angrily toward the cabin.

Chapter 11

Richie snorted. "Cher, I don't need a gun to take that sorry excuse of a human down."

She glanced at him as they walked hand in hand to the cabin. "Yeah, I guess you wouldn't. How did you know he was here? Did you hear the splashing or smell him, or something?"

"I was fixing the salad when I had a vision. Normally, I get them in advance, but this one seemed to be happening in real time."

"How far in advance do you see things?"

"It varies, sometimes hours, but usually days." He wanted to warn her about the vision of her being shot. The problem was, he knew she wouldn't listen and if she tried to avoid the event all together, he wouldn't know what to watch for so he could intervene. If he told the person involved, the outcome remained the same. Only someone else interfering without knowledge of the vision could change it. No, he needed to let the scene unfold so he could be there to save his mate.

"I'm betting the visions feel like both a blessing and a curse. If I knew something bad would happen to a friend or family member and I couldn't prevent it, I'd feel terrible."

V.A. Dold & Tori Austin

Richie sighed. "It's difficult to live with and I've had to learn the hard way to allow fate to unfold. I rarely attempt to change the outcome anymore."

She pulled him to a stop just inside the door. "Something terrible happened because you tried to step in," she stated knowingly as her eyes scoured his expression for the answer.

"Yes," he said quietly, not looking at her.

He felt her finger pressed under his chin forcing him to meet her gaze. "What happened?"

"I saw my best friend Armand Le Beau killed by a gang of humans. After I warned him, he took my advice and walked home using a different route. The gang was sitting on the porch of an old shack. I mistakenly sent him right to them. He was beaten to death."

Piper gasped and he saw tears fill her eyes. Then she wrapped her arms around his waist and held him. "I'm so sorry, Richie."

"Thank you, mon amour." He savored her warmth and then lightened the mood with a playful swat to her rump. "Get in the shower, woman. You smell like rotten gator bait."

"You don't like it? Eau de gator is the latest thing in perfume."

Richie laughed and shook his head as she walked away. Damn, she had a nice sway to her hips. Shaking off the image of her wet, slick body and the desire to follow her, he walked to the back door. For a full three minutes, he watched and listened. There was no sign of Qball. Maybe he'd

RICHIE: Le Beau Series

drowned. Then again, the man seemed to have nine lives. No, he wouldn't stop looking over his shoulder until a body was recovered or Qball showed himself.

He'd put Piper through a lot today, and he'd meant what he'd said about taking time to know each other. Silently, he vowed, he would honor his promise to slow things down. They would spend the rest of the day talking and he would keep his lips to himself.

Meanwhile at the Le Beau plantation.

Emma Le Beau was deep in meditation when the Goddess shimmered into form before her.

"Blessed be, my daughter," Luperca greeted her in her soft, peaceful voice.

"Blessed be, Mother. I would like to thank you again for your continued blessings of my family and our friends."

"You are more than welcome. It pleases me to see my children happily mated and starting families of their own. That is in fact, why I am here."

Emma became alarmed. "Has something happened?"

"No, my daughter. Everything has gone as planned." Luperca laughed softly. "I have another name for you."

"You do?" Emma asked excitedly.

"Yes. Seth, your adopted son has done a great service for me, and as such, has suffered. He has closed himself off from all human and shifter contact and I fear for his personal safety. He needs his mate to complete and heal his ragged heart and soul. Killing rogues, a few who had been his friends and family, over such a long period, although necessary, has taken a terrible toll on him.

"The least I can do is assist him in finding his mate. I am only sorry he did not find her sooner," the goddess said sadly.

"What would you like me to do? How may I be of service?" she asked in rapid succession.

"Seth is destined to meet his mate Sara Adams in Minnesota. A rogue went on a killing spree June tenth and killed Sara's brother. She's a murder investigator with the Richfield police department, but as a family member of the victim, she has been denied access to the investigation.

She is a tenacious woman and has taken it upon herself to find the killer on her own. Seth must go to Richfield and help her take the rogue down before she gets herself killed. If she dies, all hope to save Seth will be lost."

"So if I am understanding you correctly, you would like Isaac and me to get Seth to go to Minnesota after the rogue. Other than getting him to Richfield is there anything we should do?"

"In order for him to meet her, he must agree to work with her to kill the rogue. He has never worked with a partner and definitely never a human. It will not be easy. He will want to hunt the rogue on his own and return home."

Emma thought about that for a bit. "I think I know how we can force him to take her as a partner in this. Leave it to Isaac and myself, we will get it done one way or the other."

RICHIE: Le Beau Series

The Goddess's eyes twinkled with amusement. "I believe you will. I leave this in your capable hands. Blessed be, daughter, and good luck."

"Thank you. I'm sure we'll need a little luck this time. Blessed be, Mother."

Emma watched her fade from view, chewing her lip worriedly. *How are we going to pull this one off?*

Her heart was a roiling brew of delight and sorrow. Seth had been home for only a week or so, and now they were sending him away again.

*****

Richie turned from the screen door to finish the salad. Chopping and slicing was mindless work and allowed him to think.

He'd heard his good friend, Seth Le Beau had returned to the family's plantation and it was time he got some backup.

Dinner was ready. All he needed was to grill the steaks. Now was a good time to call his friend, while Piper was still in the shower.

"Hello?"

"Hi, Seth, it's Richie. Welcome home."

"Hey, Richie, what's up? I've missed you, man."

"I missed you, too. We need to get together at Logan's soon."

"Logan's? What's that?"

"That's right, you probably didn't hear about the change. Julia sold out to Logan."

"Really? I never thought I'd see the day. I'd love to get together, but I'm not sure about a bar. I'm out of practice socializing."

"Then Logan's might be the best thing for you. You need to rejoin the real world, bro."

Richie heard a deep sigh from the other end of the line and pictured Seth raking his fingers through his hair.

"Yeah, maybe."

"We can talk about that later. Do you have a minute?"

"I have a lot of minutes. I left the hunters, so I'm kind of between jobs."

"Cade may have told you my mate came home with me and is at the cabin. She's a bounty hunter and the murderer she's after is trying to kill her. She fought him in the water near my pier and knocked him out. He went under, so he may have drowned, but I doubt it. Just in case, I could use your help."

"Do you want me to take care of him?" Seth growled into the phone.

"No, she'd skin me alive if I did that. What I really need is an extra pair of eyes. He knows where we are and came after her today. I need someone to stand watch while we're sleeping."

"I'll be there after sundown, you won't see me, but I'll be there. I won't let him get to your mate. If he shows up, what do you want me to do?"

"Detain him. Piper wants to take him in alive if at all possible."

RICHIE: Le Beau Series

"Done. And, Richie," there was a long pause, "you're right. I need to rejoin the world. But I'm afraid it isn't going to be easy. I've become rather uncomfortable around people after living alone for so long. To be honest, you and my family are the only people I have any interest in having near me. I'm not stupid; I know how unhealthy that is. Seeing my brothers mated, and now you...
Well, it gives me hope. When this is over, we should go to Logan's and see if I can handle it."

"Thanks, Seth. Once Qball is in jail, the drinks are on me."

"Sounds like a plan. Let me know if you need anything else."

"Will do. Thanks again and I'm really glad you're home."

"You and me both, brother. You and me both."

Richie heard the shower turn off and ended the call.

*****

While she'd showered, Piper mulled over what she knew about Richie. Everything Anna and he told her rang with the clear tone of truth. She'd already admitted she loved him, so now it was time to put her big girl pants on and deal with all the shifter stuff.

With her mind set to a path, she could move forward. That meant getting to know him better.

V.A. Dold & Tori Austin

Of course that line of thought had her fantasizing about being with him again. The one night in the hotel had only whetted her appetite.

She smiled to herself, and her chest fluttered with anticipation. Her own personal wet-dream had saved her from the bad guy, was a supernatural sex god, and wanted to spend the rest of his life with her. She couldn't make this stuff up.

Now that she'd made a decision, she was going to seduce Richie. Tonight.

As they ate dinner, she barely tasted the food. She was too distracted visualizing him naked and at her mercy. God, she wanted him with a fierceness that thrilled her. In all her life, she'd never wanted a man so badly.

Richie studied her face. For once, he didn't know what Piper was thinking. Her walls were up and solidly in place. He relaxed and grinned happily when he noticed the interesting gleam in her eyes. Obviously she was less apprehensive than she'd been before her shower. She was still rather quiet, so he thought it might be best to leave her to her thoughts. Rather than make small talk, he took her hand, kissed her knuckles and brushed his thumb along the back.

The dinner was eaten and he was drying the last plate. He felt her arms wrap around him from behind as he was placing it in the cupboard. Turning, he searched her eyes.

Dammit. He was struggling to honor his decision to behave gentlemanly and respectfully.

RICHIE: Le Beau Series

But his mate needed comfort. He could do this. He could kiss her once and then just hold her. Clothes would remain in place, and there would be no roaming hands. A simple sweet kiss fit within the parameters of the rules.

"Come here, cher." He pulled her lips to his. He'd meant his kiss to be comforting and reassuring. Honestly, he did.

Instead, she turned the tables and claimed him. She thrust her hands deeply into his hair, kissing him with such passion, she left him quivering with need. Piper laid her stamp of ownership on his heart and soul as surely if she'd completed the ritual. He ached to lose himself in her heat, but he'd wait for her to take that step. As of that moment, he decided, Piper would call all the shots in this courtship and he was along for the ride.

"You know the cliché movie scene, 'I just almost died and I need to feel alive, let's have sex'?" she asked.

"Yeah."

"It's not such a cliché. I want you to make me feel alive and help me stop thinking so much. At least for tonight."

His arms tightened their hold on her as the air around them sizzled with energy. The tight hold he'd had on his body snapped. His heart hammered and his manhood was instantly rock hard. Richie didn't make a move though. She needed to be sure this was what she wanted.

He searched her expressive blue eyes for a long time, then said, "Piper, I want you to be very sure. I'll give you all the time you need, mon amour. If what you really want is to be held, I'll hold you until the cows come home."

He watched as her throat worked up and down with a hard swallow. Then her tongue shot out to lick her lips.

"I'm very sure. I need you Richie."

The flash of her tongue drew his gaze and almost took him to his knees. The memory of her incredible mouth had him licking his lips in return.

Piper added pressure behind his neck and urged him down to her. As if pulling him by an invisible leash, she closed the distance.

She needed this. No, she needed him. It would be an understatement to say, all the strange and fantastical things she'd learned today had been a lot to take. That Richie was one of the strange and fantastical things was beside the point. If she weren't already going crazy with desire for him, she would still want him to make her feel normal, to feel good. She needed to feel and not think. Who better to 'feel' with than the man who was rapidly stealing her heart?

She pressed against him, caging him between the counter and her body.

Acting upon the longing that had been building since her struggle with Qball, she pressed her mouth against his, hungry for him. With a ravenous groan, she slipped her tongue between his lips and explored his mouth. Her thumbs smoothed

RICHIE: Le Beau Series

back and forth across his jawline as she held his face in place. Their mouths fused, and when he returned the kiss as adamantly, she released the last threads of her control. Soft rumbles and growls rose from Richie's lips.

He grabbed her hips and pressed her tightly against his erection. Damn, he felt so good. She ground against him, needing more.

"Do you like that, cher? Let me see if I can help you out."

She held on as he shifted his weight, and pressed one heavily muscled thigh between her legs. Then cursed the barrier of her jeans when he applied pressure to her damp, aching center. She needed relief so badly she could taste it, and the denim was in the way. Piper started to slowly ride his thigh, taking what little stimulation she could get.

Her hands slid from his jaw to his chest, then lower to his jeans. The button popped easily as she worked to remove his clothes. She wanted to scream in frustration when she pulled his T-shirt loose and began working it up his body and he broke their kiss.

His lips hovered above hers and his heavy breath fluttered her hair. The warm chocolate of his eyes glowed with golden flecks of smoldering promise. "Let's take this to our bed."

Her voice came out no more than a whisper. "Excellent idea." She pulled from his arms, then took his hand and led him from the kitchen.

Once in the bedroom, Piper quickly began to strip. She paused when Richie asked, "Would you like to see it done the shifter way?"

Chewing her lower lip, she grinned. "Yeah, I think I would."

His lips slowly spread into a smoking hot, sexy grin. With a thought, Richie stood before her gloriously naked and unashamed. And oh lord, that man certainly had nothing to be ashamed of. He was absolutely gorgeous; simply looking at him made her mouth water and her pulse race.

He reached for her jeans and popped the button. "Let me help you out of those."

As she stripped her shirt and bra away, Richie knelt and reached for the zipper. The touch of his hands as he undressed her, made the butterflies in her stomach flutter faster.

With burning hunger in his eyes, he slid her jeans to her ankles. Freeing her feet, he wrapped his fingers around her calves before he skimmed them up her legs to her hips. His fingers slipped into the waistband of her panties, and they followed the path of her jeans.

Reaching for her hips, his hands slowly slid around to cup her buttocks and urge her toward his seeking mouth. He leaned forward, and encouraged her to widen her stance. Richie breathed her in before taking one slow lick.

Piper sighed and laced her fingers into his hair, holding him to her.

Growling his approval, he stroked the glistening lips protecting her womanhood, gently parting them.

When he took her into his mouth and stabbed deep, her legs almost buckled.

RICHIE: Le Beau Series

"Richie!"

There was a catch in her voice. A tremor. He couldn't get enough, licking and sucking, in total bliss until she bucked against his mouth, needing more. Her taste was heaven on his tongue.

Sliding one finger into her warm, weeping channel, she elicited a soft moan. His wolf rumbled his pleasure as her hips rocked in time with his fingers. Licking and suckling her clit, he added a second finger, filling her. Richie pushed her climax higher and higher. Piper's moans and mews increased as he quickened his thrusts. He tightened his hold as she pressed his face harder against her heated core.

She was getting close. Her eyes were glazed and her breath was labored. He could feel her muscles tightening around him as her rhythm faltered. Not missing a beat, he took control, pistoning into her, as her body gripped him hard until he felt sweat beading on his brow.

"That's it, mon amour, cum for me."

Seconds later, she threw her head back and cried out his name with a mind–blowing orgasm.

Richie slowed his fingers and gazed up at her lovely face. She was so beautiful with heavy lidded eyes and that sated expression.

With one last lick, he kissed his way to her breasts, stopping to lick and suckle each nipple. Pausing, he captured her gaze and with a sweltering look, licked his fingers clean, then claimed her mouth and plunged his tongue deep. Sharing the taste of her on his lips.

V.A. Dold & Tori Austin

With one hand laced in her hair and the other cupping her backside, he pressed her hips firmly against him, gently thrusting his engorged shaft between her thighs.

She molded against him, giving herself over to his magical mouth and hands. Their tongues danced and caressed in an erotic frenzy. Breathing hard, Richie kissed her softly one last time, then blazed a trail of hot kisses across her jaw and down the side of her neck.

In a guttural voice Richie asked, "Where do you want me, mon amour?"

Piper blushed slightly. "Could you sit with your back against the headboard? I'd like to be on top this time."

"Yes, ma'am." He hopped onto the bed and positioned himself exactly as she'd directed.

Piper swung a leg over his hips and straddled him. Her heated core, slick with her need, rocked slowly up and down his straining erection.

"I need to kiss you again." Her mouth claimed his, tongues gliding and tangling.

Richie kissed her back with equal abandon as he palmed her warm soft flesh. Each gentle stroke of Richie's thumbs across her hardened nipples increased the ache growing in her core.

When she released his mouth to explore his chest, she felt his lips on her neck, nibbling and lathing. Damn, that man had talent.

She leaned away just enough to explore his incredible chest, but not so much as to interfere with what he was doing. Softly she brushed her palm

RICHIE: Le Beau Series

across his pecks, causing his nipples to harden and a rumble to fill the room.

His hands skimmed down her waist and tightened on her hips as he kissed his way to the swell of her breast. She arched her back, begging him with her body to take possession of her aching nipple, and suck it into the heat of his mouth. Piper loved the feel of her distended peak brushing his lips, but she needed more relief than that offered.

Helpless moans escaped her throat. She was breathless with both hands bunched in Richie's hair. He was slowly killing her with pleasure.

Richie was painfully aroused. He rubbed his thick, hot shaft through the slick lips of her opening, seeking relief. His body throbbed with desire for his mate, her moans driving him to press harder against her core.

Hungrily, he switched to the other breast as he slid one hand up her thigh to brush his thumb over her glistening center.

Her rocking motion made his cock jerk in anticipation of her moist, tight heat. "You're so wet for me, mon amour."

Panting, she grasped his hands and placed them on the bed. "My turn to touch."

She rubbed her thumb across his stiffened nipple and then rolled it between her thumb and forefinger gently. He closed his eyes and groaned, his breathing labored.

With a feather–light touch, she skimmed her fingers down his six–pack, inching ever lower.

The further she went, the brighter Richie's eyes glowed, and the faster his breathing became.

Her fingers caressed their way down the downy hair of his happy trail and followed it with her fingertips until she reached the tip of his rock hard, aching erection that poked from between her thighs. His cock jumped, weeping in preparation for her.

His mind stuttered to a screeching halt when her fingers wrapped around his thick length. She held his gaze, and licked her lips as she smeared the pre–cum across the head with her thumb, swirling circles around the tip.

Finally, she stroked her fist to the base and back again. Repeating the action several times. Richie rumbled in relief. It felt so good, she sent him into a growling frenzy, arching off the mattress, and pressing harder into her hand.

Then, she leaned into his chest and licked his nipple and he nearly exploded. Mindlessly, he pumped his hips, thrusting into her fisted grip. Damn, her hand felt like heaven.

He wanted to shout for joy when she spoke the six words he'd been praying for.

"I need you inside me. Now."

He watched her face as she carefully guided him, one torturous inch at a time. Slowly, she lowered her body until he was fully seated in her hot channel. "Oh… baby, you feel so good."

She pressed into him, rubbing her pebbled nipples against his chest and kissed him. The sensation about short-circuited his brain. He took long deep breaths and clenched his jaw with the effort to harness his control and not thrust like a crazed lunatic.

RICHIE: Le Beau Series

This was for her. His job was to please her in any fashion she wished. With his body buried deep, he gripped her hips gently and waited for her direction.

She began a slow sensuous ride. Her hair swayed in a tousled 'I've been loved well' mess around her shoulders. The silken strands brushed and teased his sensitized skin. Richie sucked in a breath, taking her scent deep into his lungs. Relished the feel of her heartbeat pounding in time with his own.

Piper lifted his hands from the mattress and brought them to her breasts. "Touch me, Richie."

His hands cupped her, stroking and caressing. Silently, he thanked the Goddess for the sitting position Piper had chosen. Leaning forward slightly, he captured a tantalizing nipple and took a strong pull.

"You feel so damn good," he said around her engorged flesh before recapturing the pleasured peak.
Suckling and scraping his teeth over the nipple as he gently thrust into his mate's sweet heat.

He enjoyed the sound of her moans and the way she looked with arousal heavy lidded eyes.

His wolf howled when she threw her head back and gave herself up to the sheer pleasure they were giving her. This was what she said she needed, to lose herself in sensation. And he and his wolf were more than happy to meet their mate's needs.

He gritted his teeth as he let her set the pace. She rocked slowly at first, lifting slightly and pressing back down. Then he saw an end to her marvelous torture when she took hold of the headboard, braced herself, and began riding him in earnest.

Richie was enthralled with his mate. Piper was resplendently flushed with passion. She rode him unashamedly, unembarrassed to show her appreciation of his body with every caress, and every response.

Barely able to speak, he said. "Damn, woman, you're killing me.

Piper felt his large, warm hands grip her hips, helping her rise and dropping her down on his steel shaft. Head thrown back, mouth open and panting, she took him hard and deep, over and over.

"Oh, God. Yes, Richie. Yes, yes!"

She was getting close. He could feel her muscles tightening around him as her rhythm faltered. Not missing a beat, he took control, pistoning into her, as her body gripped him hard until he felt sweat beading on his brow. Her eyes were glazed and her breath was labored.

One stroke of his thumb over her sensitive center and Piper cried out his name, her body clamping down on him. He felt wave after wave of pure pleasure flow through her.

Her orgasm rolled over him, drawing his balls up painfully. Richie thrust one last time. Blinded by the force of his release, a single joyful howl filled the room.

"You're unbelievable," she whispered, collapsed on his chest.

RICHIE: Le Beau Series

Richie rubbed his nose in her hair, trying to catch his breath. "Just kill me now and I'll die a happy man." He panted a few times. "Give me a minute and I'll get a warm washcloth to clean you up."

Piper tried to raise her head, but it required more energy than she had. "You don't have to do that."

"You're my mate, Piper. It's my pleasure and duty to care for you."

She didn't argue further, simply snuggled into his chest and smiled to herself.

If Richie had resisted her seduction or mistakenly felt as if she were using him, she would have settled for snuggling in his arms. But he wasn't like that. He'd known even though she needed this to shut her mind down, she also wanted him because she had feelings for him.

The first time in the hotel, she'd been having sex. A basic human need. This time she was making love with a man she cared for. It was astounding how emotions enhanced the experienced and took it from satisfying to mind blowing. They fit not just physically, they fit emotionally as well.

She was beginning to see how everything Anna and Richie told her was true. Being with this man was like coming home.

Chapter 12

Next Morning

Piper awoke to sunshine peeking between the storm shutters, happy and enjoyably sore. She was encased like a sausage in the softest sheets imaginable. Smiling, she reached for Richie, then stiffened. He was gone. Had he gotten what he wanted and split?
Don't be stupid. He wouldn't do that. He's not Jeff.
With a little effort she worked an arm loose from the human burrito she'd become, and snagged Richie's pillow. She pulled it to her nose and grinned.
Damn, he had the best scent ever.
She managed to work her other arm free and began working the sheet loose. How the heck had she managed this mess? Then she blushed, remembering what she'd done last night.
Erotic images flooded her mind and her smiled widened. Of course, Richie had followed up an hour later with his own demands. Fair is fair after all. No wonder the bed was such a mess.

RICHIE: Le Beau Series

Once she was free of the bedding from hell, she flopped back and laughed. For the first time in longer than she could remember, she was happy, truly happy. It had been a very long time since she'd look forward to the future. And that was what Richie represented, the future.

She sat up again and gave the room a quick once over. Where the heck were her clothes? It looked like she would have to go searching.

There you are!

Somehow her things found their way under the bed. A few minutes later, she was dressed. Coffee. She needed coffee.

She padded on bare feet to the kitchen and found that empty, too. The house was quiet, too quiet. Where had Richie gone?

Piper carefully touched the glass carafe of coffee, still warm. He hadn't been gone long. She walked to the door and checked the yard. No one there either.

Huh.

Two kitchen cupboards later and she had a coffee cup in hand. Whoever picked the first coffee bean and roasted it was a genius.

Mm... Nectar of the gods.

She was pouring her second cup when she stilled. Something felt off. Closing her eyes, she sent herself out. There was nothing in the immediate yard or the dock. Richie's boat was still here, but there was a second boat. It was hidden in low hanging branches just downstream.

Piper's heartbeat thundered. Was Richie hurt? Did he need her help? Coffee forgotten, she crept quietly across the yard to the edge of the trees. There she sent herself out again searching the area. It wasn't long and she located Richie and another man.

She was about to creep up on them and try to listen, still unsure if Richie was in danger when he spoke in her head.

Cher, what are you up to?

Sneaking up on you. Who is that with you?

Seth Le Beau, Cade's brother. Come on out so I can introduce you.

Piper stood and stepped from the heavy undergrowth she'd been hiding behind. Still keeping a close eye on the stranger, she took Richie's outstretched hand.

"Seth, I'd like you to meet, Piper, my mate. Piper, this is my good friend, Seth."

Seth took Piper's proffered hand, inclined his head, and kissed her knuckles. "It's a pleasure to meet you, Piper."

"And you as well, Seth."

Richie tucked her under his shoulder and smiled brightly. "I've asked Seth to stand guard when we're sleeping. I don't want to give Qball any advantages."

"Really? Have you filled him in? Does he know how dangerous Qball is?"

"Yes, cher. But there is no need to worry over Seth's safety. He's a shifter and one of our elite hunters. If Qball shows his face, he won't stand a chance."

RICHIE: Le Beau Series

Piper gave Seth another once over, this time with a bit of admiration in her eyes. "So, you're kind of a badass, huh?"

One corner of Seth's mouth quirked up. "I suppose you could say that." Then he glanced at Richie. "You're right. I like her."

Piper frowned at Richie. "What have you been saying about me?"

He kissed her nose and grinned. "Nothing but compliments, I assure you. Seth and I were planning when he'd be around. I wanted to make sure we know when Seth would be here so you don't accidentally shoot him."

Piper smacked his chest. "I wouldn't accidentally shoot him. If I shot him, it would be on purpose."

Seth cleared his throat, promptly ending their argument. Then he cocked a brow and grinned. "I'm not entirely comfortable with all this talk of shooting me. Do I need to purchase a bulletproof vest?"

Piper rolled her eyes. "Very funny. And by the way, I like you too."

Richie walked her out of range of Seth's hearing and stopped. "Seth is very capable of handling Qball. As one of the elite rogue hunters, he has extra gifts. Even more than an average shifter, which is considerable."

"More gifts?"

"He can control another's mind, see even more deeply into his mate's mind than I can with you, and he's a master healer."

"Wow, why does he get extra gifts?"

"Hunters live alone most of the time. And when they battle a rogue there is rarely anyone around to provide healing so they have to do it themselves."

"It sounds like a terribly, lonely existence," she said sadly.

He pulled her into his arms. "It is."

She looked up at him. "What exactly is a rogue wolf?"

"When a shifter mate dies, normally the other mate will die also. The soul is knit together during the ritual and the terrible experience of having the soul torn in half is more than most can bear. A rogue is a shifter that survives the death of its mate and goes insane. Seth is a rogue hunter. He is tasked with killing the rogues before they go on a rampage of death and destruction, exposing shifters to the world."

"That must be horrible for him. What if he had to kill a friend or family member?"

Richie's eyes welled with tears. "Sadly, he's had to kill a few friends over the years. He's retiring though. I can tell killing has taken a huge toll on him, but I think with rest and support, he'll be all right."

"I hope so. Maybe I'll have a talk with him. Bounty hunting and rogue hunting have a few things in common. It might help him to talk to someone who understands what he's been through."

He leaned away and looked her straight in the eye. "You'd do that for him?"

RICHIE: Le Beau Series

"Of course, he's our friend."

"Goddess, I love you," he groaned, as he pulled her in for a toe-curling kiss.

Three days later

Piper sat at the kitchen table staring out the window at the beautiful sunrise playing out over the slow moving river. The third beautiful sunrise she'd enjoyed since Qball's attack. The third beautiful sunrise without a sign of her bounty.

Maybe he had drowned? Somehow, she didn't believe that. No, he was out there, biding his time. Why, she had no clue. The insane didn't play by the rules of normal human behavior. She needed to do something or she'd go crazy herself.

Richie returned from his daily debriefing with Seth, grinning ear-to-ear "Piper? Are you ready for a day of fun?"

His deep sexy voice goosebumped her arms and skittered excited energy to her belly. Three days and nights of the hottest sex she'd ever had, wasn't even close to enough.

She glanced toward the screen door, and licked her suddenly dry lips. Dressed in a T-shirt and jeans, he was the sexiest thing she'd ever seen. "Day of fun?"

Richie pulled her into his arms and kissed her breathless. "Grab your sunscreen, sunglasses and purse. I'm taking you to the French Quarter."

"Are you serious?"

"As a heart attack. I can feel your restlessness and need for action. Since waiting around here isn't bringing Qball into the open, I thought wandering around the city might do the trick."

Piper gulped the last of her coffee and ran for the bedroom. She needed to change her clothes and fix her hair. She was finally doing something productive and she didn't want to wait another minute sitting in the kitchen.

Ten minutes later, she pushed her sunglasses on her face, then grabbed her purse with the tracker inside. She was about to see the famous French Quarter for the first time!

Richie looked up from the magazine he was flipping through and grinned. She wore a shoulder holster with her favorite gun, and he caught a glimpse of a throwing knife when she bent to slip her tennis shoes on.

Yeah, she may be sweet and sexy as hell, but she didn't need his protection, not that she wasn't going to get it anyway. Except for the anomaly in his vision, he wouldn't lose a minute's sleep over her ability to take care of herself. Proudly, he held out a hand and escorted her to the boat. Damn, he loved his warrior woman.

Richie parked the car in the Hotel Monteleone's parking garage on Bienville Street. It paid to have friends throughout the French Quarter. He had a standing invitation to park in the convenient ramp from his buddy, Jed. He would have to buy Jed a drink the next time he stopped in at the Brewhouse.

RICHIE: Le Beau Series

"So, what's the plan?" Piper asked as Richie helped her from the car.

"I thought we would get a Café au lait at Café Beignet and take a stroll down Royal Street. You can't visit the Quarter and ignore Royal Street. We have some of the best window-shopping in the world. Then we can check out the Oyster Fest. It's a two-day festival down by the river. There's live music and oyster shucking and eating contests, but the highlight is the oyster and wine tasting competition, where celebrity judges decide the best pairing of half a dozen Gulf oysters paired with white wines. It's a lot of fun."

"That sounds great. Anything you want to do will be new to me, so lead on."

He felt her happiness over being out of the house. He could suggest they spent the day feeding pigeons in the park and she'd probably be thrilled.

He patiently watched as she did a quick weapons check to verify everything was out of sight, then he led her to the street. They only had a short half block walk before they were on Royal Street.

Richie quietly watched his mate drool over a simple yet elegant antique engagement ring. A stunning three and a half carat natural octagonal sapphire nestled in a square filigree setting. The gem was so extraordinary; to clutter the ring with additional stones would have been a crime. This was a unique statement ring that perfectly fit his one of a kind mate. A secret text message to James, the shop owner, and the ring was his. His excitement was palpable.

V.A. Dold & Tori Austin

As they strolled toward Canal Street, Richie spotted Café Beignet. "Would you like a Café au lait, or are you caffeined out?"

"Yes, please! I'm dying to try one."

"They have beignets too, if you care to try them."

She grinned brightly. "Even better!"

By the time they'd walked up and down Royal Street, it was only late morning. There was still time for a brunch cocktail.

"Let's head toward the Oyster Festival on Decatur Street. We can stop for Bloody Marys at Pierre Maspero's and check out their menu for dinner later."

They strolled slowly and still it only took a few minutes to reach the restaurant. The waiter placed their drinks on the table and Piper took a sip of her cocktail of gigantic proportions, and moaned, "Mmm, this is the best Bloody Mary I've ever had!"

"I thought you'd enjoy it. Out of all the bars in the city, this is where I come for a Bloody Mary. Don't tell my manager," he whispered and leaned forward to kiss her sweetly.

He grinned as Piper studiously read her menu. "If we come back for dinner, I think I'll have the Red Beans and Rice with Andouille and Alligator Sausage."

"That sounds good. I'll get the Shrimp and Grits and we can share. That way you can try more than one thing."

"Thanks, Richie. That's very sweet."

RICHIE: Le Beau Series

They finished their drinks and slowly strolled toward their destination, the parking lot of Jax brewery. The Oyster Festival would be in full swing by the time they got there.

At first, Richie tried to get them beers at one of the tents, but the line was twenty people deep. He looked over his shoulder at the entrance to the Brewhouse a half block down, where only a few people waited.

"Cher, let's get a beer at my bar and I'll introduce you to my friends."

"Okay, I'd love to see where you work. Give me a minute to check the area." Richie helped her search the crowd for Qball's face. So far, nothing.

When they walked through the open double doors of the restaurant, you would swear royalty had entered the building. Everyone seemed to know him.

Hellos and nice to meet yous were repeated several times before they each held a beer to go and headed back.

"Wow, popular much?" Piper teased him as they walked back to the festival.

"Naw, I've just worked there a long time, so a lot of people know me."

They had been enjoying the live music for a while when Richie suggested a walk along the river at Woldenberg Park. They had walked for about a block when he stiffened. His eyes glazed over in a far off stare.

"Richie? Are you all right?" Piper asked with worry in her voice.

He didn't answer. Didn't blink. Just stared into nothingness.

V.A. Dold & Tori Austin

Richie was trapped in the vision of Piper again. He saw both him and Piper in what looked like an old burned out building. They were on the ground floor. He could see vehicles outside the empty gaping holes that used to be windows. It was incredibly dark, making it hard to identify where the vision was taking place. Add to that, all of the debris scattered throughout the space, and he couldn't see much. But he heard a scuffling sound and heavy breathing.

The entire vision played out and ended once again with him watching in horror, as a man he assumed was Qball, stood and fired. Piper was thrown sideways to the ground with a gaping gunshot wound over her left breast. The light faded from her eyes and her last breath left her lungs.

Why was he being forced to watch his mate die again? He never saw the same vision twice. Frantic to get the horrifying picture out of his mind, he shook his head and struggled to breathe. His heart was crushed in a vise and his lungs refused to work. Fraught with fear, he needed to assure himself she was actually alive and still with him. He hauled her against his chest and held her tightly.

Piper let out an "oomph."

He couldn't speak he was so shaken. After a long minute, he took a shaky breath and buried his nose in her hair.

"Never leave me, Piper," he choked out.

"I wasn't planning on going anywhere. What just happened to you?"

"A bad dream. A really, really bad dream I will never allow to happen."

RICHIE: Le Beau Series

After several more minutes, Richie loosened his hold and allowed Piper to step away. It was one of the hardest things he'd ever done and his wolf didn't like it one bit. "Let's walk a bit more, then I'll take you to Bourbon Street for a stroll before dinner. We can try out one of the rickshaw bikes."

"Okay. But are you sure you're all right? You're still very pale."

"Yes, cher. I'm fine." The last thing he wanted to say out loud – EVER was that he'd seen her death in a vision. Some days his gift sucked gophers.

They turned away from the quiet of the river at Bienville Street and slowly walked toward the hustle and bustle of the French Quarter. Piper had only taken a few steps when she grabbed Richie's arm and hissed through unmoving lips, "Qball - eleven o'clock."

Richie gave her an almost imperceptible nod and continued to walk. They gave no indication of knowing he was there, yet something spooked Qball. He took off like the hounds of hell were on his tail.

Piper tore after him, never letting him leave her sight. Richie easily paced beside her. She may want to take Qball down, but he needed to ensure she survived the ordeal.

Thankfully, it was a short chase or she may have lost him in the crowd. A half block down, Qball ducked inside a burned out four story building under construction after years of neglect on the parking lot by N. Front Street and Bienville Street.

Unnecessarily, Richie pulled her to a stop as if she would charge blindly into the building. Apparently he didn't understand, she was a seasoned hunter, she knew better than to do that.

Annoyed, she frowned at him, but didn't give her position away by speaking. She took advantage of the deep shadows just inside the gaping vacant doorway to look and listen. Nothing stirred.

Piper, promise me you'll be careful and not do anything foolish. You're a professional and I know you will put personal safety above anything else including catching this bastard. If you can't take a shot from a safe position, please don't behave rashly.

She scowled at him. *I know how to do my job.*

Richie's wolf tore at him. Raging to protect their mate. The beast wanted to drag her way from the building and lock her in a padded room where she would always be safe.

He wanted that too, but doing that would cause his vision to reach its ultimate conclusion in another fashion. One he wouldn't be prepared for. He agonized over letting her enter the building, but this was the only way he could ensure his chance at keeping her alive.

With one last push, he forced his wolf into submission and locked his fear away. He needed to focus everything on his mate and remove emotions from the equation. He was terrified his plan wouldn't work. With his mate facing her unknown death, he decided in that moment if he didn't succeed, he would follow her into the beyond. He

RICHIE: Le Beau Series

didn't want to live without her. That left only one option, he had to save Piper.

Determinedly, Richie took point and silently moved forward a few feet into a pocket of cover created by a pile of pallets and burned timbers.

He cocked his head to listen. His muscles were bunched and tense, ready to explode into movement when the need presented itself.

Without looking, he knew when she quietly joined him, and after several long minutes when silence continued to reign, he felt her impatience and knew by the shifting of her weight from one foot to the other she meant to move further into the structure.

With his shifter speed, he snaked a hand out and stopped her. *Use your gift before you move.*

He watched her closely as she slowly studied a ten-foot area around them, any further than that and it was too dark for a human to see. He did a search of his own. Nothing. That could be good or bad. They had no way of knowing what Qball's line of sight was. If she tried to move, he might see her without her knowing she'd given away her position. That was too risky.

I checked the immediate area and didn't see him. He must be further in. Do you think he found a way to an upper floor?

Richie gave the structure a closer look. The fire had burned out the entire interior. From what he could see, there wasn't a staircase leading to the upper floors, but if Qball slipped out a window, he could utilize the scaffolding. No, he would have heard soled shoes on metal. He hadn't gone up.

V.A. Dold & Tori Austin

Unless he escaped out a window, he's here somewhere on this level. I'm going to work my way to the pallets on our left. Stay here until I have a chance to test the position.

Test the position? Are you using yourself as bait?

Richie didn't respond to her outrage. Of course, he was the bait. He was a shifter, she a human. His odds of surviving an attack were ten times greater.

Piper wanted to smack him. The aggravating man had no sense of self-preservation. She watched as he shifted to his wolf and silently crawled on his belly. She knew his heart rate remained slow and steady, because she felt each beat as her heart tried to match his. His breathing was relaxed, too. The man had nerves of steel. He could have been lying on his dock at the cabin, taking a nap for all the lack of stress he exhibited. For the first time, she saw Richie for what he was, a deadly predator.

Damn, that's hot.

Piper gradually slipped from protective cover, making slow, smooth movements so as not to draw the eye.

What are you doing? Are you trying to get killed? Move your ass before you get yourself shot he snarled into her mind.

His anger and lack of confidence in her abilities amused her. She didn't rush to heed his demand, but continued in her well-honed manner of moving silently. Three carefully placed, extremely slow steps and she hunkered down behind his cover. She grinned triumphantly. *Happy now?*

RICHIE: Le Beau Series

Abruptly the smile left her face as she glanced through charred slats toward the sound of gravel underfoot. Qball was nearby—and on the move.

She tensed to rise and track Qball. She needed to flank him. Before she could move she felt Richie's warning hand on her arm.

Wait for him to take cover. We might be able to pinpoint his position without giving ours away.

She nodded and relaxed back on her heels to wait. About twenty seconds later, silence filled the dark interior again.

Piper, he's behind the metal door leaning against a pile of debris. Can you see him?

No.

From the angle of his cover, we can move to our left without being seen unless he raises his head above his hidey-hole. I'll cover you while you make your way over there. Once there, verify there's room for both of us. I won't have you separated from me. Understand?

She did the equivalent of a telepathic eye roll and growled. *Got it, O' Bossy one.*

Damn, her confidence and ability to tease him under pressure was sexy as hell. Who knew a warrior woman would be such a turn on? And she'd sexy growled at him. SEXY GROWLED in the middle of a life-threatening situation.

He heard Piper giggle in his mind as her body tensed to make her move.

Richie mentally gave her a snort and patted her ass quietly. *Behave yourself.*

V.A. Dold & Tori Austin

She'd just made cover and signaled him to follow, when Richie heard Qball on the move. It was now or never. Dammit, this could be it and they were separated again. Richie used his shifter speed to close the space between himself and Piper.

He steadied the mountain of pallets they hid behind. In his haste, he'd almost sent the entire pile to the ground. *Do you have his location?*

Of course.

He smiled at her cool, almost bored attitude. *Where?*

Seven feet left of where he was before. He seems to be working his way toward the entrance so he can make a break for it.

Right. Okay, I'm getting back up. We need someone to watch that door incase he gets past us.

Piper frowned at him. *Who?*

I know some people, he grinned as he sent a text and pocketed his phone.

*****

Nick, I have a situation at the burned out building on the parking lot at N. Front Street and Bienville. Please come immediately.

His fingers moved with such speed over the screen of his smartphone, it took but a second to type the text. A heartbeat later, it vibrated with a response.

Help is on the way, he whispered in her mind.

RICHIE: Le Beau Series

Richie knew Nick was rushing toward his location and would more than likely have Derick with him. The vampires were Rose's brothers for all intents and purposes. When he'd first met them, they'd been called, Jack and Michael. But with their conversion from human to vampire, their human existence was no more and as such, they'd taken on new identities. Once changed, the new vampire had one year to create a new identity. It was the way of the vampire.

Technically, all human ties, including familial were cut and ceased to exist. Nick and Derick were an anomaly since their only family was a shifter. Etienne, the vampire king, allowed the relationship to continue since humans weren't involved. No other vampire in history had ever been allowed ties to their previous existence that Richie knew of.

His phone silently vibrated in his hand again.

We're outside, what do you need us to do? Nick sent.

Guard the door. There's a man in here that needs capturing and he's attempting to escape.

We will take care of it. He won't get past us.

While he'd been texting he knew Piper hadn't moved her eyes off the last position Qball had taken. What the devil was he trying to accomplish? It had been sometime since he'd moved or made a sound. If his goal was to kill Piper, what was he waiting for?

V.A. Dold & Tori Austin

He handed his phone to Piper and kept watch on Qball while she read the text conversation. She glanced at him and nodded once as she handed it back to him.

I'm going to use my gift. I need to get a look at his position.

Richie had every sense he possessed on high alert. Piper was doing her out of body experience in the middle of a deadly situation. This was more danger than his wolf could stand.
The beast fought to surface and protect its mate, but Richie held it in check. From the fierce pain he was in, his guts were shredded.

Piper's patience was at an end. If Qball wasn't going to make a move, she would. With a determined expression, she took Richie's hand, closed her eyes and sent herself out to find out what Qball was up to.

Her invisible self, floated across the space to peer around the barrier Qball hunkered behind. He was there, sweating like a pig and fumbling with his gun. It looked like the piece wasn't working right, as if it was jammed.

She floated closer for a better look. Qball's lips were drawn tight, and his breathing was harsh. He was obviously, panicking. This was her chance to take him. With his unusable weapon she had the advantage.

Chapter 13

To Richie's horror, Piper suddenly stood, stepped from behind their cover, and began walking across the room. You would have thought she was on a Sunday stroll instead of taking down an armed serial killer.

He scrambled to catch up to her. This was too close to his vision for comfort. They were a few feet away from Qball's foxhole when he feared his nightmare was about to play out in real-time.

Using his heightened shifter senses he listened. He heard humanity on the sidewalk, distant music playing, a car horn honk…and the rasp of metal on metal followed by a snick. The distinctive sound of a gun being cocked.

Richie's body tensed, heart stopped, and lungs burned from lack of oxygen. He'd never been more petrified, or had more to lose in his life. He didn't doubt the vision he'd had or his shifter speed. What terrified him was the uncertainty he could change Piper's fate.

He'd never successfully thwarted fate, and not from lack of trying. He prayed this would be the first time. Forcing a ragged breath, he watched every twitch and shift of her body posture, waiting for what he knew was about to happen. She would shift right to skirt the pallets as Qball rose and fired. He would have to intercede at precisely the right moment.

He blinked, and there it was. Piper shifted her weight to take that fateful step. As if in slow motion, the top of Qball's head appeared above his hidey-hole. As she turned right, Qball's arm came up, and Richie launched his body in front of her. The last thing he heard was the bullet exploding from the gun.

Piper caught his movement out of the corner of her eye and turned as his body jerked, the air whooshed from his lungs, and he slumped into her arms.

Qball locked shocked gazes with her. It was plain as day, he'd thought he'd had her that time. The crease in his brow spoke of his confusion as to how Richie had gotten in front of the bullet. What he'd seen wasn't humanly possible, but then he didn't know Richie wasn't human. It was a few seconds before he gathered his wits to take another shot.

Piper used those precious heartbeats to leverage Richie against her chest and work her right hand free to return fire. Qball recoiled and her bullet went wide, finding purchase in his shoulder. She'd been aiming for his heart. It was the first time she'd ever gone for a kill shot, but dammit, he'd shot Richie!

The hit spun Qball to the floor and out of sight. Shit. She loaded another round and readied for him.

RICHIE: Le Beau Series

The gunfire drew Nick and Derick from their position. One second they were leaning on the brick opening and the next they were there. She had no idea who was who, but they were definitely her allies.

"Secure that bastard!" the one snarled at the other, his guttural, angry tone contradicting the gentleness by which he wrapped an arm around Richie to help prop him up as they headed for the door.

Richie moistened his lips and looked down at Piper's lovely face. *What's wrong, cher? You look so worried.*

Don't try to talk. You're going to be fine. You have to be fine.

Subconsciously, he knew he'd been hit. Hell, he'd expected it. That was the plan. But the pain had yet to register with his brain, and his inability to focus his thoughts confused him.

He'd moved faster than he'd ever moved in his life. Vaguely, he remembered the sound of the gun as Qball fired, but after that everything was a bit fuzzy.

He allowed Piper to help him stay on his feet. The last thing he wanted was to fall on his face in front of his mate. He was pretty sure Nick was helping, too. *Wasn't he supposed to guard the door?*

Her body was so soft and warm. He wanted to snuggle closer and take a nap. Richie shook his head, his scattered mind was jumping all over the place. It was impossible to maintain a single coherent thought. Shit! Why weren't they in a building, stalking Qball? He needed to focus so he could protect Piper, not think about snuggling up to her curves. What was wrong with him?

When they reached the charred opening that once was the main entrance, he stumbled to a halt and swayed.

Confused by her scent of panic, he took a good look at her in the light of day. She was distressed. He couldn't stand for her to be so upset. Without thinking, he let go his hold on Nick to rub at the frown line between Piper's eyes.

Bad idea. He went down hard. Like a giant cyprus felled in the swamp. Without the added support, his legs gave out and he was flat on his back, staring up at Piper and Nick in surprise.

Piper fell to her knees next to him as Nick took up a protective stance. A crowd was beginning to form and it wouldn't be long before police showed up.

"Richie!" He was losing too much blood and his breathing was ragged. Piper raised her shaking hands to cup his face and gasped. Terror pierced her chest. He was so cold.

She watched him struggle to take a breath and whimpered in despair.

He turned his nose into her palm and tried to rumble. "I'm fine, mon amour. It's just a scratch."

"Don't talk, babe. Help is coming." She glanced up at the man standing above her. She prayed help was coming.

Then a thought occurred to her, if she could talk telepathically to Richie, maybe she could reach Seth. Richie said he was a healer.

RICHIE: Le Beau Series

Piper took several deep breaths like she did to clear her mind when she meditated. Then she let herself leave her body. But instead of going across a room, she went into Richie's mind.

Slowly she reviewed the web of threads. She hadn't expected this to be so complicated. Some of the fine silk filaments glowed brighter than the others, which had to mean something. Telepathy was a psychic gift, which as far as she knew was of the light so to speak. It could be argued the brighter threads were connected to that gift. Okay, here goes. She reached out with her spirit hand and gripped the brightest thread.

Seth? Seth can you hear me? She shouted the thought as loudly as she could.

Excuse me, but who are you? a strange voice responded.

I'm Piper, Richie's friend. I need Seth. Do you know him?

Yes, I do. I'm his father, Isaac. Why do you need him?

Richie has been shot, and he's lost a lot of blood. I need a healer before it's too late! Her voice was rising as she thought about the state Richie was in.

Breathe, Piper. I need you to remain calm and describe his condition. Tell me everything you can.

She took a steadying breath and became all business. *I'll need to return to my body, and I'm afraid I'll lose the connection.*

V.A. Dold & Tori Austin

Don't worry, I have you now and I'll hold the link.

She returned to her body and studied Richie closely, gently checking his chest, then rolled him slightly to see his back. He moaned when she moved him, but other than that remained quiet.

It looks like a through and through. He was shot in the chest at fairly close range and the bullet exited his back. Based on his labored breathing it may have hit a lung. He's lost a lot of blood, and his skin is cool to the touch. He's still conscious, but that could change at any moment.

Good job, Piper. Give me a minute.

She waited for what seemed like hours before Isaac spoke again.

I relayed Richie's condition to Seth. He followed you to the French Quarter and is only a few blocks away. Expect him in a minute or two.

She was surprised Isaac hadn't questioned how she'd been able to contact him. Instead of interrogating her he asked. *Is there anyone else there to help you? Do you need me to send protection?*

Richie called two of his friends to help us before he was shot. They're here with us now.

Good. That's good. Try to keep him awake and talking.

Piper stiffened, stopped breathing, and analyzed what she was suddenly experiencing. She was seeing things without seeing them, at least with her eyes. It was as if she was seeing them play out in her mind. Was this clairvoyance? It must be.

RICHIE: Le Beau Series

Then her heart stuttered. She could see Richie slipping away from her. It looked like he was backing into a shadowed area. What if he disappeared into that void? Would she be able to bring him back?

What's that shadow I see near him? She choked out in panic.

Whatever you do, don't let him go into the shadow! He's strong and deeply connected to you. Call to him. Demand he stay with you. Tell him something, anything to keep him with you until Seth can get there. Isaac's voice was tinged with alarm, booming loudly in her mind.

Piper framed his face with her free hand while maintaining pressure on the wound. She pressed her forehead to his and put every bit of force she had into her voice. *Richie!* she commanded. *You aren't allowed to leave me without a mate. Seth is coming, so hang on... for me. If you go, I go with you. Do you want me to die today?*

NOOOOO! He suddenly bellowed in her mind and she saw him trying to move away from the shadow.

Richie's lashes fluttered as he strained to resurface, but he didn't have the strength to open his eyes.

For a heartbeat, Piper was sure he'd open them and stay with her, but he was too weak from loss of blood. Dammit! Where was Seth? Richie was fading fast and her hold on him was tenuous at best.

V.A. Dold & Tori Austin

Panic welled in her chest and mind. Pushed to her limit, she grabbed him by the shoulders and wailed as her heart shattered. "Don't you dare die on me! You don't get to take the easy way out and leave me here alone. Open your eyes and look at me. Right now." Crushed by grief and despair, Piper laid her cheek on Richie's chest and wept. "Dammit. I need you to open your eyes."

If she'd been looking at his face, she would have seen his eyelashes flutter. Her heart leapt with encouragement as he pushed and fought to come back to her. She could feel him struggling to reassure her, giving it everything he had, but all he accomplished was a gasp from his efforts.

She was losing him!

"Please, Richie. I need you," she choked out.

She felt his chest rise and then a shuttering breath left his lungs. She waited.

Nothing.

No inhale.

"NO!"

From out of nowhere, a man appeared at Richie's side and began checking his heart rate and breathing.

"Don't give up yet, cher. There's still a chance. This isn't the first time I've had to work a miracle."

Piper's initial reaction was to defend Richie from an attacker. But then she realized who had pushed her aside. She fell back, shocked by Seth's sudden presence and smooth baritone voice in her ear.

RICHIE: Le Beau Series

Her eyes widened once her brain kicked in, and she scrambled to give Seth all the space he needed.

Seth smiled as he urgently worked on Richie. She hadn't freaked out over Richie's condition or gotten in his way; he'd known she wouldn't. Piper was made of tougher stuff. She was every bit as courageous as any shifter he'd met. His friend was a very lucky man.

Knowing he didn't have a second to lose, he'd gone immediately into healer mode. Richie wasn't breathing and he couldn't hear a heartbeat, not even a flutter. It couldn't have been much worse.

He could smell Piper's profound gratitude that he was there to help Richie. He was sure she didn't realize it, but she was mumbling, praying that he would be able to work the miracle he'd promised. From what he could see Richie was going to need one.

The woman was incredible. She stayed close, ready to lend a helping hand if he asked for it, yet never once got in is way or broke his concentration.

His healing energy was helping and Richie's color was a little better. His cool skin and gray pallor showed hints of beige here and there. But it wasn't enough, there had to be internal damage.

"Hold his spirit to you, or we'll lose him."

"How?"

Seth frantically worked to stabilize Richie as he said, "Join with him telepathically. Feel your connection, heart to heart, mind to mind. Once you've got a solid link, imagine taking hold of his spirit with your hands and hold on tight."

Once again, she amazed him. She didn't hesitate or distract him with questions or arguments over what must have sounded like a ludicrous idea of holding someone's soul with her hands. She simply closed her eyes tightly and did as she was told.

"Hold them back, boys. I need to give Richie my complete attention."

He knew Nick and Derick would follow his orders and maintain their defensive positions, forcing the growing crowd to stay to the sidewalk.

Normally, a vampire so young wouldn't be able to withstand the rays of the sun, but the king of the vampires, Etienne, had countless tricks up his sleeve and their new ability was only one. Goddess bless, Etienne.

Seth took a deep breath and closed his eyes. With his palms flat on Richie's chest, he sent his spirit inside. Heat flowed from his healing spirit form. One after another, he sealed arteries and veins to stem the blood loss. Then he used the intense magic he'd been gifted as a rogue hunter to force Richie's body to produce blood at an unnaturally high rate.

*****

Piper? Richie slurred in a weak voice. *Piper, I'll always love you.* And then he was gone.

Piper gasped and shook uncontrollably, but she held it together and tightened her hold on his soul.

Minutes that felt like hours, ticked by.

RICHIE: Le Beau Series

"He's fighting me, trying to regain consciousness. Keep him under and dammit, make him lie still," Seth barked, more out of shock than anything else.

Richie, baby. You need to lie still and be quiet. Seth is trying to heal you and you're not helping. Please, sugar, for me.

I can feel your heartache and fear.

If you want me to calm down, you need to let Seth heal you. She couldn't quite hide the distressed pleading in her voice.

Stay with me? he asked weakly, and then he was gone again.

Piper was terrified for Richie, but she stayed strong. Her heart hammered, her chest felt bruised and battered.

*****

Seth had never been ejected from a body before. Richie in his desperation to get to his grieving mate had literally thrown him out.

Once Richie was quiet and creating rather than losing blood, Seth turned his attention to Richie's heart and lungs. Visualizing a hand made of healing energy, he squeezed the heart gently, over and over, palpating the silent muscle. Once he had a normal rhythm he sent a jolt of energy into the heart to jump start the organ. A beat and a miss. He jolted the heart a second time. Another beat and a miss.

Come on, dammit! Seth snarled.

V.A. Dold & Tori Austin

He feared hitting Richie's heart with more voltage, too much and he would destroy the heart rather than heal it, but it had to be done. He gathered a little extra energy and shocked it again.

The weak, yet steady beat was the sweetest sound Seth had ever heard.

Next, he went after Richie's lungs. He surrounded them with healing energy and forced air into them. He watched as one expanded, but the other remained flat like a deflated balloon. There had to be a tear. Carefully, he examined the lung. On the left side near the top was a ragged hole. Concentrating all his healing energy on that spot, he slowly regrew lung tissue and sealed the gash. Once the hole was closed, he once again forced air into Richie's lungs. Both left and right inflated normally and picked up a healthy rhythm.

Seth returned to his body, exhausted and relieved. Richie would live. If he'd been a minute later, his only friend would have gone on to his everlasting reward, leaving his mate and Seth to grieve his loss. Seth wasn't sure he would have survived that final blow. His soul was too ragged as it was, full of holes and missing pieces.

Shaking like a naked man in a snowstorm, he pulled Piper into his arms and held her. "He's out of the woods. He'll make it. Thank you. Without you to hold him to this plain of existence while I repaired his body, we would have lost him."

Piper cried, shaking with relief in his arms. "I'm not sure how you saved him, but I'm forever in your debt."

RICHIE: Le Beau Series

"Is he going to be all right? Will he have any permanent damage?" She searched his eyes, her voice filled with concern.

"I don't expect him to have any lasting effects. He still has a ways to go before he's one hundred percent, but he's well on his way."

Richie groaned as his eyes fluttered open. Then in a weak voice he asked, "Piper? Seth? What happened?"

"You jumped in front of a bullet, that's what happened!" Piper growled before she could temper her tone. She wasn't really angry with him, she was merely reacting to the terror she still reeled from.

"I had no choice, it was the only way I could save you. Are you mad?"

"No, you idiot. But if you ever do anything like that again, I'll shoot you myself."

Seth let out a snort and stood. "I'll have one of the boys collect your car."

She gave Seth the information of where it was parked and Richie's keys. Then turned her attention back to Richie.

Before she could scold him further, he caught her face in his hands and pulled her lips to his.

Piper moaned and savored the incredible taste of Richie's lips and the fact he was alive. She shuddered when the reality of what almost happened finally hit her full force. She'd nearly lost him, really lost him, forever. His tongue swept against hers, turning her shudders into shivers.

V.A. Dold & Tori Austin

Piper finally broke the kiss so she could check Richie's wound and reassure herself he really was out of the woods. The bleeding had stopped and it looked like the bullet hole was scabbing over. His coloring was good and the sparkle was back in his eyes.

She looked up at Seth standing with his back to them a few feet away. "Thank you, Seth."

He glanced over his shoulder at her and grinned. "My pleasure."

Richie frowned at his friend and then asked, "What are you doing here? I thought you were guarding the cabin. Not that I'm not incredibly grateful you're here instead."

"When you left this morning, I got a very bad feeling and listened to my intuition. I'm glad I followed you to the Quarter or you'd be fertilizer right now."

"Believe me, I'm grateful you did, too," Richie said, before closing his eyes again.

"Derick should be here any minute with your SUV. Once he pulls up to the curb, I'll get you into the back seat. Piper, why don't you get in back with him? I'll drive while you keep an eye on our patient."

"All right." Then she caught sight of Qball on his knees in front of Nick. The serial killer swayed back and forth like he was in a trance. A feral snarl ripped from her lips as she propelled herself to her feet and lunged at the piece of shit.

RICHIE: Le Beau Series

Nick snatched Qball out of reach as Seth restrained Piper. "You don't want to kill the little bastard while the police are watching, cher. You'll need to learn to be covert about things like that."

Piper stiffened and glanced around. Two officers on foot were mere feet away and three additional squad cars arrived.

"Give them your statement, cher. But be very careful with the words you choose. Many in law enforcement know about us, but some do not," Seth whispered in her ear before releasing her.

Piper showed the police officer in charge her credentials and the bounty order for Qball. Two officers took Qball into custody as the others took statements from the rest of them.

The process took longer than Piper liked, but the officers were professional and thorough. They agreed her gunshot wound to Qball was an obvious case of self-defense. Besides, as the bounty hunter of the fugitive, she was authorized to use deadly force.

Seth squatted next to Richie and lifted him easily into his arms. "It's safe to move you now."

"Really? You have to carry me? This isn't embarrassing at all, Seth."

His lips twitched into a mischievous grin. "You can't walk yet, and you know it, so be still."

"Way to make me look weak in front of my mate," Richie grumbled.

"Knock it off, wolfman. You're the toughest, sexiest man I know." Piper grinned and threw him a kiss.

V.A. Dold & Tori Austin

Richie groaned, but stayed quiet.

Finally, they reached the vehicle and Seth helped Richie lie across the backseat while she held his head in her lap and stroked his hair. Under her palm, Richie's body vibrated from his wolf's rumble.

Piper held Richie's hand and brushed the hair from his face as they drove from the French Quarter. She was exhausted, the tension from the day settled on her shoulders like a ton of bricks. "When we get you home and into bed, I'm going to sleep for a week."

"I'm a bit tired myself," Richie joked without opening his eyes.

He was beyond tired and his chest hurt like a mother. She knew because she could feel the pain as an ache in her own chest.

Richie had just fallen asleep when Seth began to speak. "Piper, I sense your need to flee the situation. This wasn't your fault."

She shook her head as silent tears tracked down her face. "Yes, actually, it was entirely my fault. I'm sure he won't want to see me anymore. It would be best if I left and made it easier on him. He's too gallant to tell me to go."

"You couldn't be more wrong. That's not how mates work. Besides, you'll cause him an immense amount to pain if you leave."

"How would I possibly do that?" she asked incredulously.

RICHIE: Le Beau Series

"With the mating incomplete, it will be downright painful for him if you are more than a mile or two apart. He'll experience debilitating physical pain, not to mention his wolf will be nervous and pacing. He won't be able to rest and if you try to leave, the idiot will get his half dead self out of bed and go after you."

"You must be joking."

"No, cher. I couldn't be more serious. Please, stay with him until you can talk this out."

She gave him a single nod. "All right, I'll stay for a while longer."

They rode in silence for a few miles when she wondered something. "Seth, why did Qball look and act so strangely? I only nicked him with my shot."

"Nick and Derick are vampires. Nick had him in a trance."

"Vampire? No, don't tell me, I don't want to know."

Chapter 14

Weak though he was, Richie walked slowly from the bedroom. He couldn't spend one more second flat on his back. This morning he was rejoining the world. Not only was he going stir crazy, Piper's sorrow and guilt were beating at him like the rug beater his mother used on him as a child. He grinned to himself, recalling all the shenanigans he'd gotten into with Seth and the rest of the gang. He was the first to admit, he'd been a hellion.

Over the past three days, she'd hovered close, stayed by his side comforting him. But this morning when Seth came to do his daily healing session, she'd left the room and hadn't returned.

Richie found her staring out the front window at the river, quietly weeping. Her sadness was so intense, his chest felt like an elephant was napping on it. He stood behind her for a moment to allow her time to sense he was near. He wanted to comfort her, not startle her. When her body relaxed and she breathed a little sigh, he wrapped his arms around her. Held her back against his front, and rubbed his stubbled chin through her hair.

"What's wrong, mon amour? Your tears are breaking my heart."

RICHIE: Le Beau Series

"Seth told me you're almost completely healed. I've stayed to make sure you'd be all right. Now that you're out of the woods, I should go."

Richie's temper flared. "You've tried to push me away long enough, Piper. You're not leaving me. I won't allow it."

She sighed, but didn't turn around. "I pushed you away so you wouldn't get hurt. I know how dangerous my job is and I was trying to protect you. Then, I did something completely out of character and left the protection of cover. I stupidly made myself a target and nearly got you killed. You must hate me for that."

"You're wrong, cher. I don't hate you, I love you." He turned her in his arms and tipped her chin up so she looked him in the eye. "As your mate, it's my privilege to protect you, even with my life. I would do it again in a heartbeat. You're mine, don't ever forget that."

Piper opened her mouth to protest, but Richie silenced her with a finger over her lips.

"Do you recall when I suddenly stopped walking along the river in the French Quarter and you asked me what happened?"

She nodded, but remained silent.

"I was having a vision. I saw you die." Richie's body shook from the force of his raw emotions. "Qball shot you in that burned out building and I was forced to watch the light leave your eyes as you died in my arms. I was completely helpless to save you. I couldn't allow that to happen."

"Why didn't you tell me? I could have taken precautions and saved you from a bullet. Instead, you almost died. Because of me!"

"You're forgetting, I've tried to give others a heads up, it never worked. Do you remember my friend who was killed by the gang? I warned him and he tried to change his fate. He died anyway. I couldn't take that risk, not with you. I had to be the one to prevent your death. I knew every nuance of the vision and precisely what would happen. Only I knew exactly what to look for and what actions to take. If you'd done anything different from my vision, I needed to be there to counteract the change. There was no other way."

Piper's shoulders sagged. "I still don't like it, and it's still my fault. You should have told me and allowed me the chance to discuss it with you. I never would have let you jump in front of a bullet for me."

"And that's why I didn't tell you. You would have tried to change the outcome and I would have been helpless to save you. If I'd told you and you changed even one thing in the vision and did something other than what I saw, it would have been all over and you would have died.

"By not telling you, I minimized the possibility of your actions changing. Tiny changes, I could adjust for, but a major change, such as you rushing Qball instead of sneaking across the room would have been impossible for me to counter. Like I said, it's my privilege and responsibility to keep you safe, healthy, and happy. Besides, I, as a shifter,

RICHIE: Le Beau Series

had a ten times better chance of surviving a bullet than you did as a human. It made sense that I be the one to take the hit."

"Ah!" She snarled and smacked his arm. "You drive me crazy with your common sense." Then she waved a hand as if dismissing her anger. "It's all irrelevant now. While you were sleeping, I called my boss and tendered my final resignation. He tried to talk me out of it, but I'm done with that life. I won't ever put anyone else in danger again."

Richie grinned, happy to have won the battle. "If that's what you really want. I admit, I hated that you put yourself in danger. Now, promise me there will be no more thoughts of leaving."

"Fine. I'll stay," she harrumphed.

"Try not to sound too happy about spending time in my company," he teased sarcastically.

"That's not what I meant, and you know it. If you honestly still want me around, I'll stay."

He pulled her body flush with his. "I absolutely want that. So, what do you want to do with the rest of your life?"

Piper chuckled and a sparkle returned to her sad eyes. "I have no idea. I have enough money to last years, decades even. For now, I think I'm just going to relax and enjoy myself."

He nuzzled her neck, breathing in her scent. "I like that plan. I have more money than I could ever spend. I only work for the camaraderie and socializing. Heck, I just might quit as well, and keep you naked and tied to my bed."

V.A. Dold & Tori Austin

"The naked part sounds interesting, but you love your job. Maybe you should just take some time off. I think you're going to miss the bar and the people if you stop working." She closed her eyes and tilted her head to give him better access.

He kissed her neck one last time and gazed into her eyes smiling sheepishly. "Yeah, you might be right."

His wolf rumbled loudly, pushing him to claim his mate. "Woman, your scent is driving me crazy."

She blew out a little breath of laughter and shook her head. "I seem to do that to men. Not only do I drive them nuts, I make them lose their temper too. Apparently my personality is less than ideal."

"Your personality is perfect, but your sexy body is distracting me from our conversation. And you don't need to be affecting other men."

"I think you're still hallucinating from loss of blood. Perhaps you should return to your sickbed."

Richie's gaze heated and a fire lit in his eyes. "I assure you, I am far from delirious and I have ALL my faculties. Care to take them for a test drive?"

He watched her eyes search his. Then he felt her at the edge of his mind, trying to catch his thoughts and ferret out the truth of his words. He knew all she saw was the unadulterated desire he burned with.

"I need you, mon amour," Richie choked out, wrapping her hair around his fist and slowly inching his mouth to hers. All the while imposing his

RICHIE: Le Beau Series

dominance with the demand blazing in his glowing eyes. He would never let her go, no matter what she said or thought. She was his.

He felt her heart racing wildly as his lips skimmed lightly across hers. "You're forgetting to breathe, mon amour. Take a breath."

Piper sucked in a shaky lungful of air. At the same time, filling her nose with his alluring fragrance. "Mm, you smell so good."

"You do too. That's our mating scents. They intensify when mates are aroused to send them into a frenzy, encouraging the completion of the ritual," Richie growled and kissed her again, deeply.

His lips were demanding yet incredibly soft. The excitement fluttering in her stomach pooled low, building a slow burn in her core.

Richie's lips teased the line of her neck, nibbling tiny bites, then soothing with his tongue. His gentle persuasion was completely at odds with the fierce hunger she felt raging through his body.

The tiny sting from his fist, clutching her hair, holding her for his marauding mouth, sent another zing to her core. The other caressed her back, followed the curve of her hip, until she was pressed against his hardened erection.

"Mine," he growled, next to her ear.

Piper shivered when he nipped her earlobe and rumbled contentedly.

"Before this goes any further, I need a shower." He sniffed himself and wrinkled his nose. "I smell like a dirty wet dog. If I leave you alone out here, will you promise to stay or do I need to take you into the shower with me?"

V.A. Dold & Tori Austin

"I'll stay. Go ahead and take your shower, I need to do some thinking anyway."

Worry creased Richie's brow. "About what?"

"This and that. Go on. Take your shower. Shoo."

Richie eyed her for a moment, then kissed her nose. As he left the room, he turned. "I'm trusting you and holding you to your word, mon amour."

*****

Piper pulled her tattered notepad from her purse and drew two columns. At the top of the left column she drew a plus sign, on the right side she drew a minus sign. It was high time she decided what she truly wanted to do. Stay here in the bayou with Richie or take a little time off before heading back home.

The two columns were designed to help her make a decision. If she didn't stay with him, going home was a given.

First question: could she handle living day in and day out in the bayou. Absent-mindedly, she tapped her pen against her chin. She liked the wildlife and peacefulness. Hiking on the animal paths was good exercise. She loved living on water. Three pluses.

What about transportation? When she needed groceries or toilet paper she'd have to use a boat to get them.

RICHIE: Le Beau Series

She tapped her chin again. She would have to ask Richie how he handles that before she assigned it a side.

Would weather be a problem? She looked out the window and eyed the river. Richie's house was raised and fortified for storms. He had backup generators if all else failed. Weather shouldn't be an issue. Plus, it would be warm here in the winter. She carefully wrote weather on the plus side.

Being with Richie? Definitely plus, plus, plus.

What about emergencies or accidents? Did they have doctors in the bayou? She scratched the bridge of her nose with the nonbusiness end of her pen then wrote it down as another question for Richie.

She looked at her notepad and smiled, all pluses with two questions.

Richie walked into the bedroom, a towel slung low on his hips, rubbing his hair dry with another towel. He stopped short when he saw her sitting at the end of the bed waiting for him.

"Is everything okay, cher?" he asked apprehensively.

"I think so," she hedged, then sighed. "To be honest, I'm not sure."

"Uh huh." He wasn't sure what to do with that.

"Do you mind if I ask you some questions?" she asked in a tiny, shy voice that sounded strange coming from her mouth.

"Ask me anything," he said, as he combed his hair.

"It's embarrassing to admit, but I made a pro's and con's list for staying while you were in the shower and there are a couple of things I need to ask you about."

Panic stabbed Richie's heart. Had she come up with more pro's than con's? He swallowed hard on a dry throat. "Ask away."

She asked about doctors and he told her about the local homeopathic healers and the Traiteurs, a form of native faith healer.

When she asked about shopping Richie grinned. "I'm sorry, cher. I thought you understood. This is my cabin. I come here to relax. I have a house in the Garden District. That's where we'll live, not here. I brought you here instead of my house to draw Qball away from the general public."

Piper's mouth fell open. Now that she thought back, he had called it a cabin. She'd mistakenly assumed he only had the one place. Well, that changed everything.

"Piper?"

She blinked at him.

"Are you okay?"

She shook her head and covered her face. "I'm so embarrassed."

"Why?"

"I thought this was where you lived all the time."

"So what. That's an honest mistake. No big deal."

Piper raised an eyebrow. "Obviously, I have much to learn about you."

RICHIE: Le Beau Series

"No, not really. With me, what you see is what you get. Well, except for the part that I'm independently wealthy. Most people wouldn't guess that." He shrugged.

"So, when do I get to see this house in the Garden District?"

"How about tomorrow? I should be rested enough to close up the cabin and move home by then." Richie's eager smile lit up the room.

"Great." She smiled back. She couldn't help it. When the man smiled, he was freaking devastating.

"Do you have any other questions, mon amour?"

"Well, I was wondering about the ritual. Does it hurt? I mean is there biting and blood. Do you have to attack me or something?"

"Not in the way you're thinking. I'll bite you once, but I promise you'll like it. And then you get to bite me back. And I guarantee, I'm looking forward to that." He waggled his eyebrows suggestively.

Suddenly his face fell. "Except the conversion. I'm told that can be a bit uncomfortable. Did you have any major injuries between the ages of twenty-five and thirty-five? Other than the one knife wound you told me about?"

"I was shot once and I took a couple other knife wounds. Do they count?"

Richie chuckled and shook his head. Piper was one of a kind. Of course she would think nothing of a gunshot wound or being stuck with a knife.

"Yes, cher, they count. Rose, Anna's sister-in-law, another one of the Le Beau mates, told me she'd had a broken arm that was healed during the conversion. She said it was a bit painful, but the pain was rather fleeting, so I hope yours won't be too unbearable."

"The injuries didn't hurt much when I got them, so maybe it won't be so bad. Besides, I have a high tolerance for pain. I'm sure I'll be fine."

"Good, I was really worried for a minute. The pain during the conversion would never be more than what you experienced during the injury."

Piper racked her brain for any more questions she was forgetting to ask.

She was so lost in thought, when the bed dipped next to her, it knocked her off balance and she almost fell over backward off the side.

Richie's shifter reflexes saved her from utter embarrassment. Catching her by the shoulders before she slipped off.

"I'm so sorry! Did I hurt you?"

She clutched her chest, breathing hard. "No, I'm fine. I just need to let my heart slow to a normal beat."

Then she stood and walked to the bedroom door. "I need a little time to think, okay?"

"All right, but you're not leaving, right?"

"Richie," she smiled tiredly, "I'm in the middle of the bayou and you have the keys to the boat, where am I going to go?"

"Yeah, good point. I guess I wasn't thinking. I'll take my time getting dressed so I don't bother you."

RICHIE: Le Beau Series

She smiled again and walked away, she could feel his fear that she was going to change her mind and leave him. But she had a big decision to make.

Piper stood at the living room window looking out at the bayou. What would it feel like to run as a wolf? It looked and sounded cool, especially the part where she kept her whit's about her. She pictured herself running through the woods, leaving all her worries behind. She would bet a lot of money it would be incredible.

Then she heard Anna's voice in her head saying, "Their still regular people, just like you, only'" *An extra soul, wild animal, and crazy magic more,* she thought.

Did she love Richie? Yes, she honestly did.

Was she brave enough to take a leap of faith that she'd never regret accepting Richie? She liked to think she was.

It all came down to if Richie were just a normal human, what would she do? Would she marry him? *Yeah, I would.*

So that left the whole furry magic thing. Did she want to be able to shift? Hell yes. Did she want to live to be fourteen hundred years old and watch everyone she knew die? Her heart hurt just thinking about it. What would living that long even be like? What kind of technology and environmental changes would she live to see?

Face it, Piper, could you walk away from Richie and never look back? The honest answer was emphatically, no.

V.A. Dold & Tori Austin

So did it matter if she waited any longer and left Richie hanging? It didn't matter one bit. Her answer today was the same as it would be tomorrow.

"Richie, could you come out here?"

"You all right?" he asked tenderly, joining her at the window.

Piper turned and wrapped her arms around his waist, laying her head on his chest. "I'm more than all right. I was having a discussion with myself and I've realized something."

"What did you realize?" he asked, rubbing her back.

"I'm not afraid anymore."

"Afraid of what?" he wondered, smoothing her hair.

"Of taking the leap and becoming a shifter."

Richie sucked in a sharp breath.

Lifting her head, she met his gaze. "I love you, Richie and I never want to spend a day without you."

His heart soared with a mixture of elation and hope. Did she mean what he thought she meant?

"I've," she paused, closed her eyes and took a shaky breath. Then she met his eyes again. "I've never felt this way before, and frankly, it scares the living crap out of me. Are you absolutely sure you want me as a mate, and if we do this that you can't change your mind? I'm not the easiest person to live with," she confided in a shy voice. So unlike the courageous woman he had come to know.

RICHIE: Le Beau Series

Richie cupped her face with both hands, in his firmest, most serious voice he said, "I love you with my entire heart and soul, Piper. I've never been more sure about anything in my life. There is no way, even if I had the option, that I would ever change my mind. I want to spend the rest of my life with you."

"In that case, I think we should discuss the ritual."

"Are you telling me you're ready to accept me as your mate?"

She took a deep breath. "Yeah, I guess I am. Shocking, isn't it?"

Richie couldn't believe his luck, he flowed into her thoughts, loving her, cherishing the gift she was giving him, and determined to claim her as his mate. At the same time, his wolf danced around and howled joyfully.

Piper bit her lip adorably and gave him the sexy smile that always sent him to his knees.

"Are you ready to do this, wolfman?"

"I've been ready since the moment I laid eyes on you. But first let me explain a little about the ritual. The words I will prompt you with during the ritual itself, but there are a few things to go over. Maybe we should sit down, my legs are getting a little wobbly."

"Are you sure you shouldn't go back to bed?"

"No, I'm fine. I just need to get off my feet."

V.A. Dold & Tori Austin

Richie pulled her onto his lap on the couch and nuzzled her neck before he began. "The first thing you should know is the ritual is very private. It's performed while we make love. We must be very careful not to get carried away, though. I have to save my release for the end of the ritual or we have to start over."

She blinked innocently at him. "Well, that's not such a bad thing. Starting over could be fun."

He laughed and he swatted her backside. "Behave yourself, this is serious."

Her eyes went wide. "I am behaving."

"You keep telling yourself that. Okay, back to business. As I mentioned before, I will have to bite you where your neck and shoulder meet. It won't hurt so much as be very erotic. Then when it's your turn to say the words, you'll bite me back in the same way."

"How do I do that? I don't have wolf teeth."

"You'll get your own personalized wolf fangs during the ritual."

"You're kidding, right?"

"Nope, your canines will elongate and become very sharp." He rubbed the deep crease of concern between her eyes. "Don't worry, they recede again after the ritual. After that, they only reappear when you're in wolf form."

"Good, you had me freaked out for a minute."

"Finally, you will receive your wolf soul during the ritual and it might feel strange at first, so don't let that scare you."

RICHIE: Le Beau Series

"Is that it? I thought it would be much more complicated."

"That's it. Would you like to do it now?"

"Yes. Are you sure you're up to it?"

He used his arms to pull his aching body from the couch, then stood unsteadily for a moment as he got his equilibrium sorted out. "A pack of rogue wolves couldn't stop me from claiming you."

He pulled her to her feet and into his arms. "Goddess, I love you," he groaned and pulled her in for a toe-curling kiss.

Chapter 15

Desire shot through her, wild and hot. Now that she'd come to a decision, Piper was ravenous for him, free of fear and holding back nothing. The sensation was liberating and intoxicating.

His tongue's exploration was insistent, urging her to surrender to her mate.

Richie swept her into an existence of raw emotions and sensations unlike anything she'd ever known. The air crackled as energy laced with desire raced through her. Arcing from him to her and back again.

Her skin became ultra-sensitive, every touch of his fingers and lips vibrated through her nerve endings like a live wire. Piper molded her body to his, pulling him closer until they melded into one being.

Richie ran his hands down her back and over her hips to grip her luscious backside. His fingers flexed, molding and massaging. Rubbing the heavy evidence of his arousal against her heated core. His body was on fire.

He growled and kissed his way down her neck to the sweet spot where he would lay his mark and nipped her lightly. Stark need pushed his wolf to

RICHIE: Le Beau Series

complete the claiming immediately, but he wanted to savor his mate, so he forced his wolf into the background. "I need you, Piper. I'm struggling to restrain my wolf. I need you to tell me you truly want me, and you're ready to complete the ritual. This is your last chance to change your mind." The words were whispered against her skin, punctuated by licks and kisses.

Piper tipped her head, and stretched her neck. "Yes. I really want you and I'm ready. Are you sure you're strong enough?"

Richie kissed his way back up her throat. "Don't worry about me, I have plenty of energy and strength."

Piper stepped from his arms, and ran a seductive finger down his chest, sending shivers up his spine.

"In that case, give me a minute and then meet me in the bedroom."

Heat flared in his eyes and he knew they glowed with his wolf. "Don't take too long."

He watched as she disappeared in the shadows of the darkened hallway. A heartbeat later, he heard her giggle as her panties were tossed at him.

Richie scooped them up and pressed them to his nose, drinking in her heady scent. He counted to one thousand and couldn't wait a second longer. Two steps into the hallway, he found her bra hanging on a doorknob. It was like following an erotic trail of breadcrumbs. Grinning, he snatched up her pants next, and finally her blouse. With each piece of clothing his pulse raced faster.

V.A. Dold & Tori Austin

As he stepped across the threshold of his bedroom, breathing became problematic.

A scarlet scarf was draped over the lamp on his bedside table, softly muting the light. The fabric's creases and folds created interesting patterns and shadows on the walls. One glance at the decorations and he dismissed the ambiance. His attention was glued to his mate, lounging on his bed wearing nothing but incredibly sexy footwear and a smile.

Her knees were bent, flashing her glistening shaved mound, wearing nothing but a pair of fire engine red, three-inch stilettos.

Holding her gaze, he swallowed hard and force a breath into his lungs. Just when he thought he had his wolf and body under control, Piper nibbled her bottom lip and spread her knees wider.

He'd often fantasized about the moment he made love to his mate and completed the ritual. In his mind, he'd always been suave and charming. Creating a romantic night of candlelight and champagne.

This woman completely destroyed his plans and his gallant fantasy image. What she'd created was so much better.

With a thought, his clothes disappeared, leaving him splendidly naked for his mate's approval. And boy, from the way she licked her lips, she approved.

Without warning, Richie's wolf seized control and launched him on top of his mate. It was a good thing his injury was almost healed. A fresh gunshot wound would have bled all over the bed.

RICHIE: Le Beau Series

*****

Piper squealed and instinctively shut her eyes tight and pulled her knees up to protect herself. Her reflexive reaction did not go well for Richie. She heard him howl in agony when her left knee smashed into his balls.

When she opened her eyes, Richie lay cupping himself, gasping, unable to breathe.

"Oh my God, Richie. Sweetie, I'm so sorry. It was an accident."

Chewing her lip, she didn't know what to do to help him. She felt terrible, but she was afraid to touch him. She certainly didn't want to make it worse than it already was.

"Can I get you anything? How do I make you feel better?"

From the way he continued to gasp for air like a fish out of water and stayed in a tight ball, she knew it was bad.

"Should I call Seth?"

The only answer she received was another moan.

She considered getting her phone and making the call, but then it occurred to her, Richie would probably be mortified if his friend found him in this state.

"Should I leave you for a little while and go out to the living room?"

He could see the concern on her face and her lips moving, but he couldn't hear the words over the ringing in his ears.

V.A. Dold & Tori Austin

He couldn't form verbal words yet so he grabbed her hand, needing to comfort her. *Give... me... a.....minute.*

A few minutes passed and the pain was lessening.

"You take my breath away," Richie croaked, trying to lighten the mood.

"What can I do to help you?"

He rocked back and forth in agony. "Just give me a few minutes to recover."

Piper stayed to her side of the bed. He knew from the expression on her face, she was racking her brain for a way to ease his suffering.

Ice might help, she thought.

"I'll be right back."

She scooted off the bed and he heard the click... click... click of her stiletto's prancing to the kitchen. Then the freezer was opened.

Nice, wolfman. You have reusable ice packs.

The freezer door closed and he heard her heels clicking. Imagining the sexy sway of her hips with each step, as she walked down the hallway and stopped.

What are you doing?

I need a hand towel so I don't freeze your balls into a solid chunk of ice.

Good thinking, I have plans for them that require they be thawed.

By the time she returned to the bedroom, he was feeling a little closer to normal. He gave her a thankful smile and gratefully accepted the icepack.

RICHIE: Le Beau Series

Very carefully he placed it between his legs. The sudden chill on such a sensitive area gave him a start, but it felt so good.

Piper settled back on the bed and pulled the sheet over her nakedness. He scowled and let out a growl. He didn't want her covered up.

"I think we should do the ritual another day when you feel better."

"Hell no!" He snarled again, then when he saw her stricken expression he softened his voice. "I'll be fine in a bit. Shifter healing, remember?"

"If you say so." She didn't look convinced.

Ten minutes later, Richie was more than up to the challenge of the ritual.

Piper's eyes widened along with her smile. "Very nice."

He'd tossed the icepack aside a few minutes ago to allow his manly bits to warm up. From what she could see, he was ready for action.

"Come here, woman," he growled in a husky voice.

Happy to comply, Piper scooted into his arms. "Don't worry, cher, you didn't hurt me very badly. Besides, it was my own fault. Well, actually my wolf's fault, he was the one that tossed me at you. Your response was completely natural."

A lock of hair had flopped over his forehead and into his eyes. When Piper gently brushed it back with her fingers, he closed his eyes and rumbled happily.

Then her gaze centered on his mouth and she licked her lips. His brain instantly shut down.

V.A. Dold & Tori Austin

The sight of the tip of her little pink tongue flicking her lip drove him over the edge. He rumbled deep in his chest and crushed her mouth to his in a searing kiss.

Several long minutes passed as he explored her hot wet mouth. Goddess he loved her taste. He released her lips to slowly burn a trail of kisses across her jaw and down her neck, stopping to give special attention to the spot, which would bear his bite.

Piper tipped her head, threaded her fingers into his hair, and gently held him to her. "I love you, Richie. I can't wait to be your mate."

He raised his glittering eyes and held her gaze. "I can't wait, either, but we will only ever do this ritual once and I intend to do it well." Then he lowered his head again and resumed his tantalizing exploration.

He refused to allow his wolf to gain control and rush through the ritual. The dang beast had caused enough trouble already. He'd fantasized about claiming his mate so many times over the decades, he knew exactly how he wanted to please her, and he was determined it would go as planned from here on out. No more mishaps.

"Your body is perfection. I don't ever want you to change a thing about your soft curves. Well, except for when you're pregnant with our children. Then your body is going to be even more incredible. I can hardly wait to see your tummy grow heavy with my child. Damn, you take my breath away," Richie rumbled between kisses and nibbles.

RICHIE: Le Beau Series

Her sweet moans encouraged him to please her further. Tracing her collarbone with his tongue, he forged another trail of kisses to her left breast. Piper gasped when he flicked the nipple. With his right hand, he softly cupped the other breast, and gently stroked her aching nipple. The lightest of contact, designed to drive her wild with need.

"You're going to have to be patient about children. I want you for myself for a while." She panted as she writhed under his marauding hands and mouth.

"That can be arranged," he mumbled with his mouth full of nipple.

He reveled in Piper's moans, and her fingers fisted in his hair pressing her breast further into his ravishing mouth was a complete turn on.

His wolf made contented sounds as he leisurely licked and suckled in an unhurried exploration. There was so much more to explore. Switching to her other breast, he trailed one palm down her ribcage over her soft, round belly. Then he moved lower, running his hand down the outside of her smooth thigh to curl his fingers around her knee and pull her leg over his hip.

Richie rumbled with pleasure when he felt her fingers move from his hair to his shoulders and grip him tightly. She wanted him as badly as he wanted her.

One last flick with the tip of his tongue and he raised his head, his eyes glowing with the same intense desire she was feeling.

V.A. Dold & Tori Austin

"I could feast on you for hours."

He nuzzled her other breast, then slowly kissed his way down her ribs to her belly.

Piper sucked in a breath and held it when he slipped his tongue into her belly button. She was horrified. She hated her thick, squishy stomach.

Piper, he scolded in her mind. *I won't have you thinking badly of my mate's unbelievable body. I want your lush, curvy, womanly figure not a hard, bony, half-starved girl.*

She released the breath, wanting to believe him. He hadn't lied to her yet, so why would he now.

As he worked his way down her body, she moved her leg from his hip to his ribs. When he gently gripped her knee again and moved her leg over his shoulder, she moaned in anticipation. The position exposed her most intimate part to his exploration. Richie licked his lips at the sight of her wet for him. The display of his raw need sent another rush of her essence to her exposed core.

Desire rushed through her body to pool low as she lifted her hips, and strained toward his torturous mouth. She trembled with such intense need; she swore she'd rattle apart.

"Please," she cried.

"Please what? What do you want me to do to you, Piper?"

"Touch me."

"Yes, ma'am."

RICHIE: Le Beau Series

He dipped his head down and she felt him nipping and soothing her inner thigh with his tongue. Her arousal increased with every inch he moved closer to her center. She sucked in another breath when he glanced up and held her gaze as he took one slow lick.

Piper pressed harder against his hot seeking tongue. He was driving her insane with little flicks and licks, never giving her the penetration she needed. If he didn't fill her aching channel soon, she would go mad.

"Richie!" She grasped his hair in clenched fists and pressing his face against her tortured center. She needed more contact than he was giving her.

He chuckled and licked her again more slowly, curling his tongue around the neglected, engorged peak. She moaned, he had her so worked up, she was on the verge of begging.

"My mate will never beg for anything that I have the power to provide," his voice rumbled with his wolf.

"Yes!" she cried, when he slipped a finger into her hot, greedy channel and began to relieve the terrible pressure building there. Her hips bucked of their own accord as he stroked in and out while massaging her engorged nub.

Damn that feels good, she sighed.

Piper arched into his mouth and fingers, the ecstasy he was giving her indescribable. She never wanted him to stop. No man had ever brought her to orgasm with only his mouth and fingers. Hell, no man had ever given her an orgasm period. Not until Richie. And he was well on his way to doing just that. The man had some mad skills.

Following her lead, he added another finger and thrust faster and harder. Her bucking hips followed his rhythm as the sweet music of her moans and cries filled the room. But he wanted her screaming his name. His wolf howled its approval as they pleasured their mate.

He felt her nails rake through his hair and massage his scalp. Then she rubbed the silky strands between her fingers for a moment before massaging again. His wolf rolled onto its back, tongue hanging out in ecstasy, begging for a belly rub.

When he felt she was close, he curled his fingers to scrape the inner bundle of nerves as he brushed his thumb over her clit. "Let go for me, mon amour."

Her hips bucked and then she exploded into a million pieces screaming his name.

Richie kissed his way up her body.
"Goddess, I love hearing my name on your lips."

It took a few minutes for her breathing to even out which was just fine with him. He could spend forever worshiping his mate. He caressed and stroked every inch of her body.

Piper gloried in her sated body and Richie's kisses. And now she wanted to return the favor. She had some exploring to do as well.

He raised his head with an inquisitive expression on his handsome face when she pushed on his chest.

RICHIE: Le Beau Series

"My turn. On your back, wolfman." She fake growled and gave him a wink.

Richie's eyes glowed hotter at her demand. He was all for his mate taking charge. In a flash, he was on the bed, ready for anything.

Piper nibbled her lower lip. Now that he was flat on his back, very aroused, her bravado wavered. This was it, her entire life was about to change.

Then, Richie held out his hand to her and quietly said, "Touch me."

That little bit of encouragement was all she needed. She settled over his trim hips, one leg on either side of his, and drank him in with her eyes. She felt like she was really seeing him for the first time.

A slow smile spread across her face as she gazed into his eyes. More love and adoration shown back at her than she'd ever imagined a man would feel for her. He didn't say a word. He simply grinned and waited for her to do whatever she had in mind.

She felt her boldness return and she knew Richie was bolstering her self-confidence through their bond. Nibbling her lower lip, she began her unhurried perusal. Piper didn't want to miss a single detail.

Ever so slowly, she traced his strong cheekbones and jawline. He had such a handsome, strong, manly face. Her thumbs met over his bottom lip and stroked back and forth. The temptation was too much. She had to kiss him. She heard him groan when her weight shifted forward to claim his lips and caused her pelvis to grind on his erection in exquisite torture.

V.A. Dold & Tori Austin

Finally, she sat up, her hands on his chest, eliciting another groan from his lips.

"Is this too much for you? Are you going to be okay?"

"I'll be fine. Take your time." He clinched his teeth and gripped the sheet.

He seemed sincere, so she continued her study of her mate. She ran both palms down his body, enjoying every dip and muscle. She loved the feel of his skin. Slowly, she circled his hard male nipple with her finger. Richie let out a little growl as she rolled it. She grinned when his eyes glowed brighter with desire.

Richie's muscles quivered and clenched under her light touch, as her fingertips floated lightly over the ripples and valleys of his abdomen. Her gaze fastened on his hip area, fascinated by the deep 'V'.

By this time, she'd worked her way down his legs to sit near his knees. Her mouth watered to taste him. Holding his heated gaze, she leaned forward and ran her tongue from the top of the left side of the 'V' down to his weeping cock and gave it a lick. Then she used her tongue to trace the other side.

Richie jerked his hips so hard she thought he was going to buck her off the bed.

"I'm sorry, cher. I'll hold still. I promise." He would give her all the time she wanted, if it killed him. And at the rate she was going, it just might.

"Good, because I have to inspect this area a bit more," she teased twirling her finger over his groin in emphasis which sent him into a growling fit.

RICHIE: Le Beau Series

The pads of her fingers skimmed his cock, and she felt the hard length of him jump as he sucked in his breath. She lightly traced the length and shape of his cock and he thought he would die. The top of his head almost blew off when she wrapped her fist around him and began a mind-numbing glide from tip to balls.

He squeezed his eyes shut, willing his body to remain still. But when her hair grazed his inner thighs, and she took him into her warm, wet mouth, his hips jerked reflexively. His heart stuttered and all the air whooshed from his lungs. Damn, she was going to kill him with pleasure.

As she took him deep, all the way to the back of her throat, his eyes rolled and every brain cell exploded. With every caress of her tongue, his dick twitched and bounced. He panted and clutched the sheets in a death grip, barely holding to his resolve. The final straw was when she gently cupped his sack with her free hand.

That was it. Game over. He swallowed his tongue. He had all he could do to hold his release.

Mon amour, you need to stop right now. If you don't, I'm going to ruin the ritual.

A wicked gleam sparkled in her eyes as she released him with a 'pop.'

Before she could draw a breath, he flipped her onto her back covering her with his body.

"How the heck did you manage that?" Piper squeaked in surprise.

"I've got mad skills, mon amour." He grinned from ear to ear and winked. Then he nestled his hips between her thighs, and sat back on his heels.

Mimicking her early inspection, he trailed a finger along the side of her neck, and traced the swell of her breast. She shivered under his light caresses, which made his blood run even hotter.

Her body shook with arousal, but he didn't give into impulse and hurry. He simply continued his slow inspection from head to toe.

Piper was breathing hard. "What are you doing?"

"Like you, I'm enjoying every inch of my mate," he said as he brought his gaze back to her face. "The curve of your lips. The dusky color of your nipples when you're aroused. The way your waist dips in ever so slightly. I'm burning every detail into my mind so when I close my eyes, I can picture you perfectly, exactly as you are right now."

He licked his lips, tasting her essence there and gazed deeply into her eyes. Then eased his hips forward until the tip of his cock entered her. Ever so slowly, he rocked against her. Only making a shallow penetration. He closed his eyes and took a deep breath to calm himself and his wolf. Then he looked her in the eye again. "Are you ready, my beautiful mate?"

"Absolutely," she said emphatically.

"Do you see that sheet of paper on the side table next to you? I wrote the ritual out so you'll know what to say and when."

RICHIE: Le Beau Series

Piper picked up the paper and nodded. "Got it."

"Will you give yourself, body and soul, to complete this man and his wolf?

"Will you unite your life with mine, bond your future with mine, and merge your half of our soul to mine, and in doing so, complete the mating ritual?"

She looked at her script and read aloud, "I will give myself, body and soul, to complete you as a man and his wolf.

"I will unite my life with yours, bond my future to yours, and merge my half of our soul with yours. I will complete the mating ritual with you," she stated her answer and smiled brightly.

With the required request and acceptance completed, he bent forward, planting his strong arms on either side of her shoulders and leaned in to kiss her enthusiastically.

"You have no idea, how badly I've wanted to hear you say those words," he breathed against her lips. Then he kissed her again, his tongue danced sensually with hers, and in one thrust he was buried to the hilt. Slowly he rocked in and out, relishing the love he felt through their bond.

Richie kissed her one last time, a sweet lingering kiss. "Are you ready to complete the actual ritual, mon amour?"

"I've never been more ready in my life."

He locked his elbows and gazed into her eyes as he began. "I claim you as my mate." A breeze of magical energy caressed their skin with his first words.

V.A. Dold & Tori Austin

"I belong to you as you belong to me.
"I give you my heart and my body.
"I will protect you even with my life.
"I give you all I am.
"I share my half of our soul to complete you.
"I share my magic with you."

Richie unlocked his elbows and kissed her lips, then whispered next to her ear. "This is the part where I bite you."

Piper sucked in a breath as he nuzzled her neck. She felt him lapping at her neck where he'd said he would leave his mark. He lapped once, twice, a third time, and pierced her flesh with his elongated canines.

Piper yipped and then instantly sighed as bliss enveloped her. It hadn't hurt as much as she'd expected.

She felt his tongue as he lapped up the blood seeping from the little wound he'd made, licking gently. Then he started his shallow thrusting again.

"I beseech the great Luna Goddess to bless you and your wolf guardian.

"You are my mate to cherish today and for all time.

"I claim you as my mate."

The breeze of energy from earlier gathered power and swirled faster and faster around the room before it whooshed into the center of her chest.

Her eyes got wider than the rings around Saturn. "What the hell just hit me?"

"That was your wolf soul entering your body. Now you need to repeat the words back to me, and

RICHIE: Le Beau Series

bite me right here." He tapped his neck and waggled his eyebrows suggestively.

Piper concentrated on her script again, took a deep breath, and cleared her throat. "I claim you as my mate.

"I belong to you as you belong to me.

"I give you my heart and my body.

"I will protect you even with my life.

"I give you all I am.

"I share my half of our soul to complete you."

Richie rumbled loudly.

"Okay, now what was that?" she asked wide-eyed.

"That was our souls knitting together."

"It feels amazing. I've never felt this content and peaceful before."

"I feel it, too," he said, rubbing his chest with one hand, a huge smile on his face.

"Cool." She smiled continued. "I share my magic with you."

He lowered himself on his arms again, and exposed his neck to her. "Make me yours for all time, mon amour."

She'd never been so hesitant in her life. She really didn't want to hurt him by doing the bite thing wrong.

"Just do exactly what I did. Trust me, you won't do it wrong."

"Okay," she said quietly as she eyed his neck. Trusting him, she followed his advice, and copied him. She lapped at the spot, once, twice, and as she licked a third time, super sharp fangs erupted.

V.A. Dold & Tori Austin

"Holy shit! Are you sure you're not a vampire? These fangs are beyond huge," she lisped around her oversized canines.

Richie chuckled which caused his neck to move. "I'm sorry, I'll hold still so you can do this."

Thankfully, instinct took over, and she bit down piercing his flesh. She was sure she wouldn't have been able to do it without the extra push.

He moaned and she felt his ecstasy as her fangs sank deep. Still copying what he'd done, she lapped at the bite.

Richie's forearms quivered from the intense erotic pleasure each lick shot through his body, but he managed to hold still.

With a shaky breath, he locked gazes with her again to watch her finish the ritual.

"I beseech the great Luna Goddess to bless you and your wolf guardian.

"You are my mate to cherish today and for all time.

"I claim you as my mate."

Richie growled loudly and kissed her with more passion than he'd ever experienced. The ritual words were completed, now he could love his mate the way she liked to be loved. A little bit rough, with a truckload of sensation.

"Mine!" he howled, and thrust into her.

"Mine!" she echoed back, and met him thrust for thrust.

He gripped her hips and pulled almost completely out before slamming all the way to the hilt. With each deep stroke, he had her moaning louder.

RICHIE: Le Beau Series

He set a rhythm designed to drive her into a frenzy.

He tipped her hips to hit her inner sweet spot. "Can you feel your wolf engaging in our ecstasy?"

"I think so," she panted, and began to make a keening sound.

He had her on the edge as flesh slapped flesh in earnest.

Piper locked her ankles behind his hips, and he drove deeper. Three thrusts and her climax rolled over her like a tidal wave. Her channel clamped down on him as she screamed his name.

A moment later, he joined her in his own release.

Gasping, he managed to collapse by her side and not crush her. A huge, sated grin filled his face. He was so unbelievably content. Richie thought his heart would burst with the amount of love he felt coming from Piper.

She was grinning too, and had an equally sated expression on her face. A surge of male pride roared through him. He'd put that expression there.

"Wow," she panted, reaching blindly for his hand.

"Double wow," he panted and wound their fingers together.

Finally able to catch his breath, he growled, "I love you, Piper Majors."

"I love you, too, Richie Majors," she growled back. Then she sucked in a breath and whispered. "That's freaky."

V.A. Dold & Tori Austin

"What's freaky?" He propped himself on one elbow to look at her.

"My wolf growled through my voice and I felt her emotions."

He grinned and tucked a stray curl behind her ear. "Cool, huh?"

She grinned back. "Way cool."

RICHIE: Le Beau Series

Chapter 16

Piper had only nodded off when she woke with a start. She didn't feel well. Not well at all.

Richie tucked her closer to his side. "Are you okay, cher?"

"Not really. I feel strange and achy."

"I think that's the conversion starting," he said with a very concerned expression. "What can I do to make you feel better? Is there anything I can get for you?"

"I don't know. What do shifters do for the mate to help them through a conversion?"

Richie wouldn't look her in the eye. Her heart pounded and she started to become alarmed when a tear rolled down his cheek.

"I should have been more adamant about your discomfort when I explained the conversion to you. From what I've been told, there isn't much I can do to ease your pain."

"Shit. This is going to suck, isn't it?"

All he could do was nod.

"You said you were injured a few times on the job. I'm trying to remember if I've heard any stories of other mates besides Rose, who endured the healing of such things."

V.A. Dold & Tori Austin

She placed her hand over her stomach, as the cramps rolling in her belly, began to build. Then she felt a sharp pain that slowly eased. She looked at Richie in horror as her mid-section began to twitch and push up in sections, like something alive was trying to break out. Good lord, was the alien from those Sigourney Weaver movies in there?

Piper rubbed circles over her churning stomach. The only thing she could think to do was breathe like in the movies when a woman was in labor. Which was stupid, she'd never had a baby and had no idea if she was doing it correctly. All she accomplished was near hyperventilation.

She came up on her knees, clutching her stomach with both hands as what must have been the hundredth wave of pain in the past hour racked her body.

Richie leapt from the bed and searched for his phone. "This doesn't seem right. You're in too much pain and this is taking too long. I need to call Emma Le Beau." He searched his brain for stories of a mate not surviving the conversion. Thank Goddess, he couldn't remember hearing any.

A few minutes later, Richie skidded into the room and found her crawling across the floor. "Goddess, what are you doing?" he asked in a panicked voice.

"I'm going to throw up."

He swept her into his arms and rushed her to the bathroom. Then watched helplessly as Piper hung her head over the toilet.

"I've never been so embarrassed in my life."

RICHIE: Le Beau Series

Silently, he held her hair aside while she retched over and over. He was unable to bear the pain for her, so he sent her love and comfort through their bond.

When she felt well enough to go back to bed, he scooped her off the floor and carried her. Very gently, he laid her down before sitting next to her. "Mon amour, what have you failed to tell me? What happened to you between the ages of twenty-five and thirty-five that would affect you this way?"

Piper screwed up her face in annoyance. "I told you, I was shot and stabbed twice."

"Where and exactly what were your injuries," he demanded in an overly tight voice.

She let out a resigned breath, then admitted. "All in the stomach. And I lost my appendix and spleen to the stabbings."

Richie scrubbed his hands over his stubbled face. "You should have warned me. As a human you were obviously given medication to dull the pain. No wonder it didn't hurt too badly. For Goddess sake, Piper, you had to have gone through several operations.

"Now the damage from those wounds is healing and your organs are regrowing without painkillers. That's what's causing the excessive pain. Emma suspected something like this. She said if we'd known ahead of time, I could have had a hypo on hand and given it to you after the ritual. You could have slept through this, mon amour."

She nervously chewed her lip. "Oh. Sorry. I didn't think of that when we talked about it."

Piper rolled to her side, and began rocking back and forth.

Before he could think of a way to help her, pain etched her face again. He could see it. He sensed it. And damnation, he felt it like it was his own.

He saw the sheen of sweat dampen her hair and running down her face. That at least he could help with. He disappeared into the bathroom and returned with damp clothes and dry towels. As tender as a mother with a newborn, he bathed her face and dried her hair.

"Thank you," she said weakly.

"You're welcome, mon précieux. Is it getting any better?" She seemed to be resting more comfortably and hadn't doubled over in the last ten minutes.

"I think the worst of the pain is over. Now all I feel is dull aching in my joints and muscles. And a weird tingling all over my body."

"Normally, the regression is rather short. Hopefully, you follow the norm and it's almost done."

"That would be nice. At least I have an idea what to expect when we have a baby."

"Goddess, woman, are you trying to kill me? Let me get through this before you talk about something like that."

Piper chuckled at the dismay he evidently had displayed on his face.

Then a grin and fascination pulled at his lips, but he tamped it down and didn't say a word.

RICHIE: Le Beau Series

"What?" she asked, gingerly touching her face. "Why does my skin feel tight?"

"Your skin just smoothed out like Saran Wrap pulled tightly over a bowl of food."

"Is that what I just felt? Because I'll tell you, if felt freaky."

He grinned for the first time since the conversion began. "It looked freaky."

Piper sighed and lay back on the pillows. Suddenly Richie scowled darkly.

"Good lord! What now?"

He glared at her body. "How thin were you when you were twenty-five?"

She shrugged. "I don't know, maybe fifty pounds lighter."

Richie bared his teeth and snarled louder. "When this is over, you'll take a shower while I prepare a high calorie meal for you. I will not have a skinny mate."

Piper was astounded by his reaction. "Are you kidding? Most men want a thin, attractive woman."

"I'm not most men, I'm a shifter, and I want my mate soft and curvy with meat on her bones."

"Holy crow, I had no idea you were so attached to my love handles. Don't worry, a few days of cake and ice cream for dessert and all the weight will be back."

"Really?" he asked, much calmer.

"Really. All I have to do is think about food and I gain weight."

He crossed his arms and smiled broadly. "Excellent."

V.A. Dold & Tori Austin

"I think it's over. I don't feel any pain or tightness anymore." Her voice was almost a whisper.

Richie pulled her into his arms and kissed her hair. "Let's wait a minute to be sure."

After a few minutes, she wriggled to loosen his hold. "I need that shower you mentioned. I smell like a locker room."

Richie stood and helped her from the bed. "Do you need my help or should I make us something to eat?"

"I'm good. You're free to find something to fatten me up with," she teased, and walked from the room.

Richie breathed a sigh of relief. Her suffering was over. That had been much more difficult to bear than any injury he'd ever sustained personally. He really disliked his mate in pain.

He'd just turned to leave the room when he heard a gasp of alarm. Rushing to the bathroom, he yelled, "What's wrong!"

Piper stood before the mirror completely naked. A hand covered her mouth as she turned this way and that. "Is that really me?"

"Dang it, Piper, you gave me a heart attack," he groused in relief. Then he stood behind her and wrapped his arms around her middle. "Yes, mon amour, that's you."

She reached up and touched her hair. "I don't remember looking this good."

"You're stunning. The most beautiful woman I've ever seen." He turned her in his arms and kissed

RICHIE: Le Beau Series

her breathless, then left her to shower so he could get the food ready. She was going to be starving by the time she joined him in the kitchen. Going through a conversion left a person with a large appetite.

*****

    Twenty minutes later, he heard the shower shut off. Perfect timing. He turned the burner off on the stove, and grabbed his tongs. He grinned happily as he added a thick cut, medium rare steak to each plate and set them on the table. Now that he was taking care of his mate again, he felt better.

    She entered the kitchen and took a deep breath. "What smells so good?"

    "Steak, just the way you like it, baked potato with lots of butter and sour cream, and as you requested cake and ice cream for dessert."

    "Wow! If you are going to cook like this, I should go through the conversion every day."

    "Don't even say that out loud," he whispered as if someone would hear them.

    Piper laughed and took her seat. "I'm famished. Going through the conversion is a workout and brings on one heck of an appetite. This looks great, baby. Thank you."

    Richie smiled happily and sat across from her. "My pleasure."

    He watched as she took her first bite, waiting to see her reaction to food as a shifter.

    "Oh. My. God!" she moaned, eyes closed in ecstasy.

V.A. Dold & Tori Austin

"Good?"

"This is better than sex." When she saw the horrified expression on his face, she quickly amended her response. "Almost, and only better than sex with a human. It's not even in the same ballpark as you."

He smiled and nodded in approval. "Much better."

Her taste buds were dancing a jig in her mouth. And her sense of smell was off the charts. Shifter senses were the bomb!

"You'll hear and see better, as well. And I don't mean just in the daytime, you'll have perfect night vision, too. Did you notice you can smell and taste all the separate ingredients?"

"Is that the difference? This is great! I could have used these abilities as a bounty hunter."

"You certainly would have had a much larger advantage."

They ate happily in silence for a few minutes, and then he asked. "Have you noticed any change in your gift?"

"No. But I haven't tried to use it yet." She finished chewing then set her knife and fork aside and closed her eyes. For the first time, her spirit easily parted from her without effort and zoomed across the room where she directed it.

Piper opened her eyes and was astounded for a second time. She could use her gift with her eyes open. She'd always had to close her eyes to make it work. She watched as her spirit zoomed to wherever she directed it, and she could see everything from both perspectives at the same time. Then she tried

RICHIE: Le Beau Series

something she'd never been able to do. She directed her spirit to the river and upstream where she'd never been. In the past, she'd only been able to view spaces she was familiar with. This was a whole new ballgame.

"Wow!" she breathed, and then told him everything that had happened.

They were cleaning up when a knock came on the door.

"Seth, what brings you back?" Richie asked drying his hands.

"I'm collecting my gear from the woods. Now that Qball is in custody, I'm not needed here. Plus, Dad told me this morning, there is a rogue in Minnesota that needs killing and he asked me to handle it before I retire for good. So, I came to say goodbye."

"Shit. I'm sorry, man. I know you're really burned out and you didn't want to hunt anymore. Isn't there anyone else who can go to Minnesota?"

"According to Dad, I'm the only one he can send," Seth said tiredly. "The request came directly from the Goddess. I'm to allow a human woman by the name of Sara Adams to help with the hunt and ensure she doesn't get herself killed in the process."

Richie's eyes glowed angrily. Why were they pushing Seth when he was so close to ending his life? Couldn't they see how ragged and depressed he was? "All you have to do is say the word and I'll go with you."

Richie's fury brought a small smile to Seth's face. "I've always been able to count on you to have my back. Thank you, but no. You have a new mate to see to and I'll be fine. Besides, the female is a detective. I'm assuming she'll know how to handle herself. Who knows, it might be entertaining. I can practice talking to a human while I clean up the mess."

"If you get into any kind of a bind, you'd better call me," Richie demanded. "I don't have a lot of close friends and I can't afford to lose one."

"All right, I promise if I need back up, you'll be the first person I call." He grinned, then he pulled Richie into a man hug and pounded him on the back.

"See you soon, bro." He turned to Piper and kissed her knuckles with a twinkle in his eyes. "Congratulations, cher, and welcome to the family."

Piper gave Richie a confused look. She wasn't aware all shifters consider each other family regardless of parentage.

Once Seth was gone, Richie scooped his mate into his arms. "Would you like to learn to shift or are you worn out from the conversion?"

Piper's eyes lit up with eagerness. "Surprisingly, I feel great. What do I have to do?"

"Let's go outside where there's more room."

She grinned brightly and ran for the door like an excited child.

Chuckling, he joined her on the lawn. "Before you shift you need to know the shifter rules. Born shifters learn these as children. Our goddess decreed these laws when she created us."

"Okay." She folded her arms and gave him her full attention.

"Always put your mate before yourself.

"Respect another shifter's mate.

RICHIE: Le Beau Series

"Do nothing to expose the existence of shifters.

"Do no unnecessary harm to shifters or humans.

"And respect other nonhumans."

Piper raised her eyebrows at the simplicity of the rules. "Logical and practical. They make sense on a very basic level."

"You'd be surprised how simple some shifters are. Plus, this isn't the human world. Very little crime actually exists in our community."

"Really? I can't imagine a world without crime. It sounds surreal."

"And having shifters in the world sounds perfectly normal to you? Shifters are not humans, and as a species behave very differently."

"Put that way, I guess it's unrealistic to expect the rules of both worlds to be the same."

"Exactly. Now, the first thing you need to do is close your eyes and visualize yourself as a wolf. Picture your hands and feet as paws, feel the fur all over your body, and the sensation of having a tail. Be sure to picture your human clothing disappear so all that remains is the wolf."

She did as he instructed and squeezed her eyes tightly in concentration. A tingling energy raced across her skin and suddenly she was on all fours in wolf form.

"Good job!" Richie cheered. "You should see yourself. You're gorgeous. And as I suspected, you're a beautiful chocolate wolf."

V.A. Dold & Tori Austin

Without giving it any thought, Piper wagged her tail happily. The sensation startled her and she shot across the lawn to get away from it. The only problem was, the feeling followed her. She skidded to a halt and spun around to nip whatever had attached itself to her backside. She spun and spun again, until she realized it was her tail she was feeling. If a wolf could blush in embarrassment, she would be beet red. Best to pretend it didn't happen.

Piper's wolf held her head high and trotted back to Richie.

He held his hand over his mouth, hiding his grin. "Goddess, you are priceless."

Not another word, she growled.

I have no idea what you're talking about.

Good answer.

"Okay. Try to shift back. You'll need to visualize your human form with clothing and no fur. Be sure to be precise. If you want to be wearing underwear you need to visualize it, the same goes for socks and shoes."

Piper's glossy brown wolf sat at his feet and closed its eyes. A moment passed when suddenly his mate sat at his feet fully clothed.

He reached down and helped her to her feet, brushing dirt from her backside. "You're amazingly good at shifting. Most humans take months of practice to do it as well as you do."

"Really?" she asked with a frown. "I didn't think it was that hard."

"Don't say that in front of the women at the Le Beau plantation. You'll find yourself strung up."

RICHIE: Le Beau Series

"No way! Anna had trouble? She's so good at shifting."

"She's had over a year of practice."

"Huh. Okay, I'll keep my mouth shut. I don't want to make anyone feel bad."

"Do you want to go for a run with me or are you ready to see your new home in the Garden District?"

Piper chewed her lip and eyed the forest. "Can we go to the house now and come back in a few days to take a run?"

"Absolutely, cher."

"Let's do that then."

*****

An hour later, Richie had her luggage in the boat and they were speeding toward his SUV at the pier he used near town.

He was so excited to show her their home. He kept his Garden District mansion a well-guarded secret, going as far as maintaining a tiny five hundred square foot studio apartment in the French Quarter. He worked hard to hide his wealth from his human friends and coworkers. He'd even had a few over for drinks to the studio for good measure.

Other than the Le Beaus and a few other shifters, no one knew he owned the house. He'd had his shell corporation purchase it so it wasn't even in his name.

V.A. Dold & Tori Austin

The house wasn't far from the river and in no time, they were stopped in front of it. "I'll pull around to the back in a minute, but first I wanted to show you what it looks like from the front."

Piper's eyes widened. "Your house is perfect. I love the white color and it's not one of the overly large palatial homes I've seen in pictures. It's more of a medium-sized house, large enough to be impressive, but small enough to be a comfortable home."

"Our house, mon amour. It's our house now."

He looked at his two story, rectangular home with its fancy black wrought iron work on the second story balcony, seeing it through her eyes. The forest green shutters matched the front door and were more lovely than he'd remembered them being. He'd had them installed long ago as finishing touches to really make the house grand without shouting, "look at me."

This was the perfect house for staying under the radar and going unnoticed. That's not saying it wasn't expensive, the house was worth well over a million dollars.

"Do you like it?"

"I love it," she beamed. And he breathed a sigh of relief.

"Let's get this rig parked and I'll give you a tour."

They pulled around the back to his private garage and he ran around to her door. On the way to

RICHIE: Le Beau Series

the front door, he detoured to the side yard and showed her the private patio and pool with its fountains.

"Oh my, this is lovely, Richie," she breathed.

His wolf rumbled proudly. The beast loved pleasing their mate.

He took her by the hand again and led her to the door, unlocked it, and swept her into his arms.

"What are you doing?" she squeaked.

"Carrying my woman over the threshold of course." He walked them into the front hall and set her on her feet. "Welcome home, Piper."

"Holy moly." Her eyes grew large as she took in the antiques and artistically designed décor.

"The formal living room is here to the left and has French doors to the pool."

She stepped into the room and gaped,

"I know it's large," he said when he saw her face.

"Large? It's huge. This has to be at least twenty-five feet long. My entire apartment would fit in this room."

"If you don't like it, we can buy a different house." He worried she hated it after only seeing the first room.

"Don't you dare."

"Okay, but after you see all of it, if you don't want to live here, we'll move."

He led her to the far end of the living room and back into the hallway. "Across the hall is the kitchen and informal dining where I usually eat."

V.A. Dold & Tori Austin

"Wow, I could live in here and never leave." She ran her hands over the surfaces. "Oh my gosh, you have oak cabinets all the way to the ceiling, stainless steel appliances, and granite counter tops and floors. Richie, it's exactly what I would have designed for myself."

"I'm glad you like it." He leaned against the doorjamb and watched her excitedly examine the room. When she was finished, he took her down the hall toward the front door and up the stairs.

First, he showed her the guest bedrooms and then he dramatically opened the door to the master suite.

"Richie, It's gorgeous. And you have a huge four-poster bed I can chase you around in. Have you seen these monstrous closets?" Her voice rose an octave with each new thing she discovered.

"Yes, cher. I've seen them." He chuckled. "These French doors lead out to a balcony over the pool area and on the other side, those double doors lead to a private sitting room. But I saved the best for last. Close your eyes."

He led her to the bathroom and then said, "Okay, you can open them."

Piper's hands flew to her chest. "I've died and gone to heaven. I've never seen such a luxurious bathroom. This belongs in a spa somewhere."

He knew she was envisioning a long hot soak in the fancy marble tub. Richie pulled her into his arms and nuzzled her neck. "I'll draw you a bath later," he whispered as he peppered kisses up her neck and across her jaw. "First, I have dinner waiting in the dining room."

RICHIE: Le Beau Series

Piper frowned and looked him in the eye. "You didn't show me a dining room."

"I know," he rumbled with fire in his eyes. "I was saving it for last."

He took her hand and kissed her knuckles one by one, then led her downstairs. The table was set for an intimate dinner for two, with candles, crystal stemware, a bottle of champagne on ice, and two plates covered with sterling silver domes.

Her breath caught and she turned to stare at him. "How did you do this?"

He pulled her close and breathed into her ear, "I keep telling you, I have mad skills." Then he nibbled her neck until she squirmed.

Finally, he stepped back and pulled a chair for her. "We should eat before it gets cold."

He pushed her chair in, and then took his own.

He grinned like the Cheshire cat and watched her closely. "Let's see what Anna left us for dinner."

Piper lifted the dome off of her plate and stopped breathing all together.

The plate was empty except for the incredible sapphire ring she'd wanted so badly the day he'd taken her to Royal Street. It was artfully displayed in the very center of the china so it caught the light from the chandelier.

Her eyes shot from the ring to Richie. She was so shocked she couldn't speak.

With a smile bigger than any she'd ever seen on his face, he rounded the table, picked up the ring and got down on one knee.

V.A. Dold & Tori Austin

Eyes rounded and widened to the size of saucers, she gasped and her hands flew to her mouth.

"Piper Sinclair Majors, will you do me the honor of becoming my bride?"

Tears ran down her face and she nodded, her hands still shaking over her mouth. Apparently she was too shocked to function.

"I'm going to need your hand, mon amour," he coaxed and gently removed it from over her mouth to slip the ring into place. Then he cupped her face with both hands and poured his heart and soul into his kiss.

Finally, he whispered against her lips, "I can't wait to spend the coming centuries together. With you by my side, it's going to be an amazing adventure."

Richie eased her away from him and searched her face. "Mon amour, would you like to have a wedding with your family in attendance? Some of the women I know have enjoyed a traditional ceremony, others have chosen not to have one. I leave the choice up to you."

She seemed to consider the question. "You know, I think I would. My brother could give me away. And I would really like him and my aunt, uncle and cousin to be there. If I don't have a wedding they would be crushed."

"In that case, I would like to introduce you to the King and Queen tomorrow. Isaac and Emma would love to meet you and I'm sure they will insist on hosting the wedding at the plantation. Are you okay with that?"

RICHIE: Le Beau Series

Piper seemed to hesitate for a moment. "Okay, but I'm a little nervous to meet them."

He searched her face for a long moment, then smiled. "There's nothing to worry about, you're going to love them. I promise."

The next morning.

Richie and Piper walked hand in hand to Isaac and Emma's front step. As he raised his hand to knock the door swung open and a blur of flowing colorful fabrics and jangling bracelets launched itself at him.

"Oomph," Richie grunted. "Good morning Emma."

Emma squeezed harder. "I'm so happy for the both of you."

Isaac stood in the doorframe grinning at Piper, then he glanced at Richie and Emma. "Congratulations, and welcome to our home."

"Thank you, Isaac." Richie choked out as he struggled to breathe.

"Emma dear, you might want to loosen your hold a bit."

"Sorry, I forget myself." She released Richie and stepped back. Her eyes focused on Piper, and her cheeks pinkened. "I'm so happy to meet you." She hugged Piper and quickly stepped aside. Then, with a sweep of her arm, invited them in.

Piper grinned at Emma, and then glanced to Isaac. "It's a pleasure to meet you as well." She took Richie's hand again and followed him into the house.

V.A. Dold & Tori Austin

Once they were seated with refreshments, Richie made the formal introductions. "Piper, this is Isaac your King and Emma your Queen." Then he glanced to Isaac and Emma and said, "This is my mate, Piper."

The pleasantries were quickly dispensed and Richie got down to business. "I've asked Piper to marry me and she has said yes."

Emma's grin widened and she clapped her hands excitedly. "I adore weddings. If you don't already have a venue chosen, I would love to offer the plantation. Oh, and Rose could plan the event for you."

Piper smiled warmly at the Queen. "Thank you, we'd like that."

Emma grabbed her day planner and a pen. "Perfect, it's settled then. All I need is a date."

"That's the rub." Richie sat forward and looked Isaac in the eye. "I would like to have Seth as my best man, so we need to wait for him to return from Minnesota."

Isaac rubbed his chin and Emma suddenly found something very interesting on the floor. Finally, he spoke, "I'll stay in contact with him and as soon as we have an idea of his return date Rose and Emma can begin the planning."

Richie searched Pipers face for her reaction. When she nodded he glanced back at Isaac. "That will be perfect."

The wedding was temporarily on hold and now all they had to do was wait for Seth's return.

RICHIE: Le Beau Series

Read on for an excerpt from
SETH
Book 7
of the Le Beau Series

Prologue: The Plan

It had been about a year since Isaac and Emma Le Beau first hatched a plan to assist each of their seven grown sons in meeting their one true mate. The plan was a simple one. Emma would ask the Wolf Goddess to disclose who the mate was for each of them.

Then Isaac and Emma would ensure whichever son was matched to the disclosed mate was in the right place at the right time to meet her in person. Once they saw each other and experienced the draw of one mate to another, the unique scent one had for the other, nature would take its course. A very simple plan that had worked five times. And not only had they found mates for a few of their own children, but a niece and step-grandson as well.

V.A. Dold & Tori Austin

It all started with Isaac's fear that his sons would go through their long lives as shifters without experiencing the incredible love enjoyed between mates. Without children to love and cherish. Which would in turn mean no grandchildren for him. That was not allowed to happen. He wanted grandchildren, dang it.

It hadn't taken long for Emma, a powerful voodoo priestess, to learn the name of the first destined mate. Luperca, the Wolf Goddess told her their oldest son Cade would meet his mate Anna at the Crescent City Brewhouse. She would be there for lunch on a particular date and at a specific time. It was a rather simple matter to trick Cade into being there at the same time.

Isaac arranged for Cade to meet him for lunch at the Crescent City Brewhouse and then called and cancelled at the last minute. That left Cade free to have a long, leisurely lunch with Anna. The love affair and happy ending took off from there.

Sure, there was a bump or two in the road, but what great love hasn't had them. Harassing ex-husbands, dangerous crime bosses, and suspicious adult children have nothing on a Le Beau. Just look at Romeo and Juliet or Hermoine and Ron as examples of famous love affairs. Well, maybe not Hermoine and Ron. But you get the picture. Isaac and Emma were thrilled with the results and the boy never knew what hit him.

RICHIE: Le Beau Series

Then a few months later, the Goddess disclosed the next name. She had decided Simon had suffered more than necessary and gave them Rose's name as his mate. She was conveniently Anna's best friend in Colorado and it was easy enough to get her to come for a visit. That was happy ever after number two.

Isaac was over the moon, and best yet, Anna announced she was pregnant with his first grandchild.

It wasn't long and they were given the next name. They couldn't believe how quickly the Goddess was disclosing them. Not that they were complaining. They now knew that Stefan would meet his mate El at a charity ball that Simon was hosting. Stefan and El's courtship was a hard and very rocky one. But in the end it all worked out and now they were happily mated and married.

When a couple months later the Goddess told Emma their step-grandson Thomas would be mated to their niece Julia, they were both surprised and overjoyed. Thomas may be a grandson by Anna's and Cade's marriage, but he was theirs through and through. In their minds, he was as much Le Beau as any other family member. And Julia was one of Isaac and Emma's favorite relatives. It couldn't have worked out better.

While Thomas and Julia were dealing with his good for nothing father and her bat-shit crazy mother, Lucas returned home from traveling the world. The timing couldn't have been better.

V.A. Dold & Tori Austin

The Goddess had just told Emma that Lucas would meet his mate at a ranch he was about to purchase in Texas. Bam! Another son happily mated.

After that, Isaac and Emma were sure one of the other boys would be given their mate, but the Goddess had other plans and gave Emma the name of Richie Major's mate. Richie was a very good friend of the family, and Anna's best friend in New Orleans long before she met Cade. Not to mention their adopted son, Seth Le Beau's best friend in the world.

When they thought about it, it only made sense that they would help him meet his mate. Now Richie and Piper are happily mated and living in the Garden District.

Seth had only recently returned home after a century and a half of service to the Wolf Goddess as one of her elite rogue hunters. He'd shown up while Richie was busy winning Piper over as his mate.

Isaac and Emma only had him home for a week or so when Emma had another visit from the Goddess.

"Blessed be, my daughter," Luperca greeted her in her soft, peaceful voice.

"Blessed be, Mother. I would like to thank you again for your continued blessings of my family and our friends."

"You are more than welcome. It pleases me to see my children happily mated and starting families of their own. That is in fact, why I am here."

RICHIE: Le Beau Series

Emma became alarmed. "Has something happened?"

"No, my daughter. Everything has gone as planned." Luperca laughed softly. "I have another name for you."

"You do?" Emma asked excitedly.

"Yes. Seth, your adopted son has done a great service for me and as such has suffered. He has closed himself off from all human and shifter contact and I fear for his personal safety. He needs his mate to complete and heal his ragged heart and soul. Killing rogues, a few who had been his friends and family over such a long period, although necessary, has taken a terrible toll on him. The least I can do is assist him in finding his mate. I am only sorry he didn't find her sooner," the goddess said sadly.

"What would you like me to do? How may I be of service?" she asked in rapid succession.

"Seth is destined to meet his mate Sara Adams in Minnesota. A rogue went on a killing spree June tenth and killed Sara's brother. She's a murder investigator with the Richfield police department, but as a family member of the victim, she has been denied access to the investigation.

"She's a tenacious woman and has taken it upon herself to find the killer on her own. Seth must go to Richfield and help her take down the rogue before she gets herself killed. If she dies, all hope to save Seth will be lost."

"So if I am understanding you correctly, you would like Isaac and me to get Seth to go to Minnesota after the rogue. Other than getting him to Richfield is there anything we should do?"

V.A. Dold & Tori Austin

"In order for him to meet her, he must agree to work with her to kill the rogue. He has never worked with a partner and definitely never a human. It won't be easy. He will want to hunt the rogue on his own and return home."

Emma thought about that for a bit. "I think I know how we can force him to take her as a partner in this. Leave it to Isaac and myself, we will get it done one way or the other."

The Goddess's eyes twinkled with amusement. "I believe you will. I leave this in your capable hands. Blessed be, daughter, and good luck."

"Thank you. I'm sure we will need a little luck this time. Blessed be, Mother."

Emma watched her fade from view, chewing her lip worriedly. *How are we going to pull this one off?*

She needed Isaac and fast. The last time she'd seen him, he was heading for his study, hopefully he was still there. "Isaac!" she called and she hustled down the hall.

"I'm in the study, cher," he called back.

She plopped down into an overstuffed chair next to him, huffing and puffing from her exertion. When he opened his mouth, she held up one finger to silence his questions while she caught her breath.

"We have a problem," she finally panted out.

"What kind of problem?" he asked, leaning forward, concern etched into his features.

"The Goddess gave me another name and this one is not going to be easy."

RICHIE: Le Beau Series

"Who?"

"Seth."

"Holy cow," he breathed out and sat back in his chair. "I didn't see that one coming, not that he doesn't deserve his mate like all the other boys. But as a hunter, I assumed he'd never have a mate. It's extremely rare for the elite to settle down.
Of course, I didn't expect him to turn up on our doorstep talking about quitting the hunters either."

"I was rather shocked myself. And here's the kicker, we have to convince Seth to allow his mate to partner with him in a rogue hunt."

"Shit. That's never going to happen," Isaac growled.

"I'm pretty worried as well, but I might have an idea. It's going to require a lot of steadfast parental tough love to pull it off, though," she said sadly.

"What are you thinking?" he asked, leaning forward again and taking her hand.

"We could make it a condition of him coming home and living on the plantation. It's going to break my heart to force him to do something he is dead set against in order to come back home, but I can't think of any other way," she said with a tear rolling down her cheek.

Isaac scrubbed his palms up and down his face, racking his brain for other options. He had nothing. "I think that might be the only way. I'm going to have to put some thought into how we'll present it to him. I don't want to drive him away and screw the whole thing up."

V.A. Dold & Tori Austin

"I already thought about it and I think the only way we can do that is to tell him the Goddess requested him specifically for this last hunt and she added the requirement that he must work with the human. She specifically wants him to help her avenge her family, not just take out the rogue. We could tell him the Goddess has a plan for her and has tasked him with keeping her alive."

"That just might work. We'll emphasize the Goddess made it a requirement in order to force his compliance. Seth would never go against the Goddess's wishes."

He grinned, his eyes twinkling with excitement again. "He's gone to help Richie protect his mate at the cabin, when he returns, we will inform him he is heading to Minnesota."

RICHIE: Le Beau Series

K.I.S.S Series
LUCAS: Prelude to a K.I.S.S.
Book 1 First K.I.S.S. (Coming 2016)

Le Beau Series
Book 1 CADE
Book 2 SIMON
Book 3 STEFAN
Book 4 THOMAS
Book 5 LUCAS
Book 6 RICHIE
Book 7 SETH (Coming 2016)

And don't miss the follow up Le Beau HEA's
CADE & ANNA
SIMON & ROSE (Coming 2016)

V.A. Dold & Tori Austin

CADE

Anna James is single again, finally. In her opinion, men are self-centered and will never love her for who she is, a beautiful, plus-sized woman. All except the fantasy man that she meets in her dreams every night for last five years.

She just never expected her fantasy to be a real live alpha shifter...

Cade Le Beau isn't what he seems. He's a billionaire wolf. A Shifter. He laments his missed chance six months ago to meet his fantasy woman in the flesh. Just as his second chance presents itself, his fantasy woman, his mate, is threatened by the local mob boss and her ex-husband. Now, he has forty-eight hours to deal with this threat once and for all or chance losing her again.

Is it Anna who's in danger, or the humans who unwittingly threaten her?

The heat is on the moment they lay eyes on each other. Neither age, children, horrid ex-husbands nor mob bosses will stop this love affair.

SIMON

Four years of honorably serving his country has left Simon, Cade's younger brother, damaged and trapped in wolf form. Little did he know the only person with the ability to heal him completely would be found at home. Literally. Now that he's found her, he is desperate to claim her.

RICHIE: Le Beau Series

Rose is a beautiful, voluptuous woman with limited experience with men. Although she's confident, she still has reservations. Never having a family of her own, her fear of abandonment has her fleeing romantic relationships and doubting herself.

Travis is insane. A deadly loose cannon that a secret organization hired to destroy the Le Beau family by denying them their mates. Permanently.

Simon's dream will be lost forever unless he is able to maintain human form.

Rose needs unconditional love and a mate to create the family she's always wanted.

Travis's all-consuming drive is to take Rose for himself.

Will Simon ever be whole again, able to claim his mate, giving Rose the love and family she so desperately craves? Or will Travis destroy them both?

STEFAN

El is a beautiful, successful, plus-sized woman suffering a debilitating humiliation that has left her hating all handsome, wealthy men exactly like Stefan Le Beau. Unfortunately for Le Beau, she's known him since she was sixteen and was totally snubbed by him. To her, he's a hound dog and a man-whore.

Stefan is a playboy to the extreme with one hard and fast rule: date a woman only once, take her to bed and be gone before morning.

Until El.

V.A. Dold & Tori Austin

Stefan's dream of finding his mate comes true when he bids two hundred thousand dollars to win a date with El at Simon's charity ball. Money well spent in his opinion.

Now, if she would only talk to him. Or look at him. Or touch him, or…like him.

Can Stefan convince El he's a reformed man?

Can El learn to trust a man who is the epitome of what she avoids and could shatter her heart?

It will require drastic, strategic measures from the entire family to make this mating happen.

THOMAS

Julia is happy with her place in the shifter community as the owner of the famous shifter bar, The Backwater. But the life she's created for herself isn't enough to satisfy her crazy-ass mother, Lucinda, who shops her and her sister, Krystal, around to the pure blood shifters like pieces of meat. Only a born shifter mate is good enough for her girls.

Thomas James has his hands full as the shifter king's head of security. He certainly wasn't looking for a girlfriend during the first annual shifter gathering. He had the king and queen to protect, not skirts to chase.

A childhood of emotional and physical abuse by his birth father has left Thomas emotionally unavailable and uninterested in romantic relationships.

RICHIE: Le Beau Series

His father Tim's cruelty to his mother and brother molded him into an extremely protective person. No one messes with his loved ones without answering to him.

Even though Julia and Thomas are destined to be mates, the obstacles standing between them and their happily-ever-after seem insurmountable.

Lucinda insists Julia stay away from the filthy human.

Tim is trying to kill every one Thomas loves.

The mysterious Benevolent Sovereign, who is trying to overthrow the throne, has sent swampers to attack Thomas and destroy Julia's livelihood.

With family like theirs, who needs enemies?

Will Julia and Thomas's happiness be snuffed out before it has a chance to begin or will they forge through - obstacles be damned.

CADE & ANNA

When Dr. Marjorie schedules an ultrasound for Anna, Cade begins to go into paranoid meltdown. Something must be wrong! He's sure of it.

Seeing his daughter on the computer screen larger than life sets Cade onto a path of foolish, well-meaning choices. In a state of panic, he instigates a series of disastrous projects with the help of Simon, Stefan, and Thomas.

The final disaster lands Cade and Anna stranded on the family's island with Anna in labor and no help in sight.

V.A. Dold & Tori Austin

LUCAS

Krystal Le Beau hides a secret few know about: she is a psychic matchmaker. Little does Lucas know she's worked her magic and set him up to meet his destiny.

Lucas Le Beau's dream has come true. He owns a ranch of his own and he's moving in. He thought he had everything he wanted...until the most beautiful woman he's ever seen knocks him flat on his back.

Now he can't think of anything but making that sweet redhead his own. Lucas is one determined wolf! He's not giving up on Kensie no matter how stubborn she is.

Kensie Brown is visiting her sister Jojo, and so far, she's managed to flatten the owner of the dude ranch, make Jojo mad, and somehow fall for a damn cowboy, knowing she's leaving in a few days. What was she thinking?

Will Kensie trust Lucas to save her when her life is threatened, and she has no one else to turn to?

Will Lucas get to Kensie in time to stop the man who wants to expose her to the world and destroy her?

Mix one stubborn Yankee workaholic, a determined cowboy wolf shifter, and meddling family, stir well and you have the recipe for a wild Texas ride.

RICHIE: Le Beau Series

RICHIE

Four years ago, Richie met a group of Tulane freshmen when he saved one of them from a mugger.

Now the first of their menagerie is getting married.

Surprise of all surprises, Richie meets his mate, Piper, at the wedding in Missouri, of all places.

He didn't expect her to be a bounty hunter or that her murderous prey had turned the tables and she was now the hunted.

Will Piper apprehend her bounty or will her bounty get to her first?

Can Richie save her from the death he foresaw in a premonition?

Injuries are mounting and time is running out.

SETH

Orphaned at birth, Seth is adopted and raised by the king and queen of the shifters, Isaac and Emma Le Beau.

Circumstances and heartbreak propel him into the elite band of hunters. Shifters pledged to serve the Goddess as her right hand. Meting out justice to the shifters who go rogue.

Burned out and ready to retire, Seth seeks refuge at the plantation, but Isaac has one last hunt for him to complete.

V.A. Dold & Tori Austin

Unable to deny his father the king, and the Wolf Goddess herself, will this assignment be his undoing or his salvation?

Sara Adams is a police detective, a damn good one, too.

Ten years ago when Sara's older sister took a mate she learned all she wanted to know about shifters. Since then she's stayed out of their world as much as possible.

That is about to come to an abrupt end.
Sara's brother, Grant has been killed by a rogue and Sara will be damned if the monster sees another day.

Can Seth survive one more kill?

Will Sara avenge her brother or die trying?

Is there a sliver of common ground for them to stand on in order to get the job done?

There is a dangerous bloody future ahead where only the strongest survive.

RICHIE: Le Beau Series

About the Authors

V.A. Dold & Tori Austin are the Amazon best selling authors of the Award-winning Le Beau Series and the K.I.S.S series.

Her idea of absolute heaven is a day in the French Quarter with her computer, her coffee mug, and the Brothers, of course. Or, a night with a sexy cowboy in the hayloft.

A Midwest native, with her heart lost to Louisiana & Texas. She has a penchant for titillating tales featuring sexy men and strong women. When she's not writing, she's probably taking in a movie, reading, or traveling. Oh, and there is always the distinct possibility she's out cowboy hunting.

V.A. Dold & Tori Austin

Connect with Tori Austin and V.A. Dold:

Website http://www.vadold.com/
Like Tori Austin on Faceboook https://www.facebook.com/ToriAustinAuthor
Like V.A. Dold on Faceboook https://www.facebook.com/vickieann1
Follow Tori Austin on Twitter at https://twitter.com/ToriAustin15
Follow V.A. Dold on Twitter at https://twitter.com/VADOLD

Cover Design by Christa Reed Photography

For announcements about upcoming releases and exclusive contests:

Join my Newsletter. The link is on the home page of my website.